CURRY
THE SEARCHER

By Leonard E. Griffin

PUBLISH AMERICA

PublishAmerica
Baltimore

ISBN: 1-4241-1730-5
PUBLISHED BY PUBLISHAMERICA, LLLP
www.publishamerica.com
Baltimore

Printed in the United States of America

DEDICATION

This book is dedicated to my wife Hilda, daughter Samantha, son Michael and all those Boy Scouts who listened to my stories across the campfire.

CONTENTS

FOREWORD

In the beginning the Master of all Wizards was created from the Cosmos and he was bestowed with true Wizardry. Using only his thoughts he manipulated people and their surroundings to benefit the good. This Wizard, with a thought, conceived in the wombs of barren wives, male children who were later trained in the true way. This is the story of one of those children.

CHAPTER 1
The Mark

Murf was a Master Guard of the Rampart and of the first wall. His duties required him to train his twenty guards in the use of long bow, cross bow, side sword, dagger and pike. He was charged with insuring that two guards were always on the rampart walls of Varton Castle and that four manned the first wall. These guards were to alert the castle and cause a delaying action in case of attack.

His friend Seth was the Master Guard of the Gate. He trained his thirty guards in pike, side sword, dagger and horsemanship. He was responsible for the drawbridge operation, security of the castle and the court yard.

Murf had served the Varton nobility for twenty"two years under two Lords. Lord Varton senior entered the void nine years ago, then his son ascended the throne. Murf watched young Lord Varton grow from a child into a man. He had no reservations about kneeling before young Varton upon his father's death and swearing allegiance.

Today he was returning from Halon Village. The blacksmith there had built twenty new pike heads for Lord Varton. The new pike heads and his traveling supplies were on a pack horse that he was leading. These pike heads would later be sharpened then mounted on wooden yew staffs and used for castle defense by both the rampart and gate guards.

A pike was a short metal lance with a curved hook at the base. The pike could be used to spear a charging foot soldier or hook a passing horseman.

This was his eighteenth league of travel and he was anxious to get home. A league was the distance a castle guard could walk from dawn to dusk. A league was also referred to an amount of time it took to walk that distance. A league was broken down into ten lengths of time and a length was fifty moments.

Taking the last bite of an apple, Murf leaned forward and offered the core to his mare. The mare sniffed it, then lipped it into her mouth and began noisily chewing the treat. Closing his eyes as he road, he remembered the taste of his wife's mutton stew and his mouth began to water. Being Master Guards, it gave him and Seth the privilege of living outside of the castle with their wives. Each had a separate hut provided by Lord Varton.

Murf met Jill, his wife, twenty years ago during a castle festival. Flowers and ribbons were in her long blond hair and being fair of face and form, he knew no other man was going to have her but him.

Being in the guard for only two years he had little to offer. Fortunately she saw the potential in him because for the next twenty years they grew as close as one. He served in the guard and she was Lord Varton's primary cook in the castle.

Cresting the hill overlooking the Varton Castle, Murf dismounted and released the mare's cinch strap. Feeling along the cinch strap, then along her belly, he found two burrs picked up from the tall grass. He again tighten the chinch strap. Pulling it tight, he hesitated, then kneed the mare in her stomach. This caused the mare to release her breath so he could further tighten the cinch.

"I know your tricks, old girl. Hold your breath until I tighten the cinch then breath out so it rides loose." Tying it off with a lark's head knot he remounted.

Looking down on the castle he saw that it had been built on a peninsula that jutted two thousand paces into the Sea of Agnon. A pace being the distance a man makes when he takes two steps. Large rocks and crashing seas prevented any assault from the seaward side. Its greatest width was five hundred paces. Where the peninsula met the main part of the land it was only twenty five paces wide making it easy to defend. A high stone wall, called the first wall, was seventy five paces from the start of the peninsula and built with only a gate wide enough to allow for one cart to enter. From this gate four guards with pikes could delay any attack long enough for the villagers who lived just outside the castle to retreat into its safety. Approaching the turn into the peninsula, Murf was met with an unusual sight. Where the peninsula begins and continuing up to the first wall, all the vegetation was dead. The trees were completely denuded of leaves. Not a leaf or blade of grass lived, even the moss was dead. Crossing where the dead line began he suddenly noticed that there were no sounds. No birds, insects, frogs…nothing, only the sounds of his own breathing and that was coming quicker.

Slowly he reached down and released the pack horse's lead in case he had to move quickly. Pulling his side sword and dropping his visor, he spurred his horse towards the gate of the first wall. From high in two different trees, vines began to move and lower themselves. Being almost the same color as the dead trees he didn't see them coming at him. In an instant the vines whipped through the air and severed the mare's head along with Murf's upper torso. The pack horse smelling the blood turned and bolted for safety. Before he could take two strides the surrounding vines had slashed him into quarters. Other whipping vines fell from the trees and dismembered both horses and Murf. Along the ground, vines came and snared the pieces of warm meat and pulled them deep into the decaying woods.

Helplessly the guards at the first wall watched as the Master Guard was butchered by the vines.

Thirteen years earlier…

In the country of Carlin, of the Province of Shinning lies the Village of Winslow. Winslow being of the third generation founded by the Father, who raised his son, who in turn raised his son. When the present child becomes of age, then Winslow will be of the fourth generation.

As with all established villages in Shinning Province, the barter method was used to exist and flourish. The baker sells his breads to travelers and trades his wares to his fellow villagers for his needs. He obtained milk from the dairyman, flour from the millwright, eggs from the poultry lady and fat from the village hunter. For his family, he trades for cloth, meat and vegetables. A simple life was lead by all, no one was rich and none were poor.

A baker named Rales lived there with his wife Mimm. Rales was a man of usual height, dark hair, broad of shoulders and even broader waist. Years of kneading bread had made his forearms formidable weapons but his opponents were always loaves of dough. Never was he seen without his flour coated apron, the trademark of a baker.

Mimm was short and as round as Rales. Quick with a smile and a hug, she was always a help to anyone in need. Never was she seen without a colorful flower in her curly red hair. After years of being barren they were finally blessed with a child, a son named Curry.

Curry was a loving child and never seemed to catch colds like the other children and his bumps and bruises seem to heal quicker than others. When he was a month old, two poor traveling women came to the bakery for leftover bread.

Rales, as a youth, had been hungry on several occasions. There were times when even a crust of bread would have been a full meal to him. He vowed that no one who really needed food, would ever leave his shop hungry. To allow that person to leave with some dignity and self respect, they had to earn it by foretelling Rales's future. This way they paid for the bread with their stories. Many smiles and laughs were passed between Rales and the travelers by seeing who could tell the most outlandish lies of his future.

Just yesterday a lean man wearing tattered but clean clothes came into the shop, hat in hand, he asked if Rales had any leftover bread. It was near closing and the bread would be too stale to sell the next day. Rales told him he would trade bread for a fortune telling. In elaborate movements the man replaced his hat, covered his eyes with one hand and raised the other over his head.

"I'm receiving a vision, stand quietly." Turning his palm this way, then that, he said, "Your life will be filled with milk and honey."

Looking at the lean man, Rales said, "You old fool!, of course it will be, I'm a baker."

"Yes…yes my visions are always true," the lean man then performed a deep sweeping bow.

Rales broke into uncontrollable laughter. Recovering from his laughter, he brushed the flour from his hands onto the table, and took a loaf. Breaking it in half, he spread fresh butter from a crock sitting on the table onto both ends. Handing both pieces to the man he waved him goodbye.

Seeing the two poor traveling women entering the shop, Rales greeted them. Seeing their need he entered into an agreement with them, the trade of three loafs of bread to foretell his future. Gripping the bread tightly, fearing Rales may snatch it back, the two tattered women looked at Rales then to began walk away. Suddenly one stopped, turned and said, "Your son, he bears the Mark!" they then fled into the crowd and were gone.

Rales immediately went to the door, slamming it, he threw the bolt. Tossing his apron over the crock of butter to protect it for flies, he exited the back door. Crossing the small pasture of milking goats, Rales entered his hut and went to Mimm.

Rales told his wife of the woman's statement about their son, Curry. Mimm, with a look of dread, laid their child on the table. Quickly she removed his blanket and soiling rags. Desperately Mimm and Rales inspected the child for any blemish or mark. His front reveled nothing, as so was his back. With a sigh of relief Mimm pulled Curry to herself and began caressing his hair. He did not have the mark, the woman had lied. Why pull such a cruel joke on strangers? Mimm knew that many travelers were abused and taken advantage of, a few of the travelers she knew would sometimes seek some type of revenge. Looking into her heart she forgave them.

Rales embraced them both and touched Curry's brown silky hair. Then he noticed a discoloration just behind Curry's left ear just inside his hairline. Upon closer examination a peculiar mark was revealed. A small purple crescent with a dot between the tips. "Mimm, look behind his ear," Rales said.

Mimm, wetting her thumb, tried desperately to rub the mark off but this only resulted in causing Curry to fret and cry. She breathed deeply, looked into Rales eyes and resigned herself to accepting the mark and what the future it held.

Being barren for so many years, then being blessed with a child, they knew it was a wondrous gift. Having a child, even if it is but for one day is better than never having a child at all.

Squeezing her husband's hand she said, "We can always hope he will be released. I have heard that it has happened before." Rales didn't find much comfort in her statement.

Throughout the following years Curry was raised as best as his parents could do. Occasionally they made mistakes, as all parents do from time to time. His hair was kept a little longer than custom to help conceal the mark. If it were seen the other parents would pity them and the children would tease Curry.

With the mark being behind his ear he could not see it and was unaware of what his future held. Soon he began to ask questions that would cause his parents discomfort.

During the last month of his twelfth year, Rales and Mimm seemed to have a shadow of depression come over them. Their behavior changed, not in a bad way but strange. Longing looks, hugs which were held just a little too long and eyes that were quick to tears. To Curry this was very confusing. He kept asking why they were acting so strange, his friend's parents didn't act this way. His mind was searching for something he did or did not do that caused this and most of all how to return things to the way they were.

At the approach of his 13th birthday it became almost unbearable. Eating breakfast, his mother would burst into tears and run from the room. His Father avoided looking at him and even seemed to find reasons to not be around him. Always too busy, has to be somewhere else or was so tired and he had to go straight to bed.

This was to be the magic year in a boy's life when he became a responsible person in the village. A responsible person meant he was held accountable for his actions. Any misdeeds and he answered to the village leaders instead of his parents. The village leaders were comprised of four adults, the village hunter, a descendant of the original founder, the oldest male and oldest female. Five years from his thirteenth birthday, when he became eighteen, he would become of age. Then he would become the fourth generation of Winslow.

On the eve of his thirteenth birthday, his parents hit the apex of their bizarre behavior. The supper they had made was incredible. Rales and Minn had bartered with everyone for the best and choicest of foods and cloth. Rales baked yeast breads and pastries covered with sugar. Mimm sewed a complete outfit of gray breeches and a brown tunic. She also made a black hooded long cape with sleeves that would shed rain and the harsh winter winds. They bartered with the cobbler who made Curry new calf high boots of leather and a leather belt with a brass buckle.

The table was laid with mutton, beef, fruit and a selection of all his favorite vegetables, both of them, roasted corn and fat fried corn. This confused him and clouded his mind. His birthday was tomorrow, not tonight.

"Why the party and gifts tonight?" Curry asked. His parents just muttered and finished setting the table. If they wanted to act in this manner and it caused no harm then so be it, he thought. The meal went quietly, no words were spoken and no eye contact made. Happy birthday Curry, he told himself sarcastically.

That night as they sat before the final embers in the fireplace, Rales smoked his clay pipe and Mimm sat and caressed Curry's hair and they spoke of the past. They spoke of the good times, the funny times and the childish mischief Curry had done but this was not dwelt upon. A long yawn from Curry marked the conclusion of the night. Rales with a trembling lip and Mimm wiping quite tears from her cheeks, kissed their son goodnight and probably goodbye. Curry wished things would be different in the morning. Little did he know he would get his wish.

During the night Curry woke and something was different. The night sounds were louder and his soft hay stuffed mattress was now damp ground. He raised his head and nothing was familiar. His thirteen years of exploring Winslow revealed he knew nothing of this area. As he looked around he saw a faint glow. Looking up he checked the stars and found the star that never moved. He knew the glow was not the rising Sun, it was in the wrong direction. It had to be a fire but 0who would build a fire on this warm Summer night?

Curry approached the fire's glow. Staying just outside the radiance of the fire he saw a figure sitting on a log in front of the fire. His garments were like his own. A black hooded long cape, which he just realized, he himself was wearing. A one pace long walking staff was leaning against the log that the strange figure was sitting on. His hair was streaked with gray and no beard was on his face. The stranger also wore a leather cap that had no brim. It looked like an upside down soup bowl.

Somehow, Curry did not feel threatened so he took a step into the clearing, he then picked up the sounds of slight movement and quick breathing. Suddenly fear froze him in his tracks as he heard deep growling behind and to either side of him. Slowly turning his head he saw timber wolves. Pitch black, almost half a pace at the shoulder and it appeared that their intentions were to end the start of his thirteenth year.

From the fire a voice called to Curry, "Had it been anyone but you, they would have had their supper tonight."

Curry asked, "Anyone but me, why anyone but me? and who are you?"

"Last question first. I am Warlick a Wizard Master. The reason, anyone but you, means it is your time, as the mark decrees. I have been assigned as your mentor by Olen the Master of all Wizards to lead you into Wizardry.

"What mark are you talking about, I have no mark." Curry was becoming more and more frightened.

Warlick pulled back his left sleeve and showed Curry a small purple mark on the inside of his forearm. A crescent with a dot between the tips. "All in the Wizardry have a mark like this one. Yours is behind your ear just inside your hairline."

Curry's mind was confused and reality was slipping away. Absentmindedly he reached up and began rubbing the spot that this stranger had referred to. "I am confused, last night I slept in my bed and now I am surrounded by wolves in an area I have never seen."

Warlick answered, "Be patient my little Searcher. Join me at my fire and I will tell you of your past, what has transpired tonight and of your destiny." Curry sat next to Warlick and sensed something was not quite right around him, something was out of place and just didn't fit. He couldn't put his finger on it but would ponder it as Warlick told his story.

Warlick began..."When the Country of Carlin, the Province of Shinning and the Village of Winslow was formed, bandits, monsters and cruelty abound. There was a need for protectors of the common people. This was the time that there was a need of Wizards. Olen the Master of all Wizards had crossed the Great Sea with his student Klat who had just achieved the level of Wizard Master. Seeing the trouble in the land, Olen assigned Klat to travel the land and begin a Wizardry of Searchers and Wizards. Olen gave Klat the gift of selection.

Throughout the land Klat traveled. Using his powers, he made conditions for the people easier. A monster frozen here, bandits turned into gnomes there and an occasional castle drawbridge frozen shut until the Keeper of the Province learned compassion for his people. Alone Klat knew it would be impossible to help the whole country so using the wisdom of many years, he used the gift of selection given to him by Olen."

"Upon entering a new village Klat observed and sensed the villagers. A couple was needed that was barren. The couple must possess nurturing love for a child and be able to raise a child without prejudice. Each village gave Klat mixed emotions. On one hand he hoped to find the correct couple but on the other he knew that if he found too many couples there would be Wizards with little to do. With lack of duties, laziness and mischief develops, even with Wizards."

"He then decided that if the child was not required at that time for the Wizardry, he would be released. He would then begin learning his father's trade and never be called to the Wizardry. When the right couples were found, Klat would go to their cottages and at the time of High Arc of the Moon he would raise his staff and think the words to envelope the cottage with the gift of Selection."

"At that instant a child was conceived and in the proper time a male child would be born. Upon the child would be a Mark, the

Mark of a Wizard, a small purple crescent with a dot between the tips. In time the knowledge of the Mark would spread throughout the Country. Most new mothers looked for the Mark to see the future of their child. Some did not want to know. This gift to a barren family did have its cruel part. One of two things would happen. In the middle of the night at the beginning of the child's thirteenth birthday he would disappear from his bed to begin the study of Wizardry. He would never to return and would never remember his parents."

"Not being chosen, he would be released and wake as he had for thirteen years and his mark would be gone. If a Searcher, Wizard or Master Wizard should pass into the void, a new Searcher would be chosen to replace the Searcher moving up. Otherwise life would go on for the child."

"Klat timed the selections so he would be able to mentor one new Searcher at a time. After the initial training the other Wizards would assist in his further training. Searcher is the title given to a beginning Wizard. A Searcher's title lasts not for a certain period of time but when knowledge and certain skills are developed. Knowledge requiring memorizing aura names of everything he would come into contact with, Wind, light, trees, stones, fire, rain, in essence everything."

"The skills would be to think the aura word that surrounds and is part of each object and envelope the object with your mind and ask the item to do your bidding. No one, not even a Master of all Wizards can force anything but only ask. The Searcher's special hand staff of about the length of his forearm, contains the power of Wizardry and identifies one as a Searcher. The proper way to address auras is acquired over a long period of time and much practice."

"Many times a Searcher's ego exceeded his skills and he would have an embarrassing experience. Instead of asking properly, he would be rude or demanding. Asking rain to go around him so his cloak would remain dry, it would funnel large quantities of water upon him soaking him to the skin."

"The Master of all Wizards sensing the Searcher's mastery of the skills and the wisdom to make correct decisions, awards him with the title of Wizard if there is an opening. His hand staff then changes into a full walking staff and with it more power. As a new Wizard he would be responsible for one Providence. He deals with the serious problems and assigns Searchers the lesser ones to solve."

"The levels of Wizardry are Searchers with a hand staff, beginning at age of thirteen, who travel the whole country beginning their education. Wizards, with a full walking staff, who are assigned to one Province. One extra Wizard is assigned to the Cavern's of Sulferic to guard the dragon Kiliac's egg. He is called the Guardian Wizard. The Wizard Masters, with the cap of leather, are assigned to one of the countries of the World. Last of all is Olen the Master of all Wizards. There is only one Olen and he has here since the time of memory and he will be here until the end of memory. Klat has long past entered the void and I am the present Master Wizard of this country."

"So you see Curry, your walk of Wizardry begins now." Curry pondered this and his thoughts returned to the pack of wolves.

"What of the wolves Warlick ?" Curry asked.

Warlick replied, "We are not friends, the wolves and I, but more like a bear and a tree. The tree allows the bear to rub his back against him and the bear leaves some of his hair that repels certain insects that harms the tree. The wolves warn me if danger approaches and allows those to pass who I politely ask them to, in return I envelope their coats with black upon black which allows them to become almost invisible in the night when they hunt."

Curry began to see the merest glimpse of what was before him. Suddenly out of the corner of his eye a tiny light appeared, a flying light the color of light green, and it was headed straight to Warlick. Curry heard what sounded like a hummingbird as it approached. It circled Warlick's head once, then flew into his left ear canal. Mesmerized Curry leaned forward. He saw a tiny girl with wings standing on the bottom edge of Warlick's ear canal and appeared to be whispering in Warlick's ear.

Curry asked, "A fairy?" Suddenly the light brightened and came straight at his face. He yelled as something struck him, grabbing his face he jumped from the log, staggered and fell into the fire. Screams of pain escaped his lips as he rolled from the flames and jumped up beating at the flames of his cape. All the time Warlick sat, watched and smiled.

Curry yelled, "I fell into the fire and you did…," the words froze in his mouth. His cape was not on fire, not even warm. Slowly he reached towards the fire and then it struck him, that the uncomfortable feeling he had earlier but couldn't place was that the fire burned but there was no heat.

"Yes my young Searcher," replied Warlick. "This is a companion fire. No heat only a comforting light for company."

Curry sat again and wiped his face with the back of his hand. So much so soon, he said to himself. Looking down he saw blood on his hand. Feeling his face he found blood seeping from a small cut from his nose. "What happened?" Curry asked.

Warlick replied, "You shouldn't have called her a fairy, Searcher. A fairy plays the day away and accomplishes nothing. A Mintz carries messages and saves lives by doing so. They have their own powers and skills but only Olen knows all of all the powers they possess. Their wings beat so fast when they fly that they sound like a hummingbird and actually begin to glow. Fairies wings don't glow. Cley, my Mintz cut you nose with her dagger. Luckily for you she knew you were a Searcher or you would be blind in one eye right now. Your Mintz comes shortly. There are things you must know first." Warlick slid off of the log onto the ground and rested his back against the log.

He began, "You will name you Mintz and she will be yours forever. She is no toy but a companion and someday may become your best friend. You abuse your relationship with your Mintz and you will feel the dagger again. She is an equal with her kind as you are with yours. She will stand in your ear canal and give you a message. These messages will come from someone in the Wizardry. Always be polite and speak very quietly to her. When she finishes, tell her thank you then make a fist and put your thumb against your lips. She will alight on your forefinger and kiss your nose and leave. She will come to you if she has a message and come when you envelope her name to the wind."

"What messages Warlick?"

Warlick replied, "Your purpose is to protect the people throughout the country as a Searcher. If you advance enough in your training, Olen may promote you as a Wizard of a Providence if there is one vacant. For now the Wizard in your area will deal with the major problems and you will deal with the minor ones. The messages will be sent by that Wizard or one of another Providence, depending on the need and availability of Searchers."

"These assignments or messages will be given to you by your Mintz. You will obey, refusal is not an option. Trust her, protect her and respect her. When a Mintz grows sleepy she goes to a tree where the blue moss grows, there she has built a nest. Her nest is made from goose down that she gathered from the lakes where the geese nest. She then wraps herself in her wings, curls up and sleeps. Each morning she will fly to a flowering field and replace the petals in her skirt. Each Mintz wears a different flowering petal as a skirt."

"Olen placed one tree in each providence that grows a vegetation called blue moss. This blue moss hangs from the limbs of the tree and is the color of bluish gray. This is their only food source for a Mintz and from it they get their nourishment. The odor of the moss repels the birds and the small tree climbing animals. This allows the moss to grow and the Mintzs can rest or sleep undisturbed. They have never been attacked while in any of the blue moss trees. I know that even I would not want to upset two or three Mintzs in their nesting tree. The dagger at their waist is used as a warning, as you have found out, it is not the only weapon at their disposal."

"Their daily activities, when they are not delivering messages, is to meet with other Mintzs at the blue moss tree of their Providence or at the blue moss tree of another Providence. They tell each other of their Searcher's journeys, what skills he used and how it ended. This is not where one Mintz is telling the others that her Searcher is better than theirs. This allows all of the Mintzs to memorize the history Wizardry. They know the name of every Wizard and Searcher since the beginning of Wizardry. They know of every skill in Wizardry and all the mistakes that led to the death of the Wizards and Searchers."

"Olen hears their stories and tells me and the other Master Wizards around the World so we can better prepare our Searchers to survive until they gain the ability of their skills."

"A Mintz watches over you most of the time. If something ever happens to a Searcher or a Wizard the Mintz will go to Olen and tell him what happened. You will not see her unless see wishes it but she is there. Olen has made it so she could watch only. She cannot give help or advice only give or take messages."

Curry's head was swimming with so much to learn in such a brief period. He could only imagine what the next few years would hold on his way to becoming a Wizard.

Warlick looked up and said, "She comes, your Mintz, prepare her name." A tiny speck of light was in the tree tops and Curry watched as it approach him. Warlick told him, 'Put your hand out, palm up, the Mintz will land in the palm of your hand and trust you not to crush her and you trust her not to cut your wrist with her dagger.' The Mintz landed in Curry's hand and gazed up at him. Warlick told him to whisper her name that he had chosen for the Mintz.

Curry whispered, "Ary" The Mintz looked at Warlick then back at Curry.

Warlick told Curry, "Make a fist with your other hand like I told you and touch your thumb to your lips, if the Mintz accepts the name she will come to your forefinger and kiss your nose." Curry did as instructed and the Mintz flew to his forefinger and kissed his nose. Warlick closed his eyes and concentrated for a moment then said "Ary." Looking at Curry he said "Now every Wizard knows that Ary is your Mintz." Curry wondered how much power Warlick really did possess.

"Ary flew to Curry's ear and asked, "What happened to your nose?"

Curry told her, "I insulted Cley by my ignorance and she corrected me, I will not do it again." Ary flew to Cley they circled each other then disappeared into the woods.

Warlick said, "A Mintz rarely stops and talks, she will deliver her message and she will be gone, don't expect to ever have a discussion with her."

Curry asked Warlick, "When will they return?"

"When they have a message or when you call your Mintz, Ary."

"And how exactly do I call Ary, Warlick?"

"First you must have your hand staff, then you call her name to the wind," Warlick told him. With that Warlick reached over to his walking staff and pried a small splinter of wood from it. "Take this and place it in the palm of your hand tightly," Warlick told him. Curry grasped the splinter and held it tightly. Warlick lifted his walking staff closed his eyes then moved his staff towards Curry.

Curry felt his palm begin to warm then a vibration, the wooden splinter begin to swell. It continued to swell until it was about the length of his forearm and he could just touch his thumb and forefinger by reaching around it.

Warlick told him, "Your hand staff, like your Mintz is yours and yours alone until death. If out of reach, it will come to you when it is called." For the next two hours Warlick taught Curry how to call his hand staff, first from an inch away up to as far as he could throw it. Warlick told him that with maturity and experience the distance he could call his hand staff was unlimited.

The training Curry was receiving from Warlick was intense and continuous. The hours seemed to melt away as did the days and months. It was like learning to walk. A few steps now, then walking, one day he would learn to run. Curry knew when he obtained the rank of Wizard he would be running. There were so many things to learn. Calling of his hand staff, learning of Aura names, enveloping, remembering to ask and not demand things. Then there were the practical things, companion fire for light only, warming fire for heat, casting out of flames to slow adversaries. Self enveloping to slow his heart and metabolism for long periods of time so you could walk under a stream or lake without breathing. The speeding of his metabolism so he could remain warm in the coldest of nights when having a fire would give his position away. Intensified sleep where three hundred heartbeats of sleep would equal eight lengths of rest. His mind would be rested but not his body. Even with intense sleep he still needed to let his body rest from time to time. Self rapid healing for your injuries and injuries to others. The last two items he was taught was levitation and invisibility.

"You can be become invisible but you are not invisible," Warlick told him. "You can envelope those around you to look at you without seeing you but actually becoming invisible is impossible. Remember Searcher, if you do not envelope everyone, you will be seen. Enveloping the guards at the castle gate to go unseen will fail if the rampart guards are not enveloped. Being taught and acquiring the ability were two very different things."

Lengths of time sitting at the edge of the pond looking at his reflection trying to envelope himself to become invisible were disappointing. At best Curry could only make himself cloudy.

Warlick told him "In time, in time, training of a Searcher was recorded in accomplishments, not time. Acquiring the ability to call a hand staff may take hours or months, time means nothing, acquiring the ability is the goal."

Levitation like invisibility had the same results. At best he could only raise himself about the width of a finger.

Warlick told him, "The danger or drawback of levitation is

that you go up, you cannot walk on water because you can't touch the ground to generate speed. You can start by walking quickly or run then levitate yourself. If you try to levitate across a deep gully and the wind slows you down to a stop, well then you have no choice but to wait and either hope the wind blows you to one side or the other." With a sigh Warlick said, "Sometimes you have to lower yourself to the bottom of the gully and hope it is not a rushing torrid of water."

One night Warlick sat with Curry and told him of the major dangers to Searchers. Solemnly Warlick told Curry, "Young Searcher be aware of death, you can die."

"Can all Wizards die Warlick?" asked Curry.

Warlick replied, "All but Olen The Master of all Wizards. Some say he is immortal some say he has died and his Aura is revealed to us. I don't know, it is doubtful anyone will ever know. Also about death, you cannot raise the dead or talk to the Aura of the dead."

"You cannot directly injure anything that has blood," Warlick continued on, "Man, woman, child, bird, dragon anything with blood." Curry had a very puzzled look.

"Question Searcher?" Warlick asked.

Curry said, "I heard that a monster was frozen to death."

"Searcher pick up that rock at your feet and throw it at my foot."

Curry said "I will hurt you."

"Do it Searcher." Curry picked up the rock about the size of a lemon, drew back his arm and at the instant he willed himself to throw, a loud pounding was felt in his chest and head. Physically he could n't throw the rock. When he stopped willing himself to throw the rock the pounding stopped.

"See," said Warlick. "Now place the rock in front of my foot." Curry moved forward and placed the rock at Warlick's feet. He expected the pounding to start again, thankfully it didn't. He turned and return to his seat.

Warlick said, "You have not injured me by placing the rock at my feet, but if I stand and walk, I will trip over the rock and injure myself. You cannot directly injure anything with blood but you can cause them to injure themselves." Continuing the monster story, Warlick said, "Indeed the monster was frozen but it was not harmed for no Wizard can injure anything of blood. The monster was walking and its steps were not stopped only delayed. One day the freezing envelope will stop and the monster will continue on. Remember that you can only freeze something of blood, things not of blood are effected in different ways. All your envelopes are given with a time condition, a heart beat, a length, a league or a year but no longer, you must be selective. Too long and others will know a Wizard is in the area and many dislike Wizards for the power they have, be careful. Last of all you cannot pass anyone in need, we are here to help others in their plights."

"When enveloping always remember if the hand or walking staff is held in the right hand and the hand is released the enveloping stops. If it is given with a time condition the condition will remain until the time expires. You can only make two envelopes at once and to do so you must place both hands on the staff. Releasing either hand removes the envelope given with that hand."

"When you choose to sleep, first levitate to a safe place, either a high tree limb or an inaccessible rock ledge. Then envelope invisibility for a distance of sight. Take the hem of your cape and wrap it tightly around your hand holding the staff so you will not accidentally let it go while sleeping."

Curry asked, "But I can call my hand staff back to me, why wrap it to my hand?"

Warlick answered "If you drop the staff you will unknowingly become visible and like I said many prefer a dead Wizard over a living one."

As the night came about Curry asked, "If allowed may I asked what will I be learning in the future?"

With a smile Warlick replied, "Each level has its own abilities. The future holds for you control of animals, non living objects and eventually control over light, dark, wind and natural fire." Warlick thought for a moment and said, "Your next question is how long will it take?" Curry nodded in the affirmative.

Warlick said "So far during the past several months of training, you have spent but one heart beat of time in acquiring knowledge and matching it with ability. When a thousand of those heartbeats have passed you may be ready. Learn patience first, all will come in time."

"Last of all Searcher," Warlick began "are you hungry?" Curry though for a moment and said, "No, now that you mention it, I am not and I haven't eaten or taken a drink in months."

Warlick said "Nor will you. In Wizardry you draw from the Earth, nourishment and moisture. You can eat and drink, but you don't have to." With a smile Warlick said, "For me I enjoy the taste of a good sharp cheese and goat's milk for a treat, you will find your own treat.

Warlick knew Curry's time had come to walk alone. He had acquired enough skills to begin his first journey. With his knowledge and a little common sense he should do himself proud. Regrettably, several Searchers never finished their first journey, a mistake on their part and their auras passed into the void. Warlick had a feeling about this Searcher, a good feeling.

Tonight was the last to be spent together, someday, they may meet again. Warlick knew Curry's first challenge would come at daylight and he would have to face it alone. With his decision made, Warlick enveloped Curry with deep sleep until daylight then enveloped the wolves and asked them to watch over Curry until morning. With a last look at this new Searcher, Warlick picked up his walking staff and melted into the night.

CHAPTER 2
The Journey Begins

Morning light found Curry asleep in the deep woods. When the light swept his face he began to wake. Reaching up be began to rub his eyes, instantly he sat up a looked around him. He saw the wolves as they stood from their night bed, glancing at him they turned and disappeared into the forest. Curry knew he had been enveloped by Warlick to sleep because he had not enveloped himself.

Suddenly a vision entered Curry's mind. A faint glimpse of a man and a woman, the man having a baker's apron on. Curry did not remember ever seeing these two people before. The thought disappeared as quick as it began. This puzzled Curry, he would try and figure it out later but for now he had more pressing problems.

Looking around, he didn't see Warlick. "Warlick, Warlick," he called. Calling out his name only resulted in some crows returning his calls. Curry walked over and took a seat on the log. He pulled his hand staff from his belt and pondered his situation. "What is my next move?" he asked himself.

He didn't need food or drink and there were plenty of trees surrounding him where he could Levitate to if danger came.

Looking around he knew that staying here was not an option. As a new Searcher he had a purpose, the problem was he didn't know what his purpose was for that moment. It came to him, if Warlick was not here to give him instructions then maybe his Mintz, Ary could. Concentrating, he called the name "Ary" to the wind.

At that moment, far away a lone black caped figure stopped, turned and looked back the way he just came. Smiling he returned to his path and quickened his pace, he knew the adventure stories he would have to listen to once he sat again with his Searcher, just as he told his Wizard Master when he was a Searcher.

Through the morning mist came a distant glow, this became a small bright light as Ary approached. Stilling himself so Ary could stand in his ear canal he waited. A faint buzz of tiny beating wings, like that of a hummingbird, then a light touch as she landed.

Ary's small but pleasant voice called to Curry. "Searcher," she said, "ONLY!!! across the bridge to the village of Marth you will go, a Lady there you will make. Envelope the finding of Marth to the wind and journey."

Quietly Curry said, "Thank you Ary."

Ary winged from his ear and Curry remembered to bring his fist to his mouth. Ary lightly landed on his forefinger, kissed his nose and was gone. Curry realized that Warlick was not the only one to teach him Wizardry but Ary also by her telling him to envelope the finding. The first part of her message was pretty clear. He was to go to some village name Marth. The second part, a Lady there you will make, was nonsense. Was he to build a woman or make a Lady do something, he didn't know. When he arrived he would find out, in time.

Taking his hand staff, Curry enveloped the name of the Village Marth to the wind and motioned with the hand staff, nothing happened. Expecting a vision of some sorts, he was disappointed. Putting his hands on his hips he began looking around for some kind of sign. Then behind him he heard the rustle of leaves, turning he saw the fallen leaves parting from his feet towards the East.

"To Marth! and whatever it holds," Curry said. He then began taking long strides along the newly established path. Looking back at the place he had just spent several months of his life he saw the leaves return to their original positions. Even the rock he placed at Warlick's feet returned to it's original position. It was as if he, Warlick and the wolves had never been there.

A light wind and blue skies met Curry on his journey. As he walked he noticed that the signs he had been given by the finding to Marth began to become faint and intermittent. Enough for him to see but not enough to become obvious to anyone else should he meet them on the road. He found it amusing that as soon as he walked past a sign it returned to its normal position.

He passed fields of long grass that was used for thatch roofs of the local village huts, short shrub areas and a forest of timbers. Many, he noticed, had been felled, limbed and hauled off as building supplies. As he walked, he practiced his levitation and invisibility. It amused him to be walking along, levitate and slow down to a stop even though he was still moving his legs in a walking motion.

Dusk came upon him and he felt it would be best that he should stop for the night. He could envelope a companion fire to guide his way but the comment of Warlick's, 'Many prefer a dead Wizard over a living one,' stuck in his mind. Better to be a delayed Searcher than a dead one. Walking into the forest, Curry found a stout Oak tree, looking around for prying eyes, he then began to levitate into the branches. At about one and one half paces he faltered and could rise no further. The more he practiced, he knew the higher he would be able to levitate. Grasping a branch he climbed to a safe height and settled in for the night. He then enveloped himself in invisibility. Sleep was not needed for now so he recited to his deep memory, all the aura's he knew. Finishing this he again practiced levitation.

At first nothing happened, as he kept trying he felt himself begin to lift. Practice did increase the height but he could only go up or down. The sideways movements were beyond him…for now anyway. Of the two enveloping skills, he felt that levitation and invisibility would be the most useful in maintaining his good health.

Glancing at his hand in the moon light he saw nothing, a good sign. "Pride Stupid!, don't let your ego get you killed." As he was warned, the things that are enveloped are asked, not ordered and an improper ego will get refusals. Better to walk humbly for a long time than to strut and be sent to the void in a short time.

Very shortly dawn would break so he wrapped his hand with the hem of his cloak to secure his hand staff. Enveloping himself for an intense sleep of three hundred heartbeats, Curry withdrew into himself. What seemed like eight lengths of time He awoke, refreshed and energized. Slowly removing the levitation be began to lower himself to the ground. Stamping his feet to regain circulation from laying on the tree limbs all night he was off again on his journey.

Later in the day as he was passing through an Oak forest he heard shouting and the hoof beats of running horses. Quickly he walked towards the direction of the sounds. At the bottom of a small hill he grabbed his hand staff with both hands in case he had to perform a double enveloping. First he enveloped himself into invisibility and then directed his attention towards the commotion. He glimpsed a large beige wolf trotting down from the ridgeline to a thicket of Laura and hide. Curry noticed that the animal's lope was labored.

Five horsemen clad in half armor and blue tunics crested the hill and reined to a halt. Half armor was worn when a guard was not preparing for battle. Each wore a dagger, side sword, metal chest plate, helmet with visor and a one metal forearm guard.

The forearm guard was worn on the arm that would be used when holding a dagger. If he was engaged in a double blade fight, where he was using a side sword and a dagger at the same time, the forearm guard would give added protection to the arm holding the shorter blade.

By their extra weaponry of long bows, it was obvious they were a hunting party. This hunting party, by looking at their clothing, were out for sport and not to harvest for food. Thinking quickly he was going to try something he had never tried before. With almost a begging enveloping he called the aura of a near by bush to shake. It shook and he asked again until he gained the hunter's attention. At once they charged for Curry's location. Curry immediately enveloped a bush further away, then another. This would appear as if their quarry was running through the bushes to get away. The hunters fell for the ruse and charged after the movement over the crest of the hill and down into the valley.

After the woods fell silent, Curry moved the hand staff to his other hand and his invisibility ended. He quietly walked down to where the beige wolf had disappeared. Motioning with his hand staff Curry sent his own aura into the brush where the animal was hiding, this would allow whatever was in the bush to know he did not come to harm him. Curry then entered the brush. A small blood trail was found that showed by the splatter fingerling marks which way the animal walked.

When a drop of blood falls straight down it throws tiny fingerlings of blood in all directions from the center of the drop. If the animal or person is walking when the blood drops it leaves fingerlings from the drop only in the direction the animal is walking.

A few feet farther Curry came eye to eye with a beige wolf. This was not just a beige colored wolf, it was a cave wolf. The cave wolf was the most feared and largest predators in the country except for the bear. Standing over a half pace at the

31

shoulder he was a formidable animal. He dwarfed the timber wolves Curry had met when he was with Warlick.

Seeing the blood dripping from an arrow shaft Curry knew two things, one he could not out run the wolf, even with its wound and two he could not use any Wizardry skill to escape. The cave wolf sniffed at this man child and took his scent in.

In a desperate act he motioned with his hand staff and tried to envelope the aura of absence of pain. The snarling wolf on the verge of lunging felt the pain disappear and knowing it was because of this man child, he instantly sat on the ground then laid near Curry's knees.

Curry slowly reached out and touched the massive neck of this cave wolf. Few if any have ever touched a cave wolf and lived. Sliding his hand down, he touched the shaft of the arrow as it protruded through the foreleg of the wolf. Motioning with his hand staff, once again, He enveloped his aura onto the cave wolf and did this with intensity. Curry wanted the cave wolf to know without a doubt that he was there to help not to hurt. Ensuring that the pain enveloping was still present, Curry reached down and broke the arrow shaft near the foreleg. By breaking the shaft he wouldn't have to pull the sharp broad head back through leg causing further damage. He then quickly pulled the shaft free. Curry tore away part of his tunic and wrapped the wound to stop the small flow of blood.

Thinking slowly and carefully Curry decided to envelope the wolf with the aura of no infection and rapid healing. Being sure he made it so with the utmost respect and need. This was to prevent the foreleg from becoming infected and allow it to heal very quickly. The cave wolf was too large to carry and Curry had not learned to levitate water yet so he had to devise some way to get the cave wolf water before he left.

Crawling backwards out of the bushes, he then stood and walked a short distance to a spring. He looked around and saw a Royal Paulownia tree that had very large leaves. Taking one of the platter size leaves he folded it in half, then in half again.

Pulling an edge of the leaf outward it formed a small bowl. Curry then dipped it into the water and carried it to the cave wolf. Gratefully the cave wolf lapped it down.

Knowing that no further harm would happen to the cave wolf if he remained in the bushes, Curry said, "Remain here big one and you will be safe. The pain has been enveloped away until you heal, I am away." Mainly he said it for his benefit, with that Curry turned and began walking up to the crest of the hill.

Slowly he topped the hill and looked intently for the hunters. Seeing the empty forest he turned to look once again at the bushes where the cave wolf hid. To his surprise the wolf was behind him. His steps so quite, a cloud passing overhead would have made more noise.

The cave wolf knew that if the arrow shaft remained in his leg he would be unable to hunt. Becoming weak he would be slain by another dominate cave wolf or by a pack of smaller wolves. He owed a dept to this man child and felt an obligation, at least for now.

Kneeling and taking the beige head in his hands, Curry said, "I have no friends and no one follows me. If you follow my path know you now that you are free to turn at any time for we are but companions." Thus began the strange pair of travelers. A beginning Searcher and a full grown cave wolf.

Standing Curry brought his fist to his chest and bowed saying, "I am Curry, a beginning Searcher on the journey to one day becoming a Wizard. To whom am I addressing?" The beige cave wolf cocked his head to the side at the man child's strange behavior. "I see that you let your size do your speaking for you. With your permission, I shall call you Ral."

Curry and Ral then turned and headed West towards the setting Sun. Ral's injury missed the major arteries and veins causing only minor tissue damage. As Curry was being trained, he to, began training Ral.

Knowing that sound might give himself away at times, he devised hand signals for Ral. To Ral this was a great game to play. Shown a hand signal and demonstrating what was expected, this gave the signal its meaning. Rarely did Curry have to demonstrate the meaning of the signal twice. To Ral the purpose of the signals meant nothing. It was just simply a game to play. If it amused the man child, who had saved his life, then it amused him.

Later as they were passing a high field of new green grass, Curry heard riders approaching from around a curve ahead. Not knowing if mounted men were friend or foe, Curry took prudent actions. Giving hand signals to Ral to move to the right and into the grass, lie down and lastly to freeze. Curry moved to the left and enveloped himself in invisibility. Looking towards Ral, Curry enveloped Ral in a color of light green so as to blend in with the grass. All was green, his claws, nose even his teeth. The only tell tale sign of Ral's position were the two black unblinking eyes.

As the riders approached, Curry noticed there were five. Four in half armor with blue tunics, these were the hunters he had seen earlier. With them was a lady of regal position riding side saddle. Blond hair tied into a tight bun hugged the back of her neck. The lady wore a riding gown of orange with ermine trim. A riding gown was cut with a longer hem to insure she always had her ankles covered for modesty while riding. This was a sure sign of royalty. The expression she wore was not that of one on a daily pleasure ride, for sternness marked her face. Curry, even of his limited years, could tell that she was guarded not for protection but to restrain her freedom. He pitied her, he had only his clothes and a hand staff to his name, yet he had more freedom than she.

As they were about to come abreast of him, Curry glanced towards Ral and saw that he was still frozen. Then it came to him, if I remain here the dust from the riders will coat me and reveal my position. Quickly Curry laid on the ground so the dust would not be as noticeable as it coated him. As the horses came abreast of the pair in hiding they shied briefly, when they had picked up Ral's scent. After the riders passed, Curry stood then moved the staff to the other hand removing the invisibility. Shaking his cape of dust, he looked at Ral. Giving the come sign, Ral sprang to his side.

A look of amazement was in Ral's eyes. To lie within a pace of a rider that only a short time before had arrowed him, and not be seen, was a wonder. This man child may truly have some worth to him.

Motioning with his hand staff, Ral's coat returned to its beige color.

"I will have to work on your smell," he said. Curry noticed a strange look on Ral's face. Strange in that it looked as if Ral actually associated the hand gestures Curry gave him with a purpose, a serious purpose and not just a game.

These were not games they played but things that could save his life. Ral owed Curry his life for a second time. He decided that this man child was someone different from the ones he had encountered. He would travel with him for now, at least until the debt was repaid.

As the road topped a hill Curry viewed a valley below. A path turned off from the main road and continued to where a bridge spanned a small gorge with a village beyond. Seeing that there were no longer any guiding signs, that he had enveloped to find the Village of Marth, Curry assumed that this was Marth. Looking closer Curry saw activity at the bridge. Villagers were working on the bridge repairing some damage. Curry seeking to avoid contact with the people began to move North to find a crossing across the gorge then into the village.

He then remembered part of Ary's message, 'Searcher,' she said, 'ONLY!!! across the bridge to the Village of Marth you will journey.' He felt there had to be some reason that he had to cross the bridge and also he couldn't continue hiding every time someone came by. Knowing that a huge cave wolf would frighten the villagers, He motioned for Ral to go into the woods and hunt for his food and wait. Curry knew he didn't have to tell

Ral where to find him, his nose would do that. Failing that Curry could envelope his own aura to the wind and Ral could located him. Ral then disappeared into the wood line.

Not knowing the attitude of these people towards Wizardry, Curry tucked his hand staff into his belt and approached the bridge. The damage to the bridge was not too severe, just enough to prevent passage of travelers and carts. The worst part was at the end farthest away from the village. Curry noticed that the damage had been done intentionally by someone. It looked as if the support beams had been pulled from their footings by horses.

Giving the customary greeting to the first one he saw, Curry brought his fist to his chest and bowed his head and said, "I greet you friend." The startled look of the villager passed quickly and he returned the greeting. Curry asked, "My name is Curry, I see your bridge is damaged, what I lack in ability, I make up for in a strong back. Can I help you with the repairs?" The villager who Curry greeted was called Clas, the village spokesman. He was a large burly man with hair that had a habit of always getting into his eyes. His large callused hands told Curry this man did a man's work daily.

"Pass on lad, your offer is acknowledged and we thank you but this is more than just a damaged bridge. The Keeper of this Providence, Lord Marko, did this to remind us that our tithes to him were late and light in the purse, meaning the full amount demanded was not given. We try but the Keeper continues to raise the tithes and we cannot pay and still prosper. I will not allow the children of our village to go hungry. The limited guards the Keeper maintains does not justify the high costs he places upon us." Clas continued on, "We sent our most diplomatic speaker to voice our plea and Lord Marko sent him back here with his face branded with a hot fireplace poker. This damage to the bridge was from Lord Marko. Since I don't think you wish your face branded I suggest you be about your journey."

Curry looked up at Clas and said, "When you journey and come to a fork in the road, you either turn left or right. Then you live with your decision." Pausing for a moment Curry then asked, "Where do I start?"

Clas with a bold infectious laugh pounded Curry on the back and said, "Bless me lad, I think you walk in the boots of a man. Help pull those timbers from the hillside so we can replace them with new ones." Turning his back, Curry walked towards a nearby bush, as he walked he took his hand staff and tucked it into the sleeve of his cape then hung the cape on the bush.

The work was not mentally challenging, just physically demanding. By dusk the support beams were set, all that was required was to attach the wooden road bed in the morning and the bridge would be complete.

Clas said, "Curry you have worked hard, we are beholding to you but in doing so you have marked yourself as one of us. I hope you can still stand with your decision."

Curry thought, yes, I know something of being marked. He then went to retrieve his cape.

Following the villagers, Curry saw happy but stressed faces. The work on the bridge was not the cause of the stress. The harsh tithes had reduced the comfortable living to one where the parents always worried how to feed their children. Their options were limited. They could pay the tithes and suffer silently or refuse and face the wrath of Lord Marko. They had already had a taste of his benevolence.

He was shown to a small traveler's hut. Each village maintained a hut of this type so no one would have to take a traveler into their own home. On the door of the hut was a small coin box that the traveler would drop a copper or two. This paid some youth or widow of the village to clean the hut and restock the candles, fire starter, firewood, a pot of water and bedding after the traveler had left.

There were twenty coppers to a silver and ten silvers to a ring. A ring being the most valuable piece of money, it was actually fashioned into a ring so the owner could wear it on his hand or a string around his neck to prevent it being stolen from his purse.

Inside the hut were four beds, they were made of wood and laced with rope to hold the hay bedding. Curry was shown to this hut and Clas offered him food and drink. Excusing himself to wash up Curry knew he required no food but the smell of the sugar coated pastries had an irresistible appeal. Curry had a weakness for the sugar pastry the same way Warlick had a weakness for sharp cheese and goat's milk. He didn't need to eat, he obtained his nourishment from the Earth but the pastries tasted so good and satisfied his cravings. This would be a nice treat for the end of the day but he needed to remember to save one for Ral.

The villagers brought stools and sat around the village well as was their custom. Some ate a watery stew and chatted with their neighbors. Mothers nursed their young as they watched the children playing tag. The evening wore on, yawning spread from person to person and the people began leaving for their huts. Curry watched as the last of the villagers left for their hut.

Alone, Curry walked to the bridge to see if Ral was around. He stood and admired the work he and the villagers had performed. Curry always enjoyed learning new skills that he might have a use for later. Standing at the end of the new repairs Curry heard riders coming, then saw the firebrands they carried.

Lord Marko's guards in full battle armor were coming. All wore the items of half armor plus metal shin guards, back plates, both forearm guards and fighting axes attached to their saddles. Instead of their usual blue tunics they wore ones of red. The red would conceal the blood if they were wounded and not give their opponents a psychological edge. Four riders came, their visors lowered on their helmets and swords and daggers at the ready. Their intent was not known but suspected, Curry prepared for them.

The leader of the guards drew his horse up at the bridge, raised his visor and observed the repairs. "Torch the bridge," he ordered. Two of the guards from the rear came forward. Pulling spare firebrands from their saddles they prepared to light them. This way they would have a light to ride by after they threw the ones they were holding. They approached and prepared to toss their firebrands onto the timbers.

Curry had to act now, knowing he could not injure anything of blood he grasped his hand staff and enveloped the aura of a companion fire to each side of the horse's heads. Instantly the no heat fire enveloped the heads of each horse. Terrified panic filled each horse not to mention the riders. With fire to each side of the horse's head and none to their front, the horses bolted forward to escape the flames. All they knew was that safety was to their front. Crashing into each other, the riders were thrown from their mounts. The horses fled blindly in panic into the night, Curry moved the hand staff to the other hand stopping the companion fire. The horses would not stop until they reached the safety of their stables. The guards dazed and frightened quickly took to foot for the castle.

Curry was pleased with the night's adventure. He had utilized his newly acquired skills and had saved the hard work that the village had performed that day. Turning to return to the traveler's hut to recite his lessons of aura names he saw a massive lone figure standing at the end of the bridge. His arms were crossed and had a stern look on his face. As Curry approached, the figure spoke.

"Searcher?" Clas asked, making it more of a statement than a question.

Curry replied, "Searcher, how did you know?"

"We are aware of Wizardry here, you are too young for a Wizard and you lack a walking staff. Your display of, let's say magic, plus the hand staff identifies you as a Searcher."

"Am I friend or foe Clas?"

"Both," Clas said. "You saved the bridge that makes you

friend but how you did it will alert Lord Marko of your presence. That makes you a foe of sorts. We will suffer his wrath now that he knows we have befriended one of Wizardry."

"If I am the one who will cause you misery then I have to be the one to prevent it. I better meet with the Keeper of the Providence to explain what has happened."

Clas smiled and replied, "The most gracious and benevolent Lord Marko, who's compassion is without equal will welcome you as if you were a long lost returning son. Many of those who serve Lord Marko bear the brand on their face, and the brands were given when he was not angry. Lord Marko will welcome with open arms one who has embarrassed and defeated his guards."

Curry thought and said, "I can't stay here and do nothing and I can't leave and do nothing. I will meet with the Lord Marko tomorrow, I have no choice. The worse may that he will punish me and spare the village."

"Good luck Lad, I mean Searcher. It takes one with a stiff spine to do what you are about to do. If you are ever in need of a village to call home, Marth is yours. Best you leave at first light taking the road to the South." Clasping each other's forearms Curry thanked him and Clas returned to his hut.

Not waiting for first light, Curry took a last look at his new home and began walking South towards the castle. As he was walking he glanced at his shadow from the moon light, seeing a large shadow come up from behind him he cried out in fear. Raising his hand staff and turning quickly to envelope the casting of fire, he saw Ral. Curry had to sit on the ground for a few moments to allow his heart to slow. Looking at Ral, he said, "Unless you wish me to enter the void before my time please don't do that again." Ral just looked at Curry and though it was an excellent game to play.

Curry reached into his tunic and retrieved a sugar pastry and held it out to Ral. Ral sniffed it carefully, then slowly licked it with the very tip of his tongue. Withdrawing his tongue into his mouth Ral decided that nothing in nature had he ever tasted the likes of this. This man child does have some worth. Ral then reached out and gently took the pastry from between Curry's fingers. In two chews it was gone. Ral again sniffed the air and could not detect anymore of these sweet things. Curry stood and the two set off for the Castle.

About two lengths of time before daybreak the travelers viewed the castle. Having never seen a castle before, Curry was impressed. A wide drawbridge of heavy wood, two and a half paces wide. A drawbridge was the only access to the castle. At daybreak it was lowered and at dusk it was raised, that is unless an attack was imminent. It was lowered over the water filled moat to the dry land. Ropes lead from shackles at the end of the drawbridge up to the top of the wall through pulleys then down into the courtyard where they were attached to a winch. Turning a winch inside would lower or raise the drawbridge.

Walls were four paces high with turrets and shooting ports. The large stones of the walls were laid and set with mortar then the stone faces were then mortared again to make the wall too smooth to climb by hand. On each corner, of the top of the walls, were turrets. A turret was a small round room that stuck out from the wall over the moat. Narrow shooting ports allowed archers to shoot at any who would try climbing the wall with siege ladders.

The moat was odd to see. It had only a small amount of water, maybe a finger width deep. Curry had heard that moats were full of water to make it difficult to approach the castle wall. Taking a small stone Curry tossed it into the moat. The stone hit the water and became stuck in the deep muck of mud. Curry saw the logic of this. A man or horse could swim across a moat full of water but nothing could cross this pit of soft mud. The harder you tried the deeper the mud would suck you down.

Curry knew he had to meet Lord Marko on his own terms to gain what advantage he could. Circling the castle, Curry found the air portal for the kitchen.

A castle kitchen was extremely hot from the cooking fires and baking ovens. These fires required plenty of air plus a flow of air was needed to help cool the kitchen, otherwise it would be unbearable to work there. The portal was about two and a half paces above the moat. The opening was about a half pace wide and one pace high. A food preparation table had been built to fit exactly into the opening in case of attack. The cooks would turn the table on its end and slide it into the opening preventing any entry from the outside. Since there was no assault or threat of one at this time, Curry knew it would be open. Due to the time of night, Curry also knew that the bakers were not about their duties.

How did I know that about bakers? Curry asked himself. It was like seeing something in the fog only to loose it in the mist. He let it pass.

Curry sat on the ground and motioned Ral to his side. Urging Ral to lay across his lap, Curry enveloped levitation on them both. Curry had never tried this before. If Ral trusted him then Curry would trust in his skills to move them to the portal. The pair rose slowly but steadily. Knowing that he could levitate only up or down, he had taken a length of cord from the village when he left. This he hoped would give him the lateral movement he needed. When he reached the height of the portal he reached into his belt and pulled a thin cord that was attached to his belt. Taking the cord in his teeth he released his belt buckle and swung it towards the portal opening. On the third try the buckle caught and Curry pulled himself and Ral to the portal. Grabbing the edge of the portal with his hand he motioned Ral forward, Ral leaped into the portal. He followed then buckled his belt around his waist.

The Lord of the castle would be on a higher level and far away from the kitchen, away from the smells, heat and noise. He enveloped himself in invisibility and placed black upon black on Ral's beige coat. The two began the search for the upper levels of the castle and Lord Marko. Finding a set of stairs they ascended to the next level. Looking down the end of the hallway, Curry observed two guards at a door. This he felt was the Lord's bedchambers. A Lord who had abused so many people would think he needed guarding from retaliation.

Moving his hand staff to his other hand he lost the invisibility so Ral could see him make his hand motion to come to his side. Again Curry enveloped invisibility upon himself and Ral the two then approached the guards. The one on the right was sitting on the floor dozing and the one on the left was leaning against the wall with his back to them. Grasping the hand staff with the other hand, Curry enveloped deftness upon the guards. He knew that the heavy door would squeak when he opened it and didn't want to alert the guard who was awake. Carefully walking between them, He pushed the door open enough to peer inside.

Inside the room he observed a fireplace that held a small flame. There were two chairs carved of wood and covered in horsehair cushions. On the wall were drapes hanging next to the window and a rug on the floor. A sitting table had a brush, ribbons and a looking glass. Something about the items on the sitting table didn't seem right so he became extra cautious. Last of all was an occupied, four posted bed having a cloth canopy above it.

Only the rich or royalty had these canopies. Their purpose was to keep the droppings of roosting bats and birds from falling onto the bed.

Moving inside and closing the door, Curry moved the hand staff from hand to hand to removed the invisibility and deftness. Motioning Ral to the other side of the bed, Curry approached the near side. His Wizardry would be on one side and the other would be a full grown cave wolf. It was something he would not like see if he woke. A few feet away he saw something that made him pause, there was a chain on the floor. The chain was attached to the foot of the bed and it disappeared under the covers. Also there was the odor in the room, it didn't smell like a room that was occupied by a man. Looking closer in the dim light of the dying flames of the fireplace, he made out the features of a women with long blond hair. The items on the sitting table made sense now. He gazed closer and saw it was the same woman who he had seen earlier riding on the road with the four guards.

Pulling his hood over his head to hide his youthful appearance and to give a sense of fear, he enveloped the woman with immobility. Since it was impossible to injure anything of blood, he knew she could still breath and her heart would beat but be unable to speak or move. Reaching out Curry shook her and waited for her eyes to open. Waking to this dark apparition she had Stark fear in her eyes.

Using a deep voice, Curry said, "You will answer me truthfully or my wolf will soak the bed with your blood, do you understand?" When saying the last word he motioned Ral to stand on the bed and growl. That was all that was needed. Curry shifted the hand staff breaking the immobility and asked the woman her name.

Trembling she replied, "I am Lady Currant." Curry was running out of time, soon it would be daybreak and the castle's servants would begin working. He needed answers and needed them quickly.

Curry said "Tell me the truth or I swear by all of the auras I have sent to the void that I will hold your beating heart before your eyes." Pausing for effect he asked, "Why are you chained?"

She quickly replied, "Lord Marko chained me."

"Why?"

"He doesn't want me to tell what I know."

"What secret do you hold?" Curry asked

"He will kill me if I tell," she said becoming more frightened.

"So be it then," turning towards Ral, he motioned him to freeze and said, "Wolf, tear her throat out."

"No!, No! please I will tell, just call your off your wolf."

"Hold wolf, any lies or hesitation in answering me and I won't call him off next time."

With tears beginning to form at the corner of her eyes she said, "My lord and husband Lord Hart was murdered by his brother Lord Marko, then Lord Marko took the Keepership. As Lord Hart's wife I should have inherited the Keepership but Lord Marko claimed we wed and he took the rights of the Providence. No one knows that he murdered my husband. Since then I have been held prisoner either by personal guards or chained so I will not tell what he has done."

"Where is Lord Marko's room?" Curry asked.

"Why?"

"Wolf…"

"No, No please, it's the last room on the right as you leave." Curry told her to remain there quietly.

He turned to leave and thought, I will live longer by not being stupid, he again enveloped her with immobility and allowed it for one length of time. He then approached the bedchambers door. Enveloping the aura of sleep for a length of time through the door he heard the standing guard fall to the floor. Exiting quickly with Ral he moved to Lord Marko's door. Curry knew now that Lord Marko held the Providence in fear, no one would dare approach him as he slept. His door would be without guards and unbolted.

Walking quickly to the door he slowly pushed it open. Entering the room Curry saw the same items as Lady Currant's room. The only exception were the weapons and armor near the open window. Lord Marko was well prepared, long broad sword, two side swords, daggers and fighting axes.

Curry moved to the edge of the bed and positioned Ral on the other. Enveloping Ral in invisibility he felt that it would be more effective for an unseen terror to be in the room. He then motioned him to take and hold the Lord's throat. Gently Ral stepped upon the bed and moved towards Lord Marko's head. Leaning downwards he took Lord Marko's throat between his teeth.

Feeling the hot breath and sharp teeth on his throat Lord Marko awoke. Feeling and not seeing what was at his throat put terror into his heart. Seeing Curry's caped and hooded body, Lord Marko whispered though he pressure on his throat, "Who are you?"

Curry leaned close to his ear and whispered, "At this very moment, what is it that you want most?"

Lord Marko was silent, Curry reached across the bed and found Ral's leg. Placing his hand around his leg, he began squeezing. As he squeezed, Ral tightened the grip on Lord Marko's throat. When Curry heard Lord Marko's breath begin to struggle then stop, he released his grip on Ral's leg. Ral then allowed Lord Marko to breath again.

"I will not ask this of you again," Curry whispered. "At this very moment, what is it that you want most?"

In the barest of whispers, Lord Marko said, "To live."

"There are those in the Providence who have found you to be offensive and have asked me to present their proposal. Do you understand?"

"Yes," Lord Marko whispered.

"By the mid-day meal today your feet will not rest upon the land of this Providence. Do you understand?"

"Yes."

"By the supper meal today your feet will not rest upon the land of any Providence that borders this one. Do you understand?"

"Yes."

"Never again will your shadow fall upon this ground. If you feel this proposal is unacceptable then my friend will immediately escort your aura to the void. Do you understand?"

"Yes."

"What is your decision?" Curry asked.

Lord Marko was in a dilemma. He owned this Providence, had the title of Lord and had a future of wealth and power. If he remained here he knew he would die. If he left he would live. In desperation he looked around as best he could with the illumination of the candle at his bedside. With Ral holding his throat he was limited in his vision. He glanced at his weapons, the closed door with no guards outside and the caped figure above him. The candle bedside his bed did allow some light to penetrate to the face under the hood of the cape.

Inwardly Lord Marko smiled, he thought, this is just a mere child. He had dealt with older and better than this boy, he formed a plan.

"Please," Lord Marko said trembling and cowering before Curry, "what you have asked will be done, I will leave at once, please just let me live. I'll do anything just don't hurt me. Call off this beast at my throat and I will leave now. You have my word and my bond on it. Just release me and I will dress and leave immediately, please, please I beg of you."

Curry's ruse had worked. He didn't know if Ral would send Lord Marko's aura to the void if he was commanded to or not. Curry never wanted to find out. He knew he couldn't take another's life even if he wasn't in the Wizardry. Curry motioned Ral to release and move near the window next to the Lord's weapons. Ral still maintained his cloak invisibility.

Curry said, "Take to horse and make this Providence yours nevermore."

"Of course, I will obey at once." Saying that Lord Marco pulled his leg back and kicked Curry away knocking him to the floor and sprang upon him from the bed. Jerking the hood back he revealed Curry's face.

"How dare you, a mere child threaten me, the question is not if I will leave or not but how slowly you will die by my sword." Lord Marko turned and dashed to his weapons, reaching for his side sword he tripped over something unseen. Staggering he fell against the sill of the window and lost his balance. Grasping the drape next to the window to arrest his fall he fell over the window sill. He was held suspended for a moment by the drape then with a snap the mountings gave way from the mortar. A brief scream then a strange sound was heard as his body landed next to the castle wall.

Running to the window and peering down, Curry did not see Lord Marko's body. The only thing visible was the widening ripples of the shallow water of the moat. The force of his body hitting the mud, just under the water, sent him all the way to the bottom. Struggling as much as he could to save his life only resulted in him sinking deeper into the mud. The quieting of the ripples on the water showed he would never come to the surface again. Lord Marko's aura was now in the void.

Bile began to rise in Curry's throat, he had never seen anyone die before. He leaned against the wall and closed his eyes until his stomach calmed down. No one of Wizardry can directly injure anything of blood. It was by a stroke of luck that Curry had told Ral to stand next to the window, that resulted in Lord Marko falling.

Maybe Ral knew what was going to happen, maybe someone in the Wizardry told him to remain there, he would never know. When Curry was attacked, Ral did not come to his aid, he would never know why he remained next to the window. Ral may be more that just a cave wolf. Instead of Curry finding him wounded in the forest, maybe Ral was sent to find him.

Curry tried to end this without violence but Ral's position by the window ended that. Whether Curry could have stopped the Lord attacking him with a sword he didn't know. Ral had saved him from ever having to make that decision.

Returning to the Lady Currant's bed chambers with Ral, Curry released her from the immobility. Quickly he traced the chain from the bed post to her ankle. The key for the lock was nowhere to be found, it was probably with Lord Marko at the bottom of the moat. Curry searched his list of skills on how to remove the chain at her ankle. Fire, cold, hammer, saw, none of these, they would only injure the ankle. Curry thought and then tried something he had never attempted before. Concentrating intently on the chain Curry enveloped the chain with the aura of age. At first nothing happened, deeper he asked the aura. The chain then began to change in color, black of new oiled metal chain, to gray, to brown of rust. Flakes began to fall from the links. After a brief period the chain became dust and fell away from her ankle. Reaching down she began rubbing her ankle, then looked up at the hooded figure.

Pulling his hood back Curry exposed his youthful face.

"You are but a lad," she said. Then realization struck her, "Quickly I need to leave before Lord Marko awakes." Stepping to the floor she reached for her dressing ground and cinched the belt. Walking to her wardrobe she began gathering her traveling clothes. She chose clothing where she could straddle a saddle rather than ride it side saddle. Her interest was in speed not style and modesty.

"Wait," Curry said. "The threat to you is no more." He told her what had happened after he had left her immobile. "...and then he fell to his death my Lady, you are now the Keeper of the Providence." Bringing his fist to his chest he bowed his head. "You are now the Lady of the castle."

"I don't know who you are or why you came to my aid. Why did you do this?" She asked.

Curry said "I am a Searcher within the Wizardry, my name is Curry, My Lady. I was told to come to this castle and see if I could render aid. My intention was not to harm anyone, regrettably Lord Marko has died."

"Curry, you have avenged Lord hart's murder and released me from the torment of my husband's slayer. When they find Lord Marko missing the guards will sound the alarm, finding you they will think you had something to do with it and either they will follow you or kill you."

"I have no desire for title or wealth my Lady, and especially not my own death." Looking at the new Keeper of the Providence, he then said, "Lord Marko killed Lord Hart and claimed his throne, if Lord Marko advocates his throne and leaves during the night there would be no one, ever, to dispute your word. You will ascend the throne and become the Keeper of the Providence. Tell the castle that you were awaken during the night by Lord Marko and he advocated the throne because of the numerous death threats upon his life and he fled in the night. Those who followed him will then follow you, or they know they will be turned out of the castle or worse yet killed."

"Remarkable that one of such few years as you has such wisdom, yes that would work, that will work. "Thinking for a moment Lady Currant said, "I must satisfy my debt to you, how can I repay you? Ask and anything in my castle or in my Providence is yours, you are but to ask and the boon is yours."

Curry though for a moment and said "Two things my Lady, one, the Village of Marth is expecting an attack from the castle because I chased the guards away before they could burn the bridge." Holding up her hand Lady Currant said, "No harm will come to the village or any under my protection. Fairness will be upon all my domain." Seeing in Curry's face that this was acceptable she said, "And the second thing?"

"The second," Curry asked with a tiny grin, "do your bakers have the skills of pastries?"

Lady Currant gave a little laugh and said, "All you can carry Searcher, it is yours for the taking today, tomorrow and forever for as long as this Providence exists. It will be written so, in the chronicle's of the Providence of Toluc."

Curry said, "I will take my leave now before the castle turns out. Stand by your open door and wait for your guards to wake up. When they do, scream, shout and berate them for their incompetence as guards for allowing Lord Marko to enter and leave without their knowledge. They will spread the news that Lord Marko has left faster than a hawk on a dove.

Call the Master Guard of the Gate and demand an explanation of his men's unprofessional behavior and inadequate training. This will give you credibility as the Lady of the castle and new ruler of the Providence. Only the ruler would speak to him in such a manner.

Order him in front of his men to kneel unarmed and pledge allegiance to you or leave the castle forever. I bet a pouch full of rings he will kneel to the new Lady of the castle. If he accepts you as the ruler then the whole castle guard will also.

Lord Marko was the only one who knew of the chain and lock, so that will not be brought up by anyone."

Bowing again Curry said, "Rule justly my Lady." Motioning to Ral, the two companions left. The guards outside the door would sleep another few moments allowing Curry to leave and Lady Currant to prepare her speech.

Enveloping both himself and Ral in invisibility they went to the kitchen for the boon of free pastries and maybe a bit of mutton for Ral. A quick search found their reward. Moving quickly the companions then left the castle the same way they had entered to continue their journey.

Curry realized that when Warlick told him that a Searcher travels the whole country, this was to prepare him to gain as much experience as possible before being assigned as a Wizard for one of the Providences. Many challenges must be conquered before he would be ready, then again he may never be ready. Someday he would know, in time.

Curry had not slept since he arrived at Marth Village and was growing groggy. Up ahead they would find a shady area so both could rest and eat their treats. Later, he would decide what direction they would take, or Ary would.

CHAPTER 3
Scattering of Stones

Having levitated to a perch high in an Oak tree, Curry then enveloped invisibility and went into his intense sleep. Ral at the base of the tree was dozing in the coolness of the shade. Intense sleep gave Curry rest and made him alert but he never had any dreams.

Waking, he stretched, rubbed his eyes and began looking around. He felt it was better to know everything below before he levitated down. Seeing nothing out of place and Ral still sleeping, Curry lowered himself to the ground. Rubbing his knees then stretching his legs he slowly lost the tiny pin prick feelings in his legs. Sleeping on a tree limb did have its drawbacks but it was safe.

Looking about he saw an opening in the tree branches that gave a view of the blue sky. Running his fingers through his hair in an attempt to neaten it somewhat, he saw an unusual sight.

Something flew across the sky passing by the opening in the trees, Whatever it was it was very large. It appeared to be smaller than a Serpent but larger than any bird he had ever seen. "Come Ral," Curry called, and ran for the edge of the woods to try and get a better view. Breaking through the low brush at the edge of the field he scanned the sky. Ral trotted up next to him and he too began looking around. He didn't know why, he was just doing what the man child was doing.

In the distance Curry just made out the large flying creature and saw it was not flying, it was being carried. Six smaller flying creatures were carrying it through the air with ropes. In the Forest, just past the far side of the field, the flying creatures landed with their captive.

"Ral this is too unusual to let it go without a closer look," Curry said. Ral only stared at him and panted. Curry backed into the woods and turned to the right. He and Ral stayed just out of sight of the field so they could approach unobserved. It took a little over a length of time to approach the area where the flying creatures had landed. Curry motioned Ral to walk soft. He enveloped them with invisibility and they slowly entered deeper into the forest.

About thirty paces into the forest they were almost overwhelmed with a sickly sweet smell, almost like fermenting wine. Then they heard grunting sounds and the tearing of earth and brush. Dropping to his knees, Curry began crawling under some low bushes until he could get a clear view of where the noise was coming from.

The creature that had been carried by the flying creatures was a male wild boar. The entire area was covered with plum trees and the wild boar was tied by his hind leg to one of the trees. Many of the plums had lain where they fell an were in different stages of decay. The rotting fruit was the sickly sweet smell he had noticed. Over to the right was a large mound of leaves, it appeared they were used to cover something.

The most remarkable thing he saw were the creatures, they were Octals. Curry had heard about them but thought they were just a myth. The Octals were about the size of a two year old child. Each had wings similar to that of a bat that had the appearance of leathery skin stretched over their wing bones. They all had golden hair and the males had no facial hair. The male's skin was brown in color and the females were dark yellow. All wore a long tunics that had been cut in the back to allow for their wings. Since they had no means of making cloth, Curry felt they had raided the local clotheslines for their clothing. Tucked under their rope belts was a four pace long hemp rope and a small club. From the looks of the club it appeared to be fashioned from a pine tree lighter knot. It was heavy and would last forever.

He saw eight of the Octals, two males and six females. This was why they were called Octals. There were never more than eight of them in their nest. Curry would have left at this point but seeing the cruel way the boar was tied to the plum tree, he knew he would have to do something. He knew the boar was not being held there for food because there were no cooking pits or bones from any previous cooked boars.

Motioning for Ral to remain hidden and guard, he crawled backwards and moved to the left. Finding an opening in the bushes he pulled his hood over his head and removed the invisibility. Standing, he stepped into the clearing.

A female glanced up and saw Curry. She immediately screamed, "Ty!" One of the males looked at her, then followed her gaze until he saw Curry.

"To club!" he ordered. All of the Octals pulled their clubs and took to flight towards Curry. Flying straight at him, Curry immediately enveloped a wall of flash heating fire ten paces wide and ten paces high. The flash heating fire would only last two heartbeats and was more for effect than causing damage. Curry knew they would not come close enough to cause any injury to themselves.

Darting away from the flames the Octals hovered then slowly settled to the ground. Two Octals on each end pulled ropes from their belts and began twirling them over their heads. On the end of each rope was a noose that would grab and tighten should it land around his head or arms.

The one called Ty, took a step forward and said, "You are not of man, what are you?"

"I am of man but I have abilities not of man."

"Why have you invaded our nest?" Ty asked.

Looking towards the wild boar Curry said, "We of man do not torture animals of the forest. Animals of the forest do not torture animals of the forest. Why do the Octals punish the boar this way?"

Ty replied, "The boar protects our trees from creatures that would take our only food. We do not eat of the animals of the forest only the fruit. When the boar is too weak to guard our trees, we fly him into the forest and capture one to replace him."

"Do those boars you release, regain their strength?"

"Their life after we release them has no meaning to us. This is our only source of food and that is all that is important. Without it we will all die and the Octals would no longer exist."

Curry asked, "When the cold weather comes and the fruit stops growing why don't you die?"

Ty replied, "When the last of the fruit comes we take all from the trees and place it inside our nest over there." Ty motioned at the mound of leaves. "We feed on the fruit, gorging ourselves until it is all gone, then go into a deep sleep. The strongest eat the most and it results in one or two of the weakest shes ending up with little to eat. These weak ones die in their deep sleep."

"If they die, how do you have a nest of eight?"

Ty explained, "At the time of birthing, each female has one Octal. They are weaned early and grow quickly. Soon afterwards the offspring are forced to leave from our nest. They fly to another nest or begin their own nest near plum trees. Offspring from other nests are attracted to our nest because of the odor of the plums. Myself or Ja, the other male, picks the shes that are the strongest and the others are driven away. I have a bond with three and Ja has a bond with the other three. If I am short a she in my bond, I pick one. Likewise if Ja is short a she he will pick one."

"What of the dead Octals?" Curry asked.

Ty's arms dropped to his sides and his club fell to the ground. Looking at Curry with pain in his eyes he said, "The shes of my bond are more than just shes. I know what I will find when I wake from the deep sleep. I sometimes wish that it is I who does not wake. The shes are part of me and when I find them dead, part of me dies. It has been this way since the first eight formed the first nest, if I could change it I would but it is not possible. The sending of the offspring away is accepted way of life and none object to it. I never want to loose another she but it will happen again when the weather cools, and again and again." Ty folded his wings and slumped to the ground sobbing."

The attitude of the Octal nest changed suddenly. All knew of their future and none could hide their grief. Curry's intrusion into their nest meant nothing to them now. Curry's heart went out to these Octals. The pain they suffer each year upon awaking was too tragic for him to even fathom.

Looking around the area he saw the nest covered with leaves. Warm enough to withstand the coldest of Winters. The members of the Octals were in extreme emotional pain but they all looked healthy and strong. He could tell the females, shes as Ty called them, were close in their bonds with the males that had chosen them.

The wild boar had become quite in his captivity. He was rooting around and eating the fallen plums, apparently eating of the rotting plums agreed with him. Looking at the boar eating the spoiled fruit a small grin came across Curry's face. The grin turned into a wide smile. Sometimes the most obvious cannot be seen.

Looking at Ty sitting on the ground with his bond of three females sitting around him, Curry walked over to him and sat on the ground facing him.

"Ty, if you had food enough for the nest, that would last all through the cold weather, would it help?"

"Don't talk foolishness. Just look at the plums the boar is

eating, rotten. They will not last three arcs of the Sun before they turn to mush," Ty said in irritation.

Asking again, "Ty, if you had food enough for the nest, that would last all through the cold weather, would it help?"

"Yes, yes, if we had plums that could last, none would die in our nest, except from old age," Ty said with some sarcasm.

Curry said, "If I show you how to eat plums all year long will you release the boar and never capture another?"

"But what of the birds and creatures that will eat the plums?"

"They will not come to your fruit again," Curry said.

"If you can do this, we will never again take a boar, this I give my word as the head of our nest," Ty said.

"First gather river reed and some hemp to make string."

Ty spoke to Ja and he in turn talked with his bond. At once the eight lifted off and flew towards the river to gather the river reed and hemp. Curry looked around and found a patch of ground that had all day sunshine.

Hearing the sounds of flapping wings, Curry saw the Octals returning from the river with the reeds. Landing, the nest placed the reeds and hemp at Curry's feet.

Speaking to Ty and Ja, Curry asked, "May I instruct your bonds?" The two males were impressed that Curry would recognize their hierarchy in the nest.

"Instruct us all, we will either live or die by your instructions. The pain we suffer is unlivable," Ty said.

"First, Ty have two of your bond make hemp string. Then you, Ja and the rest cut the river reed the length that I am tall." Immediately the nest went to work.

Curry turned and walked through the bushes where Ral had been hiding. Removing the invisibility he reached down and petted Ral then motioned him to follow. The pair walked to an opening at the field and stopped. Curry sent Ary's name to the wind and waited.

Within a hundred heartbeats, Ary arrived. She was difficult to see because the Sunlight overpowered her glow. He whispered to her, she kissed his nose and flew away. "Come Ral, let me introduce you to some new friends."

Walking back to the nest, Curry stopped at a chest high bush and called to Ty, "Ty, I have with me a cave wolf. No one here will be harmed by the wolf, you have my word and bond on it. May he enter your nest?"

"One who can bring fire from the air, I doubt if you could surprise us anymore than what we are now. But I must ensure the safety of our nest. Prove he will not harm any of us."

Curry patted his thigh and Ral came and stood touching his thigh with his side. Then the two walked over to where Ty was standing. "Ty don't move." Curry motioned Ral to move forward, he walked over and stood nose to nose with Ty. Ral's head was twice the size of Ty's. Suddenly Ral licked Ty's face. Staggering backwards in fear he fell. Sitting up he looked around and began laughing.

"I have just been tasted by a cave wolf and lived. Yes, he is welcome to our nest."

Curry addressed the nest, "This is Ral, he has saved my life and I have saved his. As I am helping you he will also help if needed."

"Welcome Ral," The nest responded.

"Now to work," Curry said. "Take two reeds and have two shes hold them so they are holding opposite ends. Now lay another reed across the two they are holding and lash it tightly." Curry showed them how to make a square lashing. "Continue adding reeds until they completely cover the two reeds that the shes are holding." When they finished, Curry inspected their work. "This one is perfect, now have the bonds make more until you run out of reeds.

Ty, Ja and myself will gather stones while you lash the reeds. The three followed by Ral went into the field and began picking up stones the size of Curry's fist. After ten trips they had gather enough stones. Curry took one of the lashed reeds and placed it on the ground in the direct Sunlight. He place a stone under each corner so it was elevated above the ground. "Do the others like this one." Curry directed Ty and Ja. In about three lengths of time all the work was completed.

"Now bring some plums that are ready to drop from the trees." Two females flew to the plum trees and gathered ten plums. Curry took a piece of scrap river reed, split it twice and used the sharp edge to cut the plum and pull the pit from the center. He then laid the plum on the river reed drying rack. "Do this with all that will fall before you can eat them. The Sun will dry them and they will not rot. You will have plums for the entire cold weather. Make a pit in the center of your nest and store them there."

"What you have done is good but the boar must remain. He keeps the birds and creatures from the plums."

"The boar must be released, no bird or creature will ever bother your plums again." Ty and Ja looked into Curry's face and knew that what he said would be true, some how. Curry went to the center of the drying racks and drove a half pace long piece of river reed into the ground.

Standing, he walked towards the wild boar. As he approached the boar it began clicking his tusks and pawing the ground. Kneeling just out of reach of it's tearing tusks, Curry enveloped deep sleep upon him for one hundred heartbeats. Falling to the ground in sleep, Curry approached and untied the hind leg from the hemp rope. Standing he returned to the Octals and waited for the boar to wake. At a hundred heartbeats the boar opened his eyes, rolled onto his chest then raised himself to his feet. Glancing at the Octals, he turned and fled into the forest.

"How will you keep the birds and others away?" Ja asked.

Curry turned and faced the open field, "Patience Ja, have patience, you will know in time." The nest all stood in silence looking into the field and waited, for what, they didn't know. One thing they did know was that they would much rather have Curry as a friend than a foe.

Curry raised his hand to shield the Sun from his eyes. In the distance he saw something about the size of a dove coming towards them. The Octals saw it also and became afraid. The dove had no wings but it still flew. They began backing away and noticed that Curry didn't move. Two of the Shes, fearing the worst, fled into the nest of leaves to hid. The others waited between Curry and this approaching thing without wings. They felt that Curry would protect them.

The object came to within an arms length of Curry and stopped. Four tiny winged things carried a pouch made from a paw paw leaf. Curry reached out and took the pouch and then put his fist to his mouth. Each of the flying things went to his hand and looked like…like they were kissing his nose. Then they were gone.

Curry reached into the pouch and pulled out some blue moss from the tree that Ary sleeps in and placed it on the reed at the drying area. He then went to a tree in the center of the plum tree orchard and placed the remainder of the blue moss on that tree. No bird or climbing creature will come near these trees or drying plums because of the odor. It was offensive only to birds and crawling creatures not to Octals.

Curry said, "Your lives will be better now, I know the local boars will be."

Ty an Ja approached Curry, Ty said, "You have saved the lives of my bond and Ja's bond, how can we ever hope to repay you for this?"

Curry though for a moment and said, "Someday I may ask for your help, if I send a message would you come to my aid?"

Ty spoke with Ja then turned to Curry, "We will wait for your message. Our entire nest and all the nests along the way will respond. We will wait for your message for as long as we live and for as long as this nest exists."

Ty then asked Curry, "We ask one further thing from you."

"What thing is that?" Curry asked feeling a little defensive.

"Do us the honor by sharing our fruit and our nest for one night."

Smiling Curry brought his fist to his chest and bowed, "The honor would be mine Ty."

Ty walked towards Curry. When he was very close he told Curry to kneel. When he kneeled, Ty said, "If you ever come upon another Octal, say these words and he will know that you are one of us." Ty leaned over and whispered something into Curry's ear. Stepping back he turned and walked towards the plum trees. The other Octals followed him to begin picking ripe plums for drying. Now they had their Winter food and a new life.

As dusk came, Curry and the Octals entered the nest. Inside Curry saw that they had placed dozens of limber saplings into the ground forming a circle. The tops were all pulled to the center and joined with hemp. More thin saplings were interlaced in the sides and top before the whole dome was covered with leaves. Ral didn't care for the inside of the nest so he laid outside the entrance to protect Curry if needed. Curry laid at the point farthest from the entrance which was where the dominate male usually slept. A she from each bond passed out plums and all looked at Curry and waited.

"The first bite is yours." Ty said. Curry brought the plum to his lips and took the first bite. The males then took a bite of theirs, then the females. Even though Curry didn't have to eat, this was one of the most satisfying meals he had ever eaten.

Feeling secure in the nest with the Octals and having Ral at the entrance, Curry decided to have a normal sleep that night. This would be different from the intense sleep of three hundred heartbeats, instead he would sleep for many lengths of time. With intense sleep he didn't dream and he had really missed dreaming. Tonight he would close his eyes and let his mind go where it wanted to.

Curry thought to himself that these Octals were so happy right now, he just didn't have the heart to tell them that dried plums were called prunes. He was completely full, closing his eyes, Curry relaxed and surrendered to sleep.

"No more," he told the plump red haired lady with a flower in her hair. She continued to put more mutton and beef on his plate.

"Yes, here have some of this also," said a man in a floured apron as he placed roasted corn and fat fried corn on his plate.

"No, no I can't eat anymore. I'm too sleepy, I have to sleep." Laying his head on the table he fell asleep.

"Searcher awake, Searcher awake." They two kept calling over and over again.

"Searcher awake, Searcher awake." Curry immediately returned from depths of normal sleep and glanced about him. The Sunlight had begun to filter into the Octal's nest. He identified the voice, it was Ary.

"Welcome Ary, I hope all is well with you." Ary perched within his ear, hers was not a job of chit chat.

"To the Castle of Shan, through the Province of Catrel, journey you until the stones are scattered." With the sound of a hummingbird, Ary flew away showing the message was finished. Curry brought his fist to his lips allowing a perch for Ary. She stood on his finger, kissed Curry's nose and was gone.

Curry had learned that a Mintz never makes up a message, she delivers them from another a Wizard. This message was either from Warlick, the Wizard Master, or the local Wizard of the Providence. So far all had contained challenges or testing that he had to overcome without the advice of any of the Wizardry. Wisdom and correctness were the traits of the cape all Wizards wore.

Slowly he got to his hands and knees and crawled past the sleeping Octals, towards the entrance of the nest. Ral was laying on his stomach with his head up watching as Curry exited the nest. Motioning for silence, Curry stood and the two began walking towards the field. When they arrived Curry enveloped the finding of Castle Shan to the wind. To his left he saw the grass start to bend from an unseen force. Turning in that direction the companions began their next journey.

Ary said, "Until the stones are scattered," this puzzled Curry. As with all her messages, this would be revealed in time.

The pair had been traveling for several leagues of time. At times Ral would disappear and be gone from a few moments to several lengths of time. Returning, his muzzle would sometimes be bloodied from feeding. Ral did not have the restraints Curry did on injuring anything with blood. Coming upon a small lake within a gorge, Curry looked for a means of crossing.

Seeing a large wooden raft with hand rails floating at the shore, he investigated. When he approached he found it to be the ferry. The ferry had a sign nailed to the dock, "Rope Broken, gone for new one." The rope, as Curry knew, was tied to a stout tree on one bank, through two eyelets on the ferry itself and finally tied off at the opposite bank to another tree. By grasping the rope and walking the length of the ferry, it was pulled across the lake.

The walls of the gorge were too tall to climb and to circle around them would possibly add leagues of time to his journey. Seeing the solid wooden access gate to the ferry, Curry untied the bindings and took the gate to the edge of the lake. Calling Ral, Curry motioned him to lie on the gate. Reaching inside his belt Curry pulled the hidden cord free. Making sure the cord was still attached to his belt he tied the cord to the gate using a clove hitch. He knew this knot would not be effected by the water. It would continue to tighten and would be easy to release on the other side.

Motioning Ral to sit and freeze on the gate, Curry stepped to the water's edge. Enveloping the gate with levitation to a height of a fist distance above the water, Curry stood and watched Ral. Seeing that he would remain on the gate, Curry enveloped himself with his other hand to slow his metabolism. Slowing his need for air and blood flow, Curry emptied his lungs of air so he would sink to the bottom of the lake and began to enter the water. Pulling the cord attached to the gate where Ral rested seemed logical in this situation.

Deeper Curry walked pulling Ral behind him. The initial muck passed quickly until he reached the weed beds. Here walking became easier. One problem Curry foresaw was the possibility of running out of cord. Curry made a note to obtain a longer cord and place it in his cape somehow and also to devise some type of grappling device. His belt worked well enough at Lord Marko's Castle, rather Lady Currant's Castle now, but it may not suffice next time. Now he was confined to enveloping two skills. Maybe at a certain level of Wizardry, he wouldn't have these restrictions. For now he needed to concentrate only on enveloping two skills, anymore and accidents may occur. After a few moments the lake bed began to become steeper showing he was approaching shore.

A baker's dozen paces later...baker's dozen? Why would I think that? A dozen was twelve loaves, a baker's dozen was thirteen loaves. Once a Providence Keeper told the baker, who had been cheating him of bread, that if he ever came up short a loaf again the baker's head would replace the loaf. Since that day the baker always sent thirteen loaves in case one was lost. Curry filed this away with other puzzlements he had. When he meets Warlick again he might have it explained to him.

Breaking the surface, Curry was surprised that he was but a small distance off his mark. Turning around he saw that Ral was standing and wagging his tail, he was happy to see him come out of the water. Curry felt honored that anything would trust him this much. He hoped that he would never betray that trust. Curry stepped onto the dock and pulled Ral to shore. Nearing the shore Ral was anxious to leave the wooden gate. Tensing his muscles he leaped for the shore. The problem was the gate was levitated and when Ral pushed off, the gate was pushed back onto the lake leaving Ral suspended above the water, for half a heartbeat only. The gate had been levitated not Rals. He fell chest deep into the lake and scampered out, Curry couldn't help but laugh.

Looking at Ral, Curry said, "Ral both you and I have many things to learn. Soon you will become comfortable in being levitated, gates and other things will not be needed."

Curry enveloped, Ral in the aura of the absence of water. The water flew from Rals coat leaving him perfectly dry. Ral immediately spun around and snarled at whatever had caused the strange feeling of the water flying from his fur. Curry couldn't help but laugh again. He walked over and scratched behind his ear to calm him down. He then enveloped himself in the aura of absence of water and the water flew from his cape and tunic. He hadn't been taught this or other things he had done lately. It's as if Warlick taught him to count to ten and he was teaching himself to count higher. Curry knew he must only make small steps. Acquire the knowledge then master the skills.

"In time," Curry said to himself and Ral.

Curry pulled the gate to the dock and set it next to the other gate. Loosening the clove hitch he placed the cord inside of his belt. The two then continued on the road.

As they were walking he saw several plum trees. Looking closely he tried to see if he could see any Octals. He guessed he would always do that upon seeing any plum trees. On two occasions Curry glimpsed gnomes darting into brush thickets. Once he viewed a magnificent stag whose antler points equaled the number of his fingers. Strong of body and thick of neck the stag stood and looked at Curry. He knew that when cold weather arrives and the stag starts looking for a mate, his neck will almost double in size. Curry enveloped his aura and sent it to the stag. Clutching his fist to his chest he slowly bowed to the stag. The stag in turn, faced Curry and posturing, raised his antlers to their highest position. Slowly the stag turned and walked into the shadows of the forest. Curry knew that this would be a memory that he would recall for the rest of his life.

Just at dark, Curry smelled smoke of campfires and faint sounds of talking and laughter. Motioning Ral to avoid this area, he moved closer. Soon pinpricks of light coming through the branches of the trees turned into campfires. Closer he came until he could distinguish the people sitting around the fire. Curry learned it was better to find your foe then for your foe to find you. The question now was if these people were friends or foes. Babies and children were about, clean, well fed and they all seemed happy. Several dogs were also about, gnawing on bones that had been pulled from the stew pot.

A dog in this country was a requirement for sensible travelers. He could be trained to hunt rabbits for the traveler's meal. Smaller prowling animals that raided the food bundles, he could run off and the larger ones he would alert the camp of the danger.

Curry knew he bore a scent unknown to these dogs and when the wind shifted in their direction they would alert the camp. Enveloping the barest hint of the odor of a skunk, he sent it into the wind. The odor, so faint that it would not be noticed by the people but enough to desensitize the dog's sharp nose. It was an old hunting trick that he hoped would work here.

Into the firelight walked a man leading a horse loaded with trading wares.

"Welcome Tom," a seated man named Krik greeted the man leading the horse.

Tom drew deeply on his clay pipe, released the smoke and replied, "To all a safe night and may many friends have you all."

Kirk asked, "You close the drawbridge tonight Tom?"

"I, that I did, I was the last one ordered to leave the castle tonight, then they raised the drawbridge,"

Curry said to himself, ordered to leave? Castles with their guards were know to provide a safe haven to travelers and villagers. Within the walls were inns to sleep, fresh well water, taverns to eat and a traveler's hut. At worse a trader could sleep under his wagon of wares, as was custom to protect them from theft and be could stable his horse at the livery. This was the information that Curry was looking for. There was some kind of a problem at the Castle and now, whatever the problem was, he had to investigate it. All he had to do now was find out what the problem was.

Quietly Curry melted into the darkness. At the place where he first smelled smoke he found a tree for his intense sleep. For the rest of the night he would again recite his list of auras and ponder his future at the castle tomorrow.

Leaving Ral in the woods, Curry walked the road towards the castle. He timed it so that he would reach the castle just prior to midday so as to mix in with the traders and travelers. Approaching the Castle Shan, he noticed that it was of the same size and construction as Lady Currant's castle. He noticed that every wagon, cart and person was stopped and searched. Tucking his hand staff into the side of his belt, He crossed the draw bridge.

Two jovial and smiling guards stopped Curry and asked, "Welcome traveler, have you journeyed far?"

Curry responded, "Yes, I have passed through two Providences to reach here."

"Excellent," the larger of the two guards said, "My Lord enjoys hearing of the experiences of travelers. The Keeper of the Providence, Lord Shan, has one commandment my young traveler, no weapon shall enter these walls. This is ordered to prevent any tragic accidents between two hotheads. Only guards bear weapons inside the gate."

"Of course, I understand, I bear no weapon, not even a dagger," Curry said.

"Would you please open your cape so that I may see traveler?" Curry spread his cape and the guard looked first on one side then the other. Quickly glancing at the smaller guard he brought his open hand to his breast and bowed saying, "He is free to pass." This alone should have made Curry wary. No one issues such a salute with an open hand it was always a closed fist. The smaller guard said, "My Lord is now holding court in the great hall, welcoming all travelers and hearing of their exploits. Afterwards a great banquet will be held. Would you please allow my men to escort you before Lord Shan?" The banquet had no appeal to Curry, since he did not eat, but he knew that a visit with the Lord may answer some of his questions.

"Off we go then," Curry said. The smaller guard motioned to the guards leaning against the winch that raised and lowered the drawbridge. These two guards escorted Curry across the castle court yard. Their actions were lax in military bearing in that they did not maintain hold of their scabbard side swords and looked at each other as they spoke instead of observing the goings on about them.

Entering the great hall, Curry observed a massive fireplace two paces wide. Come Winter it would barely heat a room this size. The stone walls would actually pull the heat from your body. Only those closest to the fire would gain any benefit and that would only be half the benefit. A fire needs air to burn and a burning fire pulls air towards it. If you face the fire your back freezes from the breeze moving towards the fire and your face burns from the heat.

Tapestries covered the walls from ceiling to floor. Tables had been laid for a midday feast which put Curry at ease. It would seem his suspicions were not warranted. A traveler was speaking to the Lord of the castle as he entered. Those in attendance, being of about twelve in number, listened intently as the speaker described his travels. Finishing his story the Lord pounded his armrest stating, "Excellent! Excellent! Oh that I may travel as I did in my youth, your stories paint a picture of not only my Provenience but of those surrounding me. Thank you for sharing your story and please partake of the table behind you." The traveler brought his fist to his chest, bowed to the Lord then went to the table of food. The two guards escorted Curry before the Lord.

"From what Providence have you come traveler?" Lord Shan asked.

Suddenly for no reason at all a name came to Curry's mind,

"Shinning Providence, my Lord." He wondered why that name came so easily to his mind. He would think on it later, for now he had to deal with Lord Shan.

"Excellent!" Lord Shan shouted, "You two guards," motioning at the back of the hall, "bring a chair for my guest, I wish him to be relaxed for I do not want his stories rushed." The two guards brought the heavy chair forward and stood behind Curry. "Sit it down, Sit it down," Lord Shan ordered impatiently. When the chair was dropped the guards attacked. Two guards grabbed Curry's right hand and two grabbed the left pulling violently stretching his arms to their limits. A fifth guard rushed forward and snatched Curry's hand staff from his belt and took it to Lord Shan.

With his hand staff taken and his arms spread Curry could not envelope anything to free himself.

"Shackles and beam!" Lord Shan shouted. A guard brought a set of wrist shackles with a chain attached to each and two other guards brought a wooden beam, two hands wide by two hands wide and a pace and a half long. The shackles were locked around each wrist then two guards held each chain preventing Curry from moving either hand. The wooden beam was laid on the floor behind Curry, he was carefully laid on the floor so his arms ran the length of the beam. The chains were pulled tighter and strong spikes driven into the chain links preventing Curry from any movement. It was impossible to even call his hand staff to him.

Looking down on Curry, Lord Shan said, "Searcher, Searcher, Searcher, apparently your training has been somewhat lacking. I mean, not even a halfhearted challenge. I don't know who you are and it really doesn't matter but I know what you are." Walking to a wall covered by a tapestry, Lord Shan pulled it to the side revealing a terrifying sight to Curry. Mounted on the wall were two Wizardry walking staffs and four Searcher hand staffs. "You seem somewhat nervous lad, as you should be. Wizardry is a curse upon my Providence and my country. As you can see, I have taken steps to stamp out this cursed practice." Lord Shan continued on, "The Providences are for the Keepers to rule not for some meddling spell casters to interfere with. Yes these staffs were taken by me and yours will be added. Your future is, well let's say, it's somewhat bleak, why do you think they need new Searchers?" Lord Shan asked, "They die! In the morning your head will float in my moat and your body will fertilize my fields." With a final command Lord Shan said, "Remove him to the lower cells, call the masons and have them mortar his arms to the beam." Laughing Lord Shan added, "Have the executioner prepare his axe."

Curry was carried down winding steps to the lower cells. Into one he was taken and laid on the floor. Shortly two masons came in carrying buckets of fresh mortar and began toweling the mortar, covering his hands and arms up to his neck. The mortar set quickly preventing Curry from even opening his hands. Seeing he was without any possible movement the guards left saying,

"Enjoy the evening young Searcher, it's your last."

Curry pondered his problem, six of the Wizardry have been killed here and two of those were full Wizards. It was impossible to envelope anything or even call his staff. His position looked totally hopeless. Curry was on the verge of accepting his fate as the other six probably had done when he remembered something from his training with Warlick. Closing his eyes he said, "Ary, I need help." Twice Curry said this to the wind then waited. In the time that it would take to eat an apple, a small spark of light flew through the high barred smoke window. The smoke window was installed to allow smoke from heating and cooking fires to escape.

Coming to rest in Curry's ear he heard a voice ask, "Searcher, you called me?"

"Yes Ary, as you can see my arms are frozen and I cannot defend myself, I need help." Buzzing away from his ear to his cheek, Ary stood on his cheek and kissed his nose and was gone in an instant. Curry called after her, "Where are you going, I need help!" The Mintz did not return. Was this how it was with the others? Abandoned by even his own Mintz and defeated in the end. Curry thought back to the first night he met Warlick. What had he been taught and what had he learned in his travels could he use to free himself? Nothing, not a thing came to mind. Curry began to recite the auras to take his mind off his situation. Half way through the second set of auras Ary returned and again entered Curry's ear.

"Oh Ary, I'm so glad you have returned, can you help me?"

Ary replied, "Kiliac eats branchets, be patient."

Curry searched his memory for branchets. Then he remembered that it was a poisonous plant like a cabbage the size of his fist to the size of his head. Eating it resulted in certain death. Placing it in a pool of water would kill the fish but the flesh of the fish still could be eaten. In a flash it came to him, the only thing that could eat branchets and live was a dragon.

A dragon had two stomachs and each had its own gullet. One was for food where the dragon would consume meat and large fish and the other was for eating branchets. When the branchets reached the second stomach it mixed with the digestive acids and formed a gas. When the dragon belches, the gas meets the fresh air and instantly bursts into flames.

Suddenly Curry heard shouting come through the barred smoke window. He could almost make out the words when a rampart guard began to hammer a gong. The hammering was not done casually but done in a desperate act, an act of fear. The word spread quickly, even to the guards serving in the lower cells. "Dragon!" the cries came down the passage. All the guards ran to the ramparts to fight the winged beast.

Kiliac from nose to tail was twenty five paces long. The head was covered in shimmering aqua colored scales the size of your closed hand. Both eyes were yellow with red elliptical pupils. The teeth were of ivory and would reach from your elbow to the tip of your middle finger. The underside of the wings was made of leather like skin the color of dark yellow and outside was of over lapping scales of dark green. The whole body was covered in scales the size of three spread hands, its color was blackish blue with dark yellow stripes. The rear feet had claws the size of a forearm and the front feet had curved talons a half pace long.

The dragon had been seen before but only at a great distance and only briefly. Occasionally a cow would turn up missing but never had the dragon come towards the castle. This time the dragon's objective was the castle. The archers armed with long bows and cross bows made ready to fight off the dragon. The dragon circled the castle once, then again.

Several archers made feeble attempts to hit the dragon but the distance was too far and too high. With a half scream and half bellow the dragon swooped into the castle court yard.

Archers let their shafts fly. The metal tipped arrows hit true their mark but the scales of her hide deflected them easily. Though the arrows did no harm, they did aggravate Kiliac who lived in the Caverns of Sulferic. Turning her head she released a stream of fire enveloping all on the ramparts. The guards and the few wooden supports burst into flames. The screams of the dying guards and the smell of the seared flesh was over powering.

In a final defensive act the horsemen of the gate charged with pikes, only to meet the same fiery fate. The courtyard was littered with bodies of men and horses slowly being consumed with fire. Kiliac cocked her head first one way then the other, seeing no further threat she walked to the wall next to the great hall and began clawing at the massive support stones.

Curry felt the shock waves through the ground as the stones were being dislodged by Kiliac. The dust from the breaking mortar began to drift into the lower cell. Suddenly a stone was pulled from the wall flooding the cell with sunlight. More stones were removed until Kiliac could place her massive head into the cell.

Gingerly she grasped the mortared timber in her destructive jaws and lifted Curry up and into the courtyard. Taking Curry's encased right arm, Kiliac slowly crushed the mortar. Adjusting her position she then took the timber in her jaws and crushed the timber freeing Curry's arm and hand.

Instantly Curry called out for his hand staff. In the great hall his hand staff flew from the trophy wall of the Wizard staffs and Searcher's hand staffs and ricocheted against walls and doors seeking a path to the Searcher. Finally it smashed through a window and entered the courtyard. The breaking window caught Curry's attention and he saw this hand staff speeding towards him. Grasping his staff Curry enveloped aging on both of the shackles, in seconds they turned to rust and fell away. Kiliac released Curry's left arm from the mortar and Curry jumped up and ran to the doors of the great hall.

"No one will make a trophy out of any Wizard's staff!" Curry swore. Charging the tapestry covered wall, Curry grabbed the tapestry and ripped it from its mountings. He then began to remove the staffs.

Hearing a scream from behind him, he turned to be confronted by Lord Shan charging full speed at him with his side sword drawn. Without thinking Curry enveloped Lord Shan in levitation to a height of one pace. Curry fell flat on the floor to avoid the swinging sword blade, Lord Shan passed directly over his head, just out of the striking distance of his sword.

The speed of his charge plus the levitation caused Lord Shan to float towards the window broken by Curry's hand staff. Screaming curses, Lord Shan passed directly through the window into the courtyard. Curry tried to pass the hand staff to his other hand so as to cancel the levitation so Lord Shan would fall to his death but the instantaneous pounding in his head and chest stopped him. A Wizard cannot injure anything of blood. He had to leave the staffs and go into the court yard and deal with Lord Shan in another manner. Bolting for the door Curry suddenly halted when he heard the snapping of teeth, then a crunch.

Rushing to the window, Curry looked into the courtyard. All he saw was a sword lying on the ground and Kiliac making chewing motions. The dragon did what Curry could not do, she ended the threat to the Providence.

Curry returned to the trophy wall and secured the staffs. He then went to the abandoned courtyard and approached the dragon Kiliac. Bringing his fist to his chest and bowing he enveloped his aura towards Kiliac, thanking her for what she had done.

Curry began hearing noises within his head, it began as a humming type of a pulsating sound. The pulsating noise became slower then began to form into words. Curry realized that he had just been mentaled by Kiliac. Warlick had explained to Curry at their first meeting that mentaling was a way for unspeakers or different species to communicate. This was done primarily between man and beast.

"Searcher, I have come to your aid as your Mintz asked. I have honored the oath between I and Olen the Master of all Wizards," Kiliac continued on, "I do protect onto you, you do protect unto I."

Kiliac mentaled Curry the story of her species. "Dragons are only females, at twenty years of age they lay one egg and it takes twenty years to hatch. Twenty years after hatching the mother dies and the process continues. As you see there are never more than two dragons alive at one time.

In generations past Olen the Master of all Wizards came upon a dragon's egg. Gnomes were taking clubs to the egg to destroy the line of dragons. Olen enveloped fire around the egg to frighten the gnomes away. When my foremother returned and saw what had happened she made an oath with Olen. Anytime she was asked for help, she or one of her line would help. In return Olen had a Guardian Wizard watch over her egg within the caverns of Sulferic and to insure there was always an ample supply of branchets for fire breathing.

Olen had the gnomes, who were trying to destroy the egg, dig a cave to house the egg and the Guardian Wizard. Yearly the Guardian Wizard is replaced by another Wizard, who assumes the title of Guardian Wizard, so that first may go and serve a Providence.

Curry mentaled Kiliac for two favors. First was that this was a place of evil and must be destroyed. All the guards were either killed or fled into the forest. Take the stones and scattered them so it will never be built again. Second take the Wizard's staffs and Searcher's staffs to the Caverns of Sulferic for the Guardian Wizard to safe keep. "Please allow me one moment before you begin," Curry mentaled. He disappeared into the castle and returned carrying a long length of cord, a two prong fork and a bulging cloth bundle.

Moving to a hillside nearby, Curry called Ral and together they munched on the sugar pastries he took from the castle in the bundle. Curry was truly humbled by the power of Kiliac. Digging and pulling with her front legs she pulled the massive stones from the parapet to the ground. Reaching down with her jaws, she grasped each stone and snapping her head to the side, she released them. Some flew as far as sixty paces. After the wall was taken down and cast away, Kiliac began on the castle itself. She would pull with her front legs and push those stones away with her rear feet.

After flinging the last stone, Kiliac squatted and relieved herself. No animal or man would come and live at any place marked by a dragon. Never would this land see another castle. Curry's last view was of Kiliac winging away with the six staffs clutched in her talons to her home at the Cavern's of Sulferic.

Ary's message, 'journey you until the stones are scattered,' was clear now, as all her messages were, in time.

CHAPTER 4
Path of Vines

Days passed as Curry and Ral wandered the Provenience. When they were not on a journey they wandered. No destinations or time restraints, they could linger at their leisure. No messages from Ary had been received so the two relaxed.

Curry sat on the ground under a tall Cypress tree. He watched as Ral snapped at flies as they circled him attracted to the drying blood from his last meal of rabbit, gopher or muskrat, whichever was the slowest.

Curry was bending the tines of the two prong fork that he had taken from Shan Castle. One tine to the left and one to the right, bending them until they almost pointed towards the handle. This would be used as a miniature grappling hook, should the need arise. Considering his pass exploits, it probably would be. Then taking the cord he tied a bowline knot to the end of the handle. Curry knew that this knot would never loosen. The cord attached to the fork was three paces long, the additional cord that he could attach, if longer length was needed, was five paces long. The longer one he coiled into one pace loops. He ran the looped cord up one sleeve across the inside of the back of his cape and down the other sleeve. Should he need it, all that was required was to reach up his sleeve and pull the running end and attach it to his belt cord holding the modified fork. The cord with a fork attached was tied to his belt with a slip knot. Secure enough to hold tight but able to be released quickly with a jerk on the running end.

Having finished with his cord he sat and practiced enveloping acorns and having them move. For now the only items he could move were small ones. First he was able to move them to the left then the right. As he gained proficiency he could lift them and drop them on certain objects. On a leaf here and a stump there. With his confidence and skill increasing he was able to cast an acorn a great distance. By enveloping he not only cast the acorn but was able to guide it accurately to its target. Like the dagger that a guard carried, Curry knew he may never need this skill but the ability was there if a situation required.

Boring with this he propped his chin on his hands and watched Ral's amusing antics as he tried to catch the flies. As he watched suddenly he heard the buzz of a hummingbird. Smiling he knew that Ary was approaching. Steadying himself, he felt Ary stand in his ear canal.

He waited for her message but all he could hear was her breathing and it seemed labored. Apparently she had flown a great distance and was catching her breath. Straining he just could make out her words.

"Searcher, down the path of vines, the stag you will aid." Curry brought his fist to his lips where Ary could land on his forefinger and kiss his nose before she left. He waited then felt a light tap on his shoulder. Looking at his shoulder he saw Ary had fallen to his shoulder and was struggling to stand. She then fell and began sliding off of his shoulder towards the ground. He immediately brought his hand around and caught her before she hit the ground. Holding her close to his face he saw she was unconscious.

He began to panic, his Mintz was sick or hurt and he didn't know what to do for her. He needed help from someone and needed it quickly. Laying her on his knee he took his hand staff in both hands and enveloped to the wind, "Ary needs help, Ary needs help." He hoped the call would reach someone of the Wizardry.

He sent his aura into her to let her know he was trying to help. He then began sensing her aura. Her aura was so small and faint that he couldn't sense what was wrong with her. All he knew was that it was slowly leaving her and there was little left of it.

His eyes began to tear, Ary's tiny aura was slipping away and entering the void and he couldn't stop it. Think...think what would I do for anyone else? Grabbing his hand staff he enveloped her with the slowing of her metabolism to a point that she was just this side of the void. If she were bleeding inside it would slow the flow of blood, beyond this he was helpless and afraid. All he could do was sit and watch this tiny figure in his hand.

Curry observed she had long hair that reached almost to her waist. The color was halfway between pewter and silver. A single strand from the tail of a white horse was wrapped around her waist making a belt to hold a tiny dagger. That may explain why a horse is always swishing its tail.

The dagger had master workmanship. It's hilt and guard were of gold and the blade was made of silver. The doubled edged blade, as his nose reminded him, was razor sharp. This strand of horse hair also held a tiny skirt of daisy petals to her waist. Glancing at Ral, Curry saw his interest in Ary. Smiling Curry thought of the surprise Ral would encounter should he snap at Ary. Curry enveloped Ral with his aura and presented his feelings for Ary. Ral looked into Curry's eyes and he knew that Ary would never be harmed by Ral. In fact Ary now had a new protector, her own cave wolf, but there was nothing either of them could do to help her now.

Curry heard a loud humming sound and looked up from Ary and saw six Mintzs speeding towards him. The closest one flew straight to his ear and asked, "What happened Searcher?"

"She came to me and collapsed, I slowed her metabolism and that was all I could think to do."

"Wait," The Mintz ordered.

The Mintz flew to Curry's hand and joined the other Mintzs. Each began feeling Ary's arms, legs and body for injury. They lifted her eyelids then smelled her breath. Quickly the six held a discussion then looked at Curry. Then five of the Mintzs looked at the six one and waited. The six one looked at Curry, hesitated then flew to his ear.

"Searcher, Ary has been poisoned."

"Poisoned!" He shouted.

"Quite, speak softly, we have tiny ears. Yes she has been poisoned. Near our blue moss tree is a patch of honeysuckle vines. Sometime during the night something or someone evil came and poisoned the honeysuckle. As a treat to ourselves we cut the base of the flower and drink the sweet nectar. We didn't know Ary had drank of the nectar then left to give you a message. Olen sent a sister Mintz to tell us that the honeysuckle had been poisoned. That was when we heard your call to the wind."

"Can you help her?" he asked.

"No we can't," hesitating she added, "but you can, it may be at a price you can't afford."

"Anything, tell me and I will do it."

"Be warned, this is Wizardry poison. The curing of one may send the other to the void. Think carefully Searcher you may die saving her, is it worth it? You were chosen to become a Wizard one day. Who is more important, you or Ary?"

Without any hesitation he said, "Quickly do what is needed." The Mintzs picked up Ary and hovered in the air.

"Lie on the ground and pull you tunic away from your neck."

Immediately he laid on the ground and pulled the collar of his tunic down. The Mintzs then flew to his chest and carried Ary to his neck. One of the Mintzs told him that the poison had to be drawn from her through her skin into his and at the point where his heart beats the strongest.

They placed her in the groove between the two muscles of his neck where the beat of his heart was the strongest. The six gently pushed her down to make the best contact possible.

"Remove the slowing of metabolism Searcher." Immediately he obeyed. "Now envelope the speeding of metabolism to hasten the removal of the poison." Again he obeyed.

He slowly began to feel dizzy and developed a queasiness to his stomach. As the moments passed it became worse and worse. The forest was spinning and his stomach had horrible stabbing pains. Never had he ever felt pain like this before. He could only imagine what Ary had felt.

"Searcher you are becoming ill, do you want us to stop?"

"No, save Ary."

"Later it may be too late to stop. Are you sure?"

"Save Ary." He said weakly because his strength was leaving him.

"So be it Searcher."

Curry's conscience began to fade in and out as the poison entered through his skin and into his bloodstream. Slowly he glanced over and saw Ral watching him. "You are a good companion and we shared many good times and adventures, someday we will…," he said then a hole of blackness opened up and pulled him down into the depths.

He felt a cool breeze against his face and heard a voice calling to him. Looking about all he could see was darkness. Someone kept calling him over and over again. He was so tired all he wanted to do was sleep. "Leave me alone and let me rest," he said to the voice. Again the voice kept calling, "Searcher, Searcher come back."

Opening his eyes he saw all of the Mintzs hovering around his face cooling him with their wings. Reaching up he felt his neck. "Ary?"

"She rests yonder Searcher, she lives and you too but both of you barely escaped the void. You need to rest now."

Rolling over he saw Ary next to him sleeping on a leaf. Feeling dizzy he fell back and waited for his head to clear. Slowly he rolled over and sat back against the log. The thought of standing was out of the question for now. Raising his hand he motioned for Ral to guard him. In this condition of weakness he was having problems just trying to stay awake.

Looking over at the Mintzs kneeling around the leaf Ary was on, he saw one talk to the others then all but one flew away. The remaining one flew to him and entered his ear.

"Searcher, Ary is tired and we will take her to her nest so she can recover. The others have gone to obtain a way to carry her there. You knowingly offered up your life for one of my sisters and it will never be forgotten. The tale of this will be spread to all of the blue moss trees and to Olen. We of the Coven of Mintzs will grant you one boon.

"I didn't do this for a boon or any reward, I did this for my…" Two words entered his mind. The first word lacked the definition he needed and it had no heart in it. The second gave him satisfaction. "She and Ral are not my companions, they are my friends. I would never do what I did for a companion, only for a friend. No, I need no boon but I thank you anyway."

"Searcher, not even a Master Wizard can refuse a boon from the Coven. Coven boons are rarely given. The last boon given was two lifetimes ago. We will send this tale to all of the blue moss trees and ask what boon to give, then we will seek you out. A Coven boon is a gift we give to you, not one you ask for.

The hum of wings got his attention. Looking up he saw the Mintzs coming carrying a lily flower and some dark long objects. Three Mintzs landed and stood the Lily flower next to Ary. Two others pulled their daggers and slit the long dark objects. They were cattails bulbs and when they were slit the white soft floaters exploded out. They gathered up the floaters and stuffed them into the flower to make a soft bed for Ary. Two lifted Ary and placed her into the flower. In a coordinated effort, five others took the edges of the flower and lifted off heading for the blue moss tree.

The remaining Mintz came to his ear. "Searcher, Ary will recover soon thanks to you and your illness will also pass. Answer Ary's message when you are well and able, until then I will watch over you and Ral.

Curry couldn't argue with her if he wanted to. He looked to the right at Ral, then slide down the side of the of the log to the ground and was instantly asleep.

The Mintz left his ear and hovered in front of his face after he collapsed. She then pulled her dagger and holding it by the blade she held its hilt towards him. A red glow formed around the hilt then went out and covered his body. Immediately sweat began to leave the pores of his skin. "Come three mornings from now the poison will have left your body with the sweat. I thank you for Ary and for the Coven. Sleep well young Searcher."

The Mintz then flew over to Ral and hovered in front of his nose for twenty heartbeats. No words were passed or motions made, then she flew up and disappeared into the tree branches. Ral looked at Curry's sleeping form then walked over and laid his head on Curry's leg and waited.

Sunrise the third day brought Curry from his sleep. Slowly he stood on shaky legs as Ral watched. The poison had been hard on him and Ary. Now he needed to travel to answer Ary's message. He was weak but the strength was coming back quickly. Quick healing was one advantage of being in the Wizardry. Looking about he found his hand staff and enveloped the finding to the path of vines. He took one last look around. He didn't see the Mintz who watched over him but he knew she was near. Reaching down he patted Ral and they began walking.

Traveling quickly, the pair followed the enveloped signs of the finding to the Path of Vines. With the other messages there was a definite location either a castle or a village. Path of Vines was very vague. This journey's end had no end in sight. Remembering his teachings he recalled, acquiring knowledge was not the same as acquiring skills. Everything happens in time. He would arrive at the Path of Vines in time, so why not enjoy the journey.

Along the enveloped trail Curry met other travelers. A nod here, a spoken word there, the leagues slipped by. He passed ponds, fields of green and cleared and mature forests. Passing through a thick stand of trees with a ground covering of laurel, he felt the coolness of the shade surround him.

Suddenly without warning Curry was struck on the side of his head. Feeling his head he found a lump begin to form. Looking about he could not see his assailant. Then his ears picked up a slight crunching of leaves and a giggling sound. Ral charged into the laurel after this unseen attacker only to find the thicket empty. With a yelp he sprung from the thicket, he too had been struck in the side. Suddenly Curry was hit in his shoulder with an acorn. Immediately he enveloped all of the acorns within ten paces and levitated them two paces above the ground. Curry thought, you can't hit me with an acorn if you can't reach one.

An outburst of a squeaky, screaming voice emitted from the edge of the thicket.

"Curse you, curse you, leave me be. I ain't did you no harm, let me go," the voice wailed. Approaching carefully Curry and Ral discovered a gnome hanging in midair from his belt.

When Curry levitated all the acorns he also levitated the acorns that the gnome had in placed in his pouch. Looking on the ground under the gnome Curry saw two leather strips tied to a small pouch, the gnome's sling. That was how he cast the acorns at Curry and Ral. Retrieving the sling, Curry began questioning the gnome. "Let me go!, let me go!" the gnome yelled growing louder and louder.

"Silence!" Curry ordered, but to no avail. It only encouraged the gnome to increase his pitch and he began swinging his arms and legs in a tantrum. Curry circled the suspended gnome. As he did so the gnome always kept turning his face away so he could not look into his eyes. Suddenly an old folklore tale came back to Curry. If you lock eyes with a gnome he cannot walk away until he grants you a boon. Curry grasped the gnome's collar and forced him to look into his eyes. The gnome suddenly relaxed and became silent. Curry removed the levitation and lowered the Gnome to the ground.

Having never seen a gnome up close, Curry observed that he had a very bulbous nose and his eyes were all black with no white around them. Above his eyes were very large, bushy eyebrows and his large ears had small amounts of hair growing out of the canals and along their edges. His teeth were blunt since he only ate nuts and berries and didn't need tearing teeth for meat. His teeth were stained yellow from the use of his clay pipe that he had tucked into his pouch along with the acorns. Upon his head he had shoulder length matted brown hair and the only facial hair he wore was just on his chin. Apparently grooming was not high on a gnome's list of things to do. His height was a mere half pace and his clothing was made up of different pieces of material sewn together to make a set of breeches and a vest. He wore short boots on his broad feet and had tied a leather band about his head. Last of all was a tiny saw tucked into his belt.

Curry asked "What is your name gnome?"

The gnome said "A boon, a boon that's all you'll get from me, ask it now and let me be a going."

Thinking for a moment Curry said, "The boon I ask is for you to answer all my questions with truth."

"Fer how long do I have to answer, fer I got things to do?"

"For as long as the Sun shines today, gnome."

"Done, be a askin fer dark comes soon."

Curry asked, "What is your name?"

The gnome replied, "I ain't no name, when I be changed into

a gnome, the name I had be lost, you can call me whatever you want, fer I can't choose a name."

Curry said. "Since we do have one thing in common, I will call you Acorn."

The gnome smiled, "Good as any, it do seem to fit me well." puffing out his chest he said, "I now haven a name, I'm be Acorn!"

"Why did you attack me?" Curry asked.

"Some time back there be three of us who camped and lived in a cave near de woods a league North of here. We needs be simple, we hunted and trapped for our meat, picken what fruit we wanted and what we didn't hunt or pick we took from those who come through the woods."

"Bandits?" Curry asked.

"Yes," Acorn answered. "I be laying on the trail with a broken arrow tucked betwixt my arm and side to look like I be wounded by a bandit. When the travelers they be stoppen to help, my two friends would be a pouncen on them taking what they be wanten."

"One day we be seeing a caped figure with his hood pulled down, acoming down the trail. Taking my position we be waiten. The figure come and stopped two paces away and just be standin there. I begged fer help, fer my fake injury, but ain't nothin the figure he be speakin. I waited fer my friends Krale and Tiny to pounce but they be holdin back."

"The figure tossed his cape backen over one shoulder and said, 'Your aura does you shame, stand and drop the arrow it deceives me not.'

"I stood and throwed the broken arrow aside. The figure he be waven his stick at me and a covered with a pitch black cloud was I. When the wind it blew the cloud away, I be as you seein me now. The figure be goin on so I turned and ran into the woods to be finding Krale and Tiny. When they be seeing me, they be afraid and chunked stones at me. They told me to git going or they would be takin my life. I tried to go back several times but they be keepin chasing me away. The last time Tiny, he shot at me with an arrow." Acorn stuck his stubby finger through a hole in his vest. "Bless me, it be a close one. Since then I be livin here a league just South of dem waiting for the figure to be coming back and make them into gnomes too."

"Fer you see stranger, I be so lonely that sometimes I be a casting acorns with my sling at travelers just fer them to talk at me."

Curry asked, "The woods that your friends live in, does it have a name?"

Acorn nodded and said "Yes, it be the forest with the path of vines."

Curry asked, "How can you be so lonely with your duties to the Stags?" He knew that a gnome's only job was to tend to the stags and does of the forest.

"None about near me, they be livin to the North, so I have nothing to be keeping me busy and mischief be happening.

Curry told him, "Acorn, your boon has been fulfilled, I release you." He returned his sling to him and added, "I am traveling North about a league or so, would you care to visit your friends?"

Acorn gave a crooked smile and said, "You ain't no common traveler, least none I've ever be seenin could do what you did. You be a Wizard or something?"

"Acorn my name is Curry, a Searcher of the Wizardry."

"That mean you be a Wizard?"

"Yes, I be a Wizard."

"Well Wizard Curry, I might just be a comin along. Mind you they ain't my friends, least not til they can be standin straight up and look me eye to eye."

The three struck out North. Curry was surprised that Acorn had no problem keeping up with his pace. The journey would entail a travel of a league. A length was one tenth of a league.

At dusk when they were about three lengths from the Path of Vines, Curry told Acorn that they would settle for the night.

"I really don't care to meet strangers in the dark."

Walking into the forest Curry told Acorn to find a thicket of berries and eat his evening meal then return. After a time Acorn returned wiping his mouth of blackberry juice. Curry enveloped a small companion fire and told Acorn to remain there. "Ral will see to your safety as long as you remain here." Curry then disappeared deeper into the forest, finding a strong Oak, he levitated up into the limbs and secured himself for the night. Wrapping his hem around his hand and hand staff, he enveloped himself in intense sleep. Three hundred heartbeats later he woke and recited his growing list of auras. With the coming of dawn Curry began to plan his future encounters with Krale and Tiny.

With the breaking of dawn Curry levitated to the ground and set off to where Ral and Acorn slept. Ral, hearing footsteps in the forest, stood and sniffed the air. Identifying Curry's scent he stretched, yawned and went into the thickets to relieve himself. Curry removed the enveloping of the companion fire and shook Acorn.

Startled, Acorn jumped to his feet. "Leave me be, I ain't be doing nothing." When he saw Curry he relaxed. When Ral returned, the trio returned to the path and began the journey to the Path of Vines. Later in the day Acorn said, "We be comin to the forest where the Path of Vines is." Curry motioned Ral to move ahead and to the right of the path. Giving Ral a good head start the two continued on. Into the forest they ventured and soon the creeping vines began to appear. The deeper they went the more vines they saw. It got to the point that all they could see were creeping vines strangling the thickets and trees around them.

Whispering Acorn said, "Around the next turn be where we would do our stuff."

Curry put his hand on Acorn's shoulder and said, "Go and hide until I call." With that Curry continued on. Rounding the turn he saw a figure on the ground with an arrow protruding from his side. Closing his eyes Curry sent out his sensing for other auras. Farther and farther he sent it until he discovered the second person. Pinpointing the second attacker, Curry went forward.

Kneeling next to the prone figure Curry said, "What happened?" The figure only moaned. Curry knowing the location of the second person heard him nock an arrow. Instantly Curry raised his hand staff to envelope him in levitation, he was a heartbeat too slow, at that moment an arrow hit his hand staff knocking it from his hand. Turning, Curry dove for his hand staff, that was the last thing he remembered.

Krale stood and pitched the arrow, that he had been holding at his side, into the brush. Reaching down he massaged his foot where he had kicked Curry on side of his head. Coming up from behind him, Tiny looked down at the prone figure.

"Better get at it, he will wake soon," Tiny said. Tiny grabbed Curry under his shoulders and Krale grabbed him behind his knees. They then carried him up the hill to a small cave.

Tiny began tying him as Krale returned to the trail to retrieve the hand staff. At the cave Krale pulled the arrow from the hand staff and placed the shaft back into Tiny's quiver. Taking the hand staff over to a oak tree, Krale placed it into a deep knot hole. He then wedged a fallen tree limb into the hole and hammered it tight with a rock. Reaching up he grabbed the tree limb and tried to loosen it. Finding it tight he walked over to the cave where Tiny was tying Curry's hand to a stake that had been driven into the ground.

"Hand staff is wedged tight," Krale said.

"You sure?" asked Tiny.

"Positive, tried to pull the tree limb out, couldn't budge it. Give me some rope and I'll finish his feet." Tiny pitched him some rope and he began tying Curry's feet to stakes set deep into the ground.

"I really didn't think your idea of preparing for a Wizard was any good," Krale said, "but it looks as if it has paid off." He finished tying Curry's feet to the stakes then stood and stretched his back. "The staff is locked away and he ain't going nowhere, what now?"

"Go check the pits for supper, thought I heard something just before I shot. Anyway make sure they are covered up good and proper so no one can see them."

"O.K." picking up a small hand axe, Krale headed over the ridge to check the pits.

At the top of the ridge Krale saw three trails. One was a foot trail used by the local people when they would take a shortcut through the woods. Since Krale and Tiny had been here, it had not been used. The second was a doe trail. The leaves had been crushed to almost a powder from the constant use of going from their feeding area to their bedding area.

The last was a faint Stag trail. A trail used by one, maybe two bucks. The rubbings on the saplings showed that they only passed in one direction, probably at night.

A rubbing was when a stag would rub his antlers against a sapling. This tore the bark from the sapling and left an odor from his forehead scent gland to mark his territory. If the bark is removed completely around the tree then the stag walks the trail in both directions. If only on one side then that is the direction he travels. Most rubs are made at night.

Walking down the foot trail, Krale covered about thirty paces then stopped. Looking around for prying eyes, he knelt down and picked up a hand full of leaves. Leaning over he scattered them on the ground where a small hole was seen. The small hole was just part of a larger hole covered by river reed stalks and leaves.

This was a pit trap that Krale and Tiny had two purposes for. It caught small animals that they butchered and ate and it provided defense in case the local lord sent guards to capture them. The pit was a pace wide and a pace long. It was just over a pace deep. Many hours were spent digging these, then hauling the dirt away but they have paid for themselves many times over. Most pits had sharpened stakes driven into the bottom to impale the prey. Tiny decided not to use them. If a castle guard fell in and died then nothing would save him and Krale from the executioner's axe.

Krale then checked the stag trail. About twenty paces from the pit he saw that it too was undisturbed. Turning he walked towards the doe trail making his own trail through the woods. If he walked down the doe trail he would leave his scent from his boots, then the does would make a new trail elsewhere.

Walking up to a stump, Krale stood on it. It gave him just enough height to see over the bushes that grew next to the trail. Looking down the doe trail Krale saw the gaping hole in the middle of the trail. The trap had been sprung. Pushing through the bushes he ran to the edge of the pit and looked down. Immediately he turned and dove into the safety of the bushes at the side of the trail.

Curry was sitting on a three legged stool in a small hut. A stout man with large forearms was sitting before the fireplace, smoking a clay pipe. Across from him sat a red-haired woman of the same proportions but shorter in stature. The woman leaned over and picked a wild flower that was growing out of a crock of butter sitting in front of the fireplace. Placing this in her hair she stood and walked towards Curry. She held something behind her back. Slowly she reached out and began caressing his hair. Looking up he saw that she was smiling, suddenly she pulled her hand from behind her and in it was a double edged dagger. Swinging the dagger, she stabbed Curry in the head sinking the blade deep into his brain.

Never had Curry felt such pain. Waves of pain washed over him, nausea spread from his stomach to his head then back to his stomach. Through blurry and tearing eyes he slowly began to focus his eyes, he saw that he was looking at the ceiling of a small cave. It was daylight and he saw no one. Reaching up with his hand to rub the searing pain in his head he found that he couldn't move his arm. Turning his head and looking to his right, mistake…more searing pain and nausea. Waiting for the pain to ease, he saw his hand was tied. A very slow look around showed that he was spread eagled and staked. Slowly he began to rotate his head on his neck, this seem to help relieve the pain and help him concentrate.

Curry remembered kneeling at the prone figure on the trail, his hand staff was shot from his hand and then a foot coming towards his head. After that nothing, except for the strange dream, until now. Moving his fingers and rotating his wrist to regain circulation, he called for his hand staff. At Lord Shan's castle they had pulled his arms so tight that he could not move his hands at all to call his staff. Now he called for it but it didn't come. From somewhere outside of the cave he heard a thud like someone hitting a tree trunk with a branch. Again he called his hand staff, again the thudding sound. A large shape then stepped into the entrance of the cave.

"Wasting your time lad, the staff ain't coming" Tiny said. "You can't get to it and it can't get to you, so just rest easy."

"What do you want? Curry asked.

"Want? well lad several things. Me and my friend have held many discussions with the travelers on the road yonder. Some we robbed, some we didn't. We have learned a great deal about you Wizards. Without your staff the worse you can do is maybe kick me in the shin. With your staff, I couldn't find a place to hide from your wrath."

"Again, what do you want?" Curry asked.

"Impatient are we, O.K. here it is. We have grown tired of taking some coppers here and maybe a silver now and then. We want one good purse so we can get out of these woods and live a comfortable life. That's where you come in. About a league and five lengths from here is a castle, in the great hall is a chest that has the Providence's tithes. You get that using your Wizardry powers and we will give you your freedom."

"What makes you think I will do that?"

"Look at yourself lad, staked to the ground, you will never be found up here and you will never get loose. Yes, I know about you not needing food or water so it will be a long, long life looking at a cave ceiling. If you give your word and bond to get the tithes and never harm us we will release you and return your staff."

"I know once one of Wizardry gives his word and bond he can't go back on it. Think on it Wizard, I'll be back." Tiny then stood and left the cave. Curry heard the breaking of tree branches. It sounded like he was getting ready to build a cooking fire.

Curry knew if he gave his word and bond he would have to follow through with it. Curry began thinking through his options.

"Tiny! Tiny!" Krale shouted as he ran towards the cave. "We caught a wolf, we caught a wolf."

"Calm down, we have caught wolves before, why are you so excited?"

"It's a cave wolf, a big one."

A tanned cave wolf hide brought as much a ring or more in money. The pair had never caught one before.

"Don't worry about it, we have something better in the cave. Kill it and drag the carcass into the woods and leave it," Tiny said.

"I can't, I'm not going to try and use my hand axe, that's a little to close for comfort. Bring your bow and shoot him, then I will haul it off.

"You take my bow and do it," Tiny said

"C'mon Tiny, you know I can't draw it back."

Turning and looking at the cave, Tiny said, "Be back in a bit Wizard, make yourself to home." Then the two left.

Raising up from a small bush, Acorn watched as Krale began running back to the cave. Acorn remembered the times in the cave with Krale and Tiny. Living day to day stealing from travelers who were too weak to fight back and always dodging the Castle guards. Even as a gnome he was living a better life. He ate good and now had a real purpose in life caring for stags and does. He, Acorn the gnome, was somebody.

When Krale disappeared over the hill Acorn went and knelt at the pit and slowly peaked down. After seeing Krale's reaction he didn't know what to expect. In the darkness of the pit Acorn saw a large beige figure. A threatening growl came up from the pit. Acorn then heard the animal sniffing the air to catch his scent. Then the growling changed to a pleading whine. It was Ral, the Searcher's cave wolf.

Jumping to his feet he scanned the woods for something to get Ral out of the pit. About eight paces away, *eight gnome paces*, he saw an old fallen tree about the width of two spread hands with some of its limbs still attached. Closer inspection revealed that the limbs were spread too wide to go down into the pit. Pulling his saw from his belt he made quick work trimming the limbs. He left just enough for Ral to have footholds.

Grabbing one end of the log he lifted it to his chest then raised it over his head. He slowly walked to a nearby standing tree and placed the end against the tree. With the log leaning against the tree he crawled underneath to the balance point and shouldered its weight.

What a gnome lacked in stature he made up for with strength. Slowly walking to the pit he slid the end into the hole. When it reached the bottom, Ral took a tentative step onto one of the limbs, finding it stable he clambered out of the hole. Glancing at Acorn for an instant, he turned and sped off down the trail towards the cave.

"Your be welcome," Acorn said. He then began pulling the log from the pit. "No need telling others I be about," He said to the woods. After moving the log back into the woods, he turned from the trail and headed across the forest towards the cave.

Ral was sniffing the air as he trotted. Faintly he found Curry's scent, he also detected other man scents, and they were strong, meaning they were close by. Ral crawled under a large bush and waited. Soon two with the strange man scents approached. Tightening his leg muscles he prepared to lunge. They came close and continued down the trail. Ral's priority was to Curry, they could wait. After they passed, Ral carefully entered the trail and sped off towards the slowly intensifying scent of Curry.

Ral approached the cave and sniffed the entrance. He could tell that Curry was the only one inside. Entering he sniffed at Curry's foot then the ropes. Curry shook his left hand and called Ral to him. Ral took the hint and began to tear at the hemp rope holding Curry's hand. The rope was thick and the going was slow.

"Hurry, it's the biggest one I have ever seen," Krale told Tiny.

"It don't matter how big it is, we have something bigger at the cave."

"Look, look, see for yourself." Peering down the two looked at an empty hole. Turning Tiny slapped the back of Krale's head.

"What's that for?" he asked as he rubbed his head.

"You wasted my time, for nothing. You should have axed him when you were here. Now he's gone. You can cover it later, let's get back to the cave. I don't like leaving a Wizard alone." They turned and returned to the cave.

Ral was almost through the rope. Every few seconds Curry would snatch on the rope. Slowly it started to give. "Hurry Ral," Curry encouraged him. With a few strands of hemp left Curry snatched and he was free. Reaching over he untied his other hand then both feet. Standing he staggered, being stretched that long took some of the feeling from his limbs.

Stepping outside he looked for Tiny and Krale. Not seeing them he called for his hand staff. He heard the thumping sound beside the cave. Turning, he called again then listened intently. The thumping was heard again. He located the sound. The hand staff was hitting itself against the inside of a tree. Running to the tree he grabbed the tree limb wedged into the knot hole and began jerking on it. This failing he began beating it with his hands but the limb was too tight. Looking down he saw a large rock. Picking it up he began pounding on the side of the limb to loosen it. He didn't care how much noise he made, he had to get his hand staff and had to get it now.

Tiny and Krale heard the pounding. "He's loose!" Tiny said and began running. As he ran he pulled an arrow from the quiver over his shoulder. He had made up his mind, this Wizard would die. He couldn't risk going up against a Wizard who had a grudge to settle. Topping the small hilltop and coming around a tree he saw Curry pulling the limb out of the knot hole. Quickly he nocked his arrow and came to full draw. This would be an easier target than the hand staff was.

Seeing Tiny coming to full draw, Krale got behind him. If he didn't kill the Wizard then maybe Tiny would stop the lightning bolts or whatever the Wizard would shoot back at them. At least it would give him some time to get away.

At the instant Tiny was releasing the arrow, Krale heard a 'thunk.' Tiny immediately collapsed to the ground. With Tiny on the ground he could see Curry plainly, Curry was staring straight at him and was holding his hand staff.

Curry had turned his head and looked up the trail as he grabbed his hand staff. Seeing Tiny at full draw he knew there was little he could do. He saw the arrow being released and prepared himself for the hit. The arrow past just over his head and then saw Tiny fall to the ground. Behind Tiny was Krale and he knew that the Wizard was not pleased. Krale immediately turned and fled into the forest, or at least he tried. All he managed to do was make running motions with his legs, he had been levitated.

Curry motioned Ral to fetch Krale to him. Ral advanced on him and gently grabbed the leg of his breeches and was beginning to pull him to Curry.

"RELEASE! DOWN!" Curry screamed as Krale began

swinging a dagger at Ral. Instantly Ral released him and dropped flat on the ground. Krale shot straight up in the air two paces. "Drop the dagger," Curry ordered. Krale's response was to tightened his grip on the handle of the dagger. Curry raised him another two paces in the air. Knowing he had no other options, Krale dropped the dagger.

Curry lowered him then Ral pulled him to the cave. Releasing the levitation he looked at Ral and said, "Guard." Krale knew it was over, shortly he would enter the void. Curry went to Tiny, levitated him and pulled him to the cave. He noticed that Tiny had a growing lump at his temple. When both were at the mouth of the cave and Ral guarding them he began looking around.

Walking back up the trail to where Tiny dropped his bow, Curry saw movement in the woods. Staring intently he saw movement again. "Acorn, step out so I can see you."

Acorn, stepped from around the tree he was hiding behind but kept one hand behind his back.

"Show your hand Acorn," Curry ordered. Acorn brought his hand out and in it was his sling. Acorn just stood there and grinned. It all came together now. Just as Tiny was going to release the arrow, Acorn had used his sling to cast an acorn and hit Tiny in the temple rendering him unconscious and sending the arrow wide of its mark.

"Acorn, come on out, you have nothing to fear from these two. Acorn put his sling away and then he walked to the cave where Curry and Ral were. Tiny sat up and began rubbing his head and moaning. Curry told them to come and sit on a log in front of the cave. Frightened they obeyed and looked upon the face of someone who could do things no human could.

Curry said, "You two have done two things of evil. One you have taken advantage of innocent travelers and stole their belongs and money. Second, and worse, you deigned help to your companion." The two looked at each other in puzzlement.

"My lord" Krale said, "I have never deigned help to Tiny."

With disgust Curry said, "It's not Tiny that I talk of." Turning, Curry said, "Do either of you recognize this gnome?"

"No my lord" they both responded together.

Acorn said, "Tiny, Krale don't you be seeing the one who use to lie on this very path a holdin a broken arrow shaft while you two be hidin?"

Looking at each other, then at Acorn they both said, "Mallow?"

"Yes" said Acorn, "that were my name and it were taken from me. When I be in need the most, you run me off. The name Mallow ain't but a word now, I be given a name of Acorn by the this here Wizard fella."

Curry looked at the two sitting figures and taking his hand staff said, "Nevermore will anyone be in fear of you." With that Curry enveloped the two with the aura of being a gnome. Instantly both were encased in a cloud of black. In a few heartbeats a breeze came and blew the cloud away leaving two gnomes sitting on the log. Similar in stature as Acorn except one had a wart here and the other had a patch of dark skin there.

Curry said, "Your future will be this: You will gather and store acorns. The stags and does of the forest will browse the tender bush and tree leaves of Spring, Summer and the first of Fall. When that is gone you will provide acorns throughout the Winter. Should the acorns be consumed you will fell saplings with your saws so the stags may eat the upper limbs. You will call and sit with does heavy with fawns. Protect, you will, those fawns from wolves, badgers and wolverines with your slings until they gain the ability to run." Continuing on Curry added, "Should two stags lock antlers while sparring you will saw the antlers with the saw at your side, releasing them. Come the Spring the antlers will grow back. Anything needed by the stags you will provide."

"I will give each of you a name now..."

"Searcher!" Acorn shouted. "Not be having a name you got to obey one who got one."

Smiling Curry said, "That would be enough restitution for what they did to you."

Acorn said, "Away we be goin, we got acorns to gather, mushrooms to dry and lichen to grow, but first." Acorn disappeared into the cave. Pulling a flat rock to the side, that tiny had been using as a back rest, he pulled out a small leather pouch. Returning from the cave he handed it to Curry, "We not be having no need of this, you be using it well Searcher. You ever be a needin gnome stuff done, Acorn be the one you send for." Acorn brought his fist to his chest and bowed, Curry returned the salute and offered his hand. Reaching up with his small hand Acorn grasped Curry's forearm then turned and melted into the thicket with the other two. Shortly Curry lost the sounds of their footfalls among the leaves.

Looking in the pouch Curry found coppers, silvers and two rings. He never had this this much money before in his life, as a matter of fact he had never seen this much money before. His needs were so simple he knew he would never be able to spend it all. Thinking for a few moments, he motioned for Ral to stay and he headed towards the village.

Curry visited several huts in the village and returned with a cloth sack containing something bulky. Returning to the cave, Curry retrieved the dagger that Krale had dropped and placed it on the sack inside of the cave and left. Just as he was almost out of sight of the cave he turned and saw Acorn waving at him. Returning the wave he and Ral continued on.

Curry had gone to the village and purchased half of a bolt of cloth, needles and thread. At another hut he bought sugar sticks and hard honey balls. At the last hut he gave the rest of the money, except for four coppers, to the owner and told him to give bread to anyone who was poor and hungry until the money ran out. As he turned to leave he saw some sugar pastries, returning to the counter he held out the four coppers and asked for the sugar pastries. The baker placed a double hand full of pastries in a cloth and pushed it and the four coppers back to Curry.

"Lad, your gift will feed many, my gift will feed one, I thank you."

Curry knew that Acorn would be able to sew himself a new outfit with the cloth, needles and thread. The dagger would be used to cut the cloth and the sweets he knew would not go to waste. Cheap price for someone who had saved the lives of a Searcher and a cave wolf. He knew that to Acorn that gift was more valuable then a hundred rings. Curry smiled at the thought that Acorn would be the best dressed gnome in the forest.

Ary's message was finally made clear, as she said, 'the stag you will aid.' Acorn and the two new gnomes would aid the stags and their does.

Turning to Ral, Curry said, "Ral it's time for us to wander, like Acorn said, 'Away we be goin.' With that the two moved along the path of vines, munching the sugar pastries, to their future in Wizardry.

CHAPTER 5

Mountain of Snow and Ice

Ral and Curry had traveled eleven leagues and being foot weary, Curry decided on a treat. Coming upon a slow flowing creek he and Ral left the road and moved a short distance down the creek to a thicket where they would have some privacy. Looking around Curry saw no one.

Closing his eyes he sent out his sensing for a distance of fifty paces. Noting no presence, Curry removed his hooded cape, belt, boots, tunic and breeches. Thinking to himself, this body has not seen the Sun since that night I met Warlick.' Walking up to a tree he hide his hand staff in a large knot hole. Insuring that it was not wedged, he turned and walked to the creek bank.

Taking a step into the water he felt the muck squirm between his toes. Flexing his toes a bit he brought the other foot into the water. Walking in up to his waist he took a breath and lowered himself completely into the water. Coolness engulfed him. All the weariness of the past eleven leagues eased away. Lifting his head from the water he saw Ral sitting on the bank watching him, he called him into the water. Ral sniffed the air then turned and trotted off into the woods. Curry thought that Ral had his own mind. He knew there was no need to enter the water so he elected to venture off in search of a new smell.

Moving to the center of the creek Curry found the bottom to be sandy. Picking up handfuls of sand he began scrubbing the road grim from himself. After cleaning himself he went to the grassy bank and sat to dry naturally. No need to envelope himself to dry this time, he felt no need to rush anything right now. His times of intense sleep fulfills his sleep requirements but there are times that he needs to rest and regain his strength.

Feeling his chin and jaw he noticed that he felt nothing, no stubble, beard or even youth fuzz. Thinking back he recalled that Warlick had no beard. From stories he had ever heard they always told of Wizards having great flowing beards and hair below their shoulders. Warlick never mentioned if Olen or Klat had facial hair. He would ask him when they met next.

Standing, he gathered his clothing and took them into the water and washed them the best he could using just water. Wringing them out he then draped them over some nearby bushes. Taking up his belt, fork and cords, Curry inspected them to insure they were all in good condition. Placing them next to his drying clothes, Curry called for his hand staff. In a blur the hand staff flew to his hand. Looking close at the hand staff Curry followed the grain as it wound around the staff. All wood grains he had ever seen ran the length of the piece of wood. This traveled in a spiral pattern and there was no indication of any knots. Peering closer he noticed for the first time that just under the wood's sheen were letters. The letters formed words but the letters and words were of nothing he had ever seen before. Possibly it could be some ancient and forgotten language spoken by the Cosmos to Olen the Master of all Wizards. Another question he would pose to Warlick.

His hand staff had given him certain powers. Even now he didn't know the full extent of its power. There were times he would try something using the staff, usually in a time of danger and what he wanted was accomplished. There were limits to what he could do. He knew he could not raise the dead and certain powers were only reserved for full Wizards. A Wizard was able to control light and dark in a limited area and be able to levitate water. Hopefully one day he would have the powers that a Wizard controls.

Curry had been practicing levitating and moving objects. The items were always small about the size of acorns. He could make the object rise and lower, then left and right. Finally he could cast the objects with extreme accuracy. With practice he was gaining strength and knew he would be able to move larger objects soon. His goal was to be able to make himself move sideways once he had levitated himself. Then he not have to carry the cords and the fork he fashioned into a grappling hook.

Sitting cross legged on the ground, he reached out and picked up a small creek stone. Tossing it up in the air and catching it a few times he thought, if I can make things go up and down, by levitation, then maybe I can make things stop that are not levitated. If I could accomplish this I could possibly stop a dagger being thrown at me or an arrow in flight.

Taking the stone in one hand and his hand staff in the other, he tossed the stone straight up over his head. It reached the top of its arc then began to fall. He ordered the stone to stop.

"Ow!" Curry yelled and grabbed his eye. Rubbing the tears from his eyes he looked around to make sure no one had seen what had happened, not even Ral. "Next time I will try it with a feather," he grinned. As with everything it will take much practice, eventually it will come, in time.

Hearing Ral bark Curry turned his head, another bark then repeated muffled barking. He smiled, Ral had stuck his muzzle into a rabbit's hole. "Seek supper elsewhere Ral, that one was quicker than you." Taking a blade of grass he began to absently chew on it.

Laying back he looked up to the clouds and searched for those that looked like animals or human faces. Curry had imagined that people had done this since the beginning of time and will continue until the end of time. Closing his eyes he relaxed and absorbed what he needed from Mother Earth.

Suddenly he heard a familiar buzzing sound, like the beating of a hummingbird's wings. His eyes shot open and he bolted to a sitting position. Unable to reach his clothing he quickly snatched his pile of cords, belt and fork to cover himself. In his haste the fork pricked his inner thigh drawing a yelp from his lips.

Embarrassment flooded his face as Ary approached. She hovered in front of him for a moment…then a moment more before flying to his ear.

Ary said, "Thank you Searcher for saving me, to the Providence of Quinen you will go and the cold killer you will kill." Ary paused for a moment then added, "Silly Searcher." Curry heard her giggling as she flew to his forefinger to kiss his nose goodbye. Curry kept his eyes closed until she vanished.

Opening his eyes Curry looked for Ary, not seeing her he got up and felt his clothing to see if they had dried. Finding the clothing dry he dressed quickly. Securing his cord and belt he took his hand staff and enveloped his aura to the wind. Ral in the distance snapped his head up from another interesting rabbit hole and ran to Curry's side.

Enveloping the finding of the Providence of Quinen to the winds, Curry and Ral set out following the faint signs. They would arrive in one league maybe thirty leagues. Only time would tell.

'Cold killer you will kill,' was Ary's message. Trying to analyze Ary's message was impossible until the time was right. A cold killer could be a hired assassin or a killer that shows no emotions. 'You will kill.' Ary knows I cannot kill anything of blood but I could cause the death indirectly. This is all too confusing, from what has happened before I have discovered that time will reveal what I need to know. With that Curry and Ral continued on, length after length, league after league.

As they traveled, the villages became fewer and smaller. Curry noticed that they were always moving upward. First the top of hills then to the top of ridges. The weather slowly began to cool. The nights at first were very comfortable. Now the nights caused a shiver now and then. Their goal, Curry feared, would be in a place he didn't care to go.

Curry never liked cold weather. The coolest he wanted to be was under a shade tree in the middle of Summer. Fortunately enveloping his metabolism would help him through this journey. Curry would make sure he kept an eye on Ral in case it got too cold. With his fur and his heritage he shouldn't have any problems with the cold.

After climbing a steep hill, Curry got his first glimpse of what cold really was. Before him was a towering mountain with steep rugged sides. Most impressive was the color, blinding white from base to peak. Glancing down he saw the faint signs were leading directly towards the mountain of snow and ice. Looking closer Curry saw a small village between him and the mountain. An excellent place to stop and get a sense of what problems are going on in the area and try and figure what he was suppose to do.

Sending Ral off to hunt, Curry made his way into the village. Smiles and laughter were few and far between in this village. Seeing a visitor's hut, Curry opened the door and entered. All villages had visitor huts. This one had only the items needed for a nights visit. Several wood frame beds laced with rope covered in fresh hay or evergreens. A fire place for heat and preparing water for tea. Firewood and on a shelf a flint and steel with a stack of cattails gathered from the marsh.

Breaking open the dark end of the cattail reveals thousands of tiny white floaters. When struck with a spark from the flint and steel it burst into flames to start a fire. A small coin box was attached to the front of the door for a minimum payment of a copper per traveler per night. The coins left, pay for a youth in the village to supply firewood, candles, fresh bedding, fire starter and water for the next traveler.

Curry met two travelers when he entered the visitor's hut. Sitting on one of the empty beds, Curry said, "Greetings to you,

I am new to this area and have farther to travel. Should I be aware of anything along the road that I will be taking?"

The two looked at each other, then at Curry and one said, "Lad have you not heard of the Providence of Quinen?"

"No...no, nothing one way or another, why?"

"This is not of legend lad but of fact." The traveler said. "About sixty leagues of time past, upon the mountain of snow and ice came a beast called a Kligget. This beast shows no mercy for animal nor man. Around the base of the mountain the remains of both have been found. The throats of the unwary have been torn from their necks and a portion of one of their limbs removed by a bite of the Kligget." Continuing on the traveler said, "Many a brave but foolish hunter or pair of hunters have climbed the mountain to hunt the prized Ice Ram that this Providence is know for but none have returned. Of the rams only mangled carcasses have been found." With a stern warning the traveler told Curry, "Please take the word of one who has nothing to hide lad, stay away from the mountain, I don't want to come upon your remains someday." With that the travelers removed their boots and laid them near the fire to dry and lay exhausted on their beds.

Curry placed his boots next to theirs, then laid on his bed. He wondered what a Kligget would look like and how he could help these people. After a brief period of time he heard their regular breathing of sleep, Curry quietly got up, retrieved his boots and left the visitor's hut. Sitting on a bench outside of the hut, he pulled his boots on and he gazed at the mountain of snow and ice. He thought, that a journey of a thousand leagues begins with one step, taking a deep breath he took the first step.

After leaving the village he sent his aura to the winds so Ral would find him. Snow on the ground crunched under his feet as he walked. The cold penetrated the leather soles of his boots and his toes began to tingle. Seeing a pile of boulders in the setting Sun on his left, he located Ral laying on the largest warming himself. Ral's panting was revealed by his warm breath meeting the cold air. Coming abreast of his friend Curry enveloped Ral to change his beige coat of fur and nose to white upon white for a period of a league. Blending in with the snow may have an advantage should they meet the Kilgget.

Five lengths they walked until they gained the base of the mountain. Curry enveloped a heating fire and they waited for daybreak. Dawn revealed that a trail circled around the mountain. A path made many lifetimes ago for a reason he did not know. Following the path Curry began to shiver. As he climbed the temperature quickly began to drop.

Enveloping his metabolism for a period of a league he increase his heat. Ral seemed unaffected by the cold, his thick coat and heritage of cave wolves sustained him in this weather. After a length Curry noticed the path always circled upward. Leaning out carefully over the edge he saw that the path he was on circled the mountain and continued about five paces above him.

Motioning Ral to continue on, Curry enveloped himself in levitation and raised himself to the next path. Taking his fork from his belt he cast it to the rock face. Snagging a rock, Curry pulled himself to the path and moved the hand staff to the other hand to release the levitation.

Standing for a short period he heard the crunching of feet on the snow. Ral's breath could be seen before his form could be made out. The whiteness of his coat blended in with the snow completely. Curry repeated the climbing levitations six more times then stopped to allow Ral to rest. Curry knew that should he or Ral confront the Kilgget, it would be only moments before the other would come to the aid of his companion.

The climb had been difficult for Ral. The steepness was not a factor just the length of the trail. Enveloping a heating fire in the shape of a circle on the ground, Curry let the snow melt into a puddle for Ral to drink. Placing his finger into the water first to insure the water was warm so as not to chill Ral's body core, he let him drink his fill. After resting Curry again motioned Ral forward. Levitating upward again Curry attained the next level.

On this level Curry saw an opening in the side of the mountain. He saw a cave a pace high by a pace wide. He again threw his fork towards some rocks next to the trail and pulled himself to a firm footing. Coming closer he looked into the depths to see how far it went inside the mountain. Seeing only black Curry decided to envelope a companion fire to get a closer look.

Half way through the enveloping he heard a snarl then the Kilgget launched himself towards Curry from the darkness of the cave. Slapping Curry with his massive paw he sent the hand staff one way and Curry to his back with such force that the wind was knocked from his lungs. Curry began sliding on the ice towards the trail's edge. Clawing with his fingernails, he tried so slow the speed of the slide, then he passed over the edge into emptiness. Below him was a drop of two hundred paces and that distance was quickly reducing.

Instantly Curry called his hand staff to him. Looking back at the edge that he had just fallen from he saw a blur of wood coming at him. Desperately he reached out and grasped the hand staff. Enveloping levitation Curry's descend stopped and began to ascend. Enveloping stronger levitation he rose faster.

When he attained the path where he had fallen, he halted the levitation. The Kilgget stood waiting for him, snarling and trying to reach out to grab Curry. The Kilgget became more frustrated and angrier.

The beast was the height of one and a half paces and covered in white fur. His head did not form from a neck but from his shoulders. To look around required him to turn his whole body. His eyes were red with black pupils. His teeth were the length of a finger, sharp and spiked as a gar fish of the river. Below his mouth to his waist was a stain of dark dried blood. His paws were of four fingers ending in black claws, a hand's width long. His feet were stubby having six short claws for climbing ice walls.

Curry was in an awkward situation. The Kilgget could only stand and growl at him and Curry could only float two paces from the edge. If he threw his fork it would allow the Kilgget to grab it and pull him to his death. If he remained where he was the wind would blow him either farther from the mountain or worse yet into the arms of the Kilgget.

Suddenly a demon force of white lunged at the back of the Kilgget. Sinking his fangs deeply into the side of its head, Ral began crushing the muscle and tendons beneath. Taking advantage of the distraction Curry quickly cast his fork and pulled himself to the path. Reaching back the Kilgget tore Ral from the side of his head tearing the muscles from his own neck. Throwing Ral against the mountain wall, Ral issued a single yelp and fell crumpled to the trail unmoving.

Turning, the Kilgget saw Curry on the trail and charged him. Curry quickly enveloped the Kilgget in levitation and raised him a hands width above the ground. Clawing and snarling the Kilgget tried with all his massive power to reach Curry. Never had he seen anything, man nor animal with so much anger. Pulling the extra cord from his cape, Curry tied the end to the cord holding the fork with a sheet bend knot and cast the fork at the Kilgget's arm. Snagging the thick fur at his side, Curry snatched the cord as hard as possible. This caused the Kilgget to begin to spin in levitation. The cord began to wind around the Kilgget and the faster he would spin the tighter the cord became forcing his arms and legs together. When he stopped spinning, Curry enveloped him with the freezing of stone for a league of time. Pulling him to the cave opening, Curry removed the levitation and the Kligget fell heavily.

Insuring the beast was frozen, Curry raced to Ral's side. Kneeling with fear on his face, he sent his aura to Ral's clouded mind to let him know that he was there to help. Enveloping his hand to sensitivity, Curry began to touch Ral's body. Checking each paw, leg, neck and head he sensed no breaks or extra warmth of bleeding inside. Feeling the backbone and ribs he only detected slight deep warmth along two ribs. He needed to keep Ral warm. Laying on the snow was draining the warmth from him and would lead to the cold sleep of death. Enveloping deep sleep onto Ral, Curry then levitated him to a height of half of a pace so he would not have to pick him up and possibly causing him further injury. He then guided Ral into the cave.

Enveloping a companion fire for a length of time, the cave filled with light. Finding a flat level rock Curry enveloped a fierce fire of heat for several moments to heat the rock. He then lower the fire temperature and moved it into a horseshoe shape to encircle the rock. Slowly he lowered Ral onto the warm rock and removed the deep sleep so Ral could awake at his own speed. Seeing his breathing was normal and resting, Curry went to the Kligget. Levitating the beast he pulled him deeper into the cave for a closer look.

Sitting at the Kligget's side, Curry slowly removed the freezing of stone state until the beast could only barely move. Defending himself would be a very simple matter with the beast in this state. Taking hold of the hand staff with both hands, Curry enveloped his aura to the beast then he sensed the aura of the beast.

Curry's brow wrinkled and there was confusion in his face. A strong fierce aura was there and a second hidden one, just barely there but able to be sensed. Curry sat and thought for a moment, a Wizard's advice would be helpful now, he thought.

He had never been confronted with two auras in one form before. He reasoned that he would have to separate the two somehow. If all else fails he could return both auras back into the form.

Concentrating, Curry called the strongest aura to him. He stayed back just far enough so the aura would not enter him. Slowly a mist began to form at the beast's feet. The haze grew thicker and thicker until he could not see through it. The cloud then began to slowly move up towards the head of the Kligget.

To Curry's amazement he saw the feet of the beast change

into a pair of brown fur boots. The cloud continued up the beast's body. As the cloud lifted, more of a human figure was revealed. Tree trunk thighs of white fur became legs of a man. Paws into regular hands and last of all the head revealed a sandy haired man of about twenty-five years.

As the cloud drifted up and towards the mouth of the cave Curry instantly enveloped it to concentrate upon itself, when it was the size of a large pumpkin Curry enveloped it with the freezing of stone for a period of a year. He didn't want this aura to escape into the freedom of the countryside. The cloud fell to the floor of the cave. A year was the maximum he could freeze something so he gave it the maximum he could.

Glancing at Ral and seeing that he was resting, Curry turned his attention to the man before him.

The man very slowly began moving his mouth. Curry removed the freezing of stone.

"Who are you?" the man asked when his mouth could move normally.

Curry replied, "I am a Searcher of Wizardry, they call me Curry. How do you feel?" The man who's body had been encased in the creature's body looked into Curry's eyes. His lip began to quiver and this turned into chest heaving sobs. Curry tightened his grip on his hand staff, never had he seen a man of his stature cry like a small child before and it frightened him.

The man slowly grew quiet and said, "For about the last sixty leagues of time I have been trapped here inside this creature. I am, or was, the village hunter. The village of Rakin which lies a league East of here is my village. I hunt the local game and barter the meat and tanned hides for what I need. My needs are simple and it allows me to do what I do best and do what I love to do, hunt.

One day I climbed this mountain, stalking an Ice Ram who's hide is sought by all in the Providence. As I came around a curve I was confronted by a figure dressed as you with a black hooded cape. Pulling his hood back he revealed dark hair to his shoulders and a full black beard to his chest. His eyes were what brought the most fear to me. Eyes, solid black and filled with pure evil. The image of those eyes have been burned into my soul. I hope never to see them again but I know they will come to me in my nightmares." Curry absorbed this, A Wizard having a beard and causing hardship to another for no reason. This I must ask Warlick about, he said to himself.

"Upon seeing me," the hunter continued, "he lifted his arms over his head and then pointed both hands at me." Taking a breath he continued, "A mist came towards me and covered me. The mist changed into a cloud then into the creature you defeated.

I was locked inside of this creature. My eyes looked through his, my arms encircled his prey both animal and man." Overcome he rested a bit, "When his teeth tore out a throat my teeth were there also." Crying again he said, "I watched as I tore the throats from two hunter friends I knew from the other villages. I could see what he was about to do but I was helpless to stop him. I couldn't even slow him down to try and allow the prey to escape." Tears were streaming down his cheeks, "Now I am free, I don't know how I can repay you. Searcher what I have is yours, what you want, I will travel the country to get. I will be indebted to your for the rest of my life. I give you my word and my bond that I will repay you one day."

Curry felt not only awkward by embarrassed at the hunter's outpouring. Curry did not do this or anything for profit, none in the Wizardry did. The occasional small gratitude of someone he had helped was payment enough. Curry tried thinking of a way for the hunter to fulfill his oath to him and still allow him to save his honor and self respect. Curry decided to try what he had done in the past.

He asked, "In your village do you have a Baker?"

"A baker, Searcher we have two families of bakers. People throughout the Providence come to my village to be trained as bakers. The bakers travel to the valley in the fall and gather acorns, these they boil in water to leech out the bitterness. Letting them dry they grind them into a flour for breads and such."

Smiling Curry asked, "Would they happen to make any pastries coated in sugar?"

The hunter said, "No, sorry Searcher, they have no sugar coated pastries." A look of disappointment covered Curry's face and his shoulders began to slump. "They do have a pastry drizzled in raw honey from their neighbor's hives. I don't like to brag on someone else but their pastries are so good that once you put it in your mouth you hate to swallow."

Curry's eyes lit up and sparkled, he said, "Fill my pouch with those and you can call your oath settled."

"My word Searcher but that will not fulfill my debt," the hunter said.

Beginning to feel uncomfortable Curry said, "If you want your debt settled, this is what you must do. Go to a certain village near here that is in need of a hunter. There do what you do best, then your debt is finished."

The hunter knew he would never be able to go home again but his word was his oath. He might be able to visit once in a while but never again would it be his home. "I will go anywhere you ask and do as you ask Searcher. What is the name of the village?"

"Rakin," Curry said smiling, "you swore an oath to obey my wishes and don't you ever try to go back on it."

Smiling the hunter said, "Thank you Searcher."

Curry levitated the hunter and slowly spun him as he retrieved his cord. Putting the cord and fork away Curry lowered and removed the levitation from the hunter.

He stood and stretched his massive arms. "Bless me, by everything good it feels marvelous to be able to control your own arms again." Looking towards Ral the hunter asked, "Is he yours?"

Curry said "He belongs to no one but himself, we are friends and his side is injured." The hunter said, "Please allow me to wrap his chest until he heals. Being a hunter I have learned more than just how to take animals." Curry agreed.

Putting Ral into a deep sleep and levitating him slightly Curry allowed the hunter to bind his side. The hunter tore his tunic into strips and wrapped Ral's side as if he had done this many times before. Lowering Ral, Curry then enveloped a lack of pain upon Ral's wound and enveloped a quick healing.

Removing the sleep, Ral stood and looked about confused. The Kligget was gone and a strange man thing was here with his friend. His friend did not give off a scent of fear so he knew this other man thing must be a friend. The three then walked out onto the trail.

Following, the hunter said, "And what of the creature's cloud Searcher?" Turning Curry walked back into the cave and picked up the frozen cloud that once was the Kligget. Walking to the back of the cave he placed it on the ground then covered it with some loose rocks.

Leaving the cave he told the hunter to back away. Enveloping a heating fire above the cave, the snow and ice began to melt and drip into the opening. The dripping turned into a flow then into a torrent of water. The water draining into the opening soon began to freeze from the intense cold. Curry continued this until the entire cave was frozen solid.

Turning to the hunter, Curry reached out and grasped a small feather attached as a decoration on his tunic. Closing his eyes he enveloped the feather with a finding of Curry's aura.

Looking at the hunter Curry said, "Should you ever see the ice and snow melt at this level pull this feather from your tunic and cast it into the wind. The feather will find me and I will return. This creature will never harm again."

The hunter looked at the frozen cave and said, "Searcher, you killed the Kligget, for that, I and my village thank you."

'Cold killer you will kill,' Ary had said. Curry thought for a moment, A Wizard cannot injure anything of blood. A mist has no blood, so a cold killer he did kill. As the three began walking down the trail Curry asked, "Hunter, by what are you called?"

"My given name is Rales," said the hunter. Suddenly a faint image of someone with massive forearms flashed in Curry's mind then was gone. Curious he thought.

"How long to the bottom of the mountain Rales?" Curry asked.

Smiling Rales said, "From here to there," pointing towards the base of the mountain."How long will it take Rales?"

Laughing Rales said, "About a league if it doesn't snow Searcher." Rales was in good sprits now that he was released from the Kligget.

"Wait Rales." Curry looked over the edge of the trail down to the base of the mountain. Turning he enveloped Rales in levitation and watched as he tried to reach the ground, a comical sight he was as his feet ran without moving. Turning to Ral he levitated him also. Pulling Ral under his arm he walked to the hunter. Grabbing the hunter's belt Curry ran to the edge of the trail and launched the three of them over the edge.

The hunter screamed as Curry weight made them fall. Enveloping himself, their fall stopped. Slowly removing the levitation the three began to sink to the mountain's base.

Laughing Curry said, "You said the mountain was from here to there. So I figured you wanted to go there." Rales kept a death grip on Curry's arm as they descended.

Occasionally they had to kick off a lower path to fall freely. In the time of a hundred breaths the three landed gently on the mountain's base.

The hunter knelt to the ground and said, "Searcher if you don't mind I'd rather walk next time."

Curry smiled, thought a moment and asked, "Drizzled in honey you say?"

With that the hunter burst into a hardy laugh. "Yes Searcher, and all you can eat, my oath on it." The three then took to foot for the village of Rakin and Curry's treat.

Rakin Village watched a dead man walk into their village. Rales's disappearance at the mountain of snow and ice coincided with the first killings by the Kligget. All knew he had been killed while hunting on the mountain for the Ice Ram. Word spread fast in the small village of his return and everyone turned out.

The twenty year old daughter of the village cobbler, a pretty girl who was just barely a pace high, glanced out the window of the hut at the commotion. Seeing Rales she jumped up from her work bench and ran from the hut.

Leaping into Rales's arms she kissed him directly on the mouth. Rales was completely flabbergasted. None of the pretty girls in the village hardly even looked at the plain hunter, let alone wanted to kissed him. Setting her down carefully, she reared back and hit him with her fist in muscular chest. Rales was shocked, first she kissed him then she hit him. This tiny thing couldn't hurt him no matter how much she tried. He was terribly confused.

"Blast you Rales," she said with tears in her eyes, "don't you ever do that to me again." Realizing what she had said and that she had kissed him for the first time in front of the whole village, she turned with a red face, and fled back into the cobbler's hut, slamming the door.

Rales turned and looked at Curry with his mouth open. He could not make any words come out of his mouth. He couldn't even form words in his mind he was so shocked.

Looking at Rales, Curry said, "Its hard to believe that a fist that tiny would knock the wind out of you and make you speechless." Winking at him he added, "I expect you'll be training a new hunter in a few years if she has anything to do with it." Rales could only blush.

Many a winter night to come will be filled with Rales's stories to the villagers about the Kligget and the Searcher who had saved him. Taking Curry to the baker's hut, he fulfilled his oath to him. Curry knew that he would have to leave, it would not be fair to these people or himself if he became attached. His was a different calling and it didn't allow for a home, at least for now.

CHAPTER 6
The Disappearing Rock

Curry said his goodbye to Rales and left the village moving East away from the Mountain of Snow and Ice and the cold. He was preparing to envelope his aura for Ral to find him when a snow bank beside him exploded. In the swirling spray of snow flakes came a solid white creature straight for him, the Kligget! Curry screamed and covered his face with his hands. Not feeling the Kligget's claws he looked up and felt foolish when he realized that it was Ral.

Taking a deep breath and letting his heart begin to slow down he remembered that he had forgotten to remove the white coloring of Ral's coat. Curry felt that Ral loved to play this game of hiding then springing at him and just to hear him scream. Taking his hand staff he returned Ral's coat to its beige color.

Ral approached Curry an sniffed at his cape.

"Do you really think you deserve something after what you just did to me?" Ral kept rooting around his cape then sat and cocked his head to the side. "Just remember there are plenty of cave wolves out there who would love a sweet treat and not try to scare me to death to get them."

These funny noises coming from the man child's mouth made

no sense but the tone showed affection. Smiling at Ral, Curry reached inside his cape and withdrew a sticky honey drizzled pastry and offered it to Ral. Sniffing once more, Ral took it gently and in two chews it was gone. Offering his hand, Ral licked the honey from his fingers. Ral's side had healed quickly and the binding was removed. Warm temperatures met them as they traveled further East.

Two lengths later the honey pastries were gone and the two travelers approached a crossroad. Glancing at the three roads that met the one they had just traveled, Curry looked down at Ral and asked, "Which way Ral?" Ral hearing his voice perked his ears and just stared at Curry. He said, "Some cave wolf you are." Picking up a pebble Curry stepped to the center of the crossroads and pitched it high into the air. The pebble fell to Curry's right. "It's decided," Curry announced, "the road to the South." Turning, the two began their journey, to where, they didn't know but it would be revealed in time.

Stopping to rest in a shady area next to a creek, Curry sat leaning against a popular tree as Ral drank from the creek. The warming weather had a relaxing affect upon Curry. The villages he had traveled through since turning South showed hard working people who were quick to smile and wave. Pleasant and friendly, these villages would offer a restful place for Curry to stay a while. The problem was that too many questions would come up about Curry. What was his trade?, Why don't you eat? and Why did a cave wolf show up when you did? Greetings and a short visit was all Curry could afford. There were those no matter how friendly, would turn in one of the Wizardry for a price of a few coppers.

He heard the sounds of a hummingbird and knew Ary had gotten better and was coming to give him a message. Looking towards the sound he immediately became disappointed. It was a hummingbird drinking the nectar from some red flowers nearby. He wondered how many people heard that sound and thought it was a hummingbird when it was actually a Mintz.

Closing his eyes he leaned back and listened to the hummingbird feeding on nectar. It felt good to be able to relax and enjoy the country side. The hummingbird sped off into the forest and everything became quite. A moment later he returned to feed again.

"Searcher awake." Curry jerked up from the tree he was leaning against and saw to his astonishment that there were three Mintz before him. One was in his ear and two hovering in front of his face.

"Is this about Ary?" he asked with mounting dread.

"She is fine, thanks to you," One said into his ear. "When we arrived at the blue moss tree with Ary we sent one of our sisters to another blue moss tree with your tale. They in turn sent out others and so on. All were asked what skill to grant you as a boon. The Coven of Mintzs has chosen your boon. This boon has never been given before and will never be given again. The Coven grants to you the skill of slowing of time.

"Slowing of time?"

"Yes Searcher, with this skill what ever happens during one heartbeat of normal time will now take six heartbeats of time to occur. Everything about you will slowdown but it will not stop, for a period of six heartbeats. You and anything touching you will not be effected by this skill. You will be able to step out of the way of an arrow, a falling rock, the bite of a snake but only for six heartbeats then everything returns to normal."

"This skill only affects an area of twenty paces. Anything outside of the area who enters will also begin to slow. To perform this skill requires that you must think of the word slow and then say the word time. Your hand staff will not be needed for this."

"My sisters will now give you this skill."

The two Mintzs in front of Curry, pulled their daggers and holding them by the blade they held the hilt towards him. From one Mintz's dagger came a blue glow and from the other came a yellow glow. These two glows came to a point about a hand's width from his face where they then came together. Where they met changed the two different colored glows into a green glow. This green glow came forward and covered Curry, in the time of ten heartbeats it faded and disappeared.

"Try tour skill now," The Mintz said.

Curry looked at the two Mintzs in front of him and thought of the word slow and said "Time." He was astonished. He could actually see their wings moving in slow motion and the sound of a hummingbird was gone. Six heartbeats later their wings returned to a blur and the sound began.

"Have you any questions Searcher?"

"Yes, do all of the Wizards and Master Wizards have this skill?"

"No, you and only you have this skill. Not even Olen has this ability."

"I thought that Olen created the Mintzs and gave them some of his skills."

"No Searcher, we were created by the Cosmos and given our own skills and abilities. The skills we give to those in the Wizardry are none they possess and it is rare that it is even given. The tale is sent out to all of the blue moss trees and if any of the sisters object, then the skill is not given. You saved Ary's life and we hope someday this may save your life. Journey well Searcher." With that the three sped off into the forest.

Curry and Ral sat there for a moment. He thought he had some idea what a Wizard could do if he became angry at you. It terrified him to think what a Mintz was capable of. He recalled that Warlick had told him that even he would not want to upset several Mintzs in their nest. He was honored by the gift of this new skill by the Mintzs and thankful he would never have to confront any of the Coven.

Standing, Curry dusted his cape and pushed his hand staff into his belt. He walked the short slope to the edge of the road. Looking both ways and seeing no one, Curry stepped onto the road. Turning South Curry began walking, hearing movement behind him, he turned and saw Ral trotting up to him. As he looked forward, suddenly Ary was in front of his face. Startled he quickly ducked, Curry took a breath and said, "Sorry Ary." She flew to his ear and said, "Thank you Searcher, to the Providence of Blour, through the Village of Sturgeon, you will disappear the depths of despair." Ary then flew to Curry's face and waited for him to make a fist.

Curry said, "Ary ask Warlick if he knows of a Wizard who's hair and beard are black and eyes are of evil." Ary stared at Curry a moment and vanished. Curry had never seen Ary move so quickly before and she didn't give him a parting kiss. This was most peculiar. He didn't know if she would give Warlick the message or if he would answer the question if she did. Hopefully soon he would find out who this bearded Wizard might be.

Curry enveloped the Village Sturgeon to the wind and watched as a small area of the grass went flat. As the two passed, the grass returned to its original position. The skies darkened and there was thunder in the distance. Curry watched as the dust in the road seem burst into tiny puffs as the rain drops formed tiny craters when they hit the road. Enveloping the aura of a shield, the rain passed around the two. It was a brief shower cooling at first, then when it stopped the humidity increased and he began to sweat.

For a league and two lengths they traveled. Curry decide it was time for Ral to sleep. Finding a quite area off of the road, Curry leaned against a log and watched as Ral laid down and slowly closed his eyes. Soon his legs were twitching and he made small woofing noises. Chasing rabbits in his dreams, he thought. Curry watched over Ral as he slept. He recited his growing list of auras and reviewed the many ways he had enveloped things and what effect it caused. After doing this he levitated a twig and moved it to a stump and dropped it there. Again and again he did this until the stump was covered. He had mastered the moving of small levitated things left and right then forwards and backwards. He only wished he could do larger things, like himself. It would be nice to not have to carry the fork and extra cord. He thought that this skill must come with the rank of Wizard or with more practice. Either way he would continue practicing.

At dawn Ral awoke, he stretched and went off to relieve himself. Upon returning Curry motioned him to guard. Wrapping the hem of his cape around his hand holding the hand staff, he enveloped invisibility and intense sleep. He knew that Ral would watch over him as he had done for Ral. Awaking three hundred heartbeats later refreshed, the two continued on their journey. As they walked, Curry motioned for Ral to hunt. Ral loped easily across a field into a thicket where rabbits like to live. Curry continued on knowing Ral would find him and if not he would sent his aura out for Ral to guide him. He hoped Warlick would sent an answer soon about this dark haired Wizard.

Eight leagues later he and Ral began to pass thicker forests. Their double and triple canopies of leaf covered branches kept any sunlight from reaching the forest floor. The smell of moist decaying leafs was staggering. No saplings or brush could grow under these conditions. Fortunately for the stags mushrooms and lichens covered everything. Seeing daylight ahead Curry and Ral quickened their pace. As they broke from the forest, Curry was amazed to find an empty lake.

The lake bed was of dry, cracked mud, it looked as if someone had laid thousands of broken clay plates on the bed. This had occurred some long time past for no signs of fish bones or algae plants were present. Not even signs of dark spots where some moisture existed. Walking across the bed Curry saw a hole in the center of the lake bed. The hole was massive, twenty paces wide and ten paces deep. The slime filled bottom held branches, sticks and decaying logs.

Continuing on, Curry saw at the edge of the lake bed, overgrown foundations of old huts. A village had been here before, then abandoned quickly. All of the huts were at the same stage of decay, showing they were abandoned at the same time. Seeing a gouge in the lake's edge Curry walked towards it. As he approached he saw that there was a valley below. The bank here had given away and allowed the water to drain out. In the lower valley was another lake that was about a thousand spaces square. To the West he saw a village, the Village of Sturgeon he thought.

Following the trail, Curry had a chance to view the impressive lake. Occasional fish leaping out of the water feeding on insects and swirls showed an active fish population. With a village name of Sturgeon he thought that fishing would be their primary trade. Looking towards the village he saw several small three man fishing boats turned upside down. This struck him as odd since the day had been clear for fishing. Curry also noticed no plots laid for gardens anywhere near by, everything seemed out of place.

He motioned Ral into the forest to remain hidden. He then continued towards the Village. As he approached the first hut Curry saw few faces and those he did see were not happy. As a matter of fact they all seemed have drawn faces of hunger. With a lake this size and the activity of the fish he saw no reason anyone should go hungry. Walking up to the primary well of the village, Curry sat on the edge and lifted a gourd from the bucket. Sipping the cool water Curry looked about him. He didn't need any water, for he had not had a drink since he first met Warlick. To walk in a just stare would be rude and very suspicious.

From the windows and cracked doorways, suspicious eyes watched him. With dusk coming Curry approached the nearest hut to ask where the visitor's hut was located. As he approached, the cracked doorway slammed shut.

Looking around in confusion he saw a man approach from around the hut. Clad in a leather vest laced up the side and breeches patched repeatedly at one knee, Curry sized him up quickly. A military man, the vest was a chafe vest worn under armor and the patched knee was from kneeling on one knee in a boat holding a line at the end of which was a chum ball. The

chum ball was a mixture of worms, grubs, flour and bee's wax. When he felt fish repeatedly biting at the chum ball he order the nets cast. This large man carried a pike in his hands. A pike was a weapon of a castle guard. The way the man carried the pike, told Curry that this man had extensive knowledge and skill with this weapon.

Approaching at the port position the man stopped and immediately went to an on guard position. "What business do you have here lad?"

Curry taken back by his rudeness replied, "I am just a traveler heading South, with night coming on and seeing your village I felt it best to sleep here for safety." Looking Curry in the eyes the man hesitated a moment then spun the pike up over his shoulder to the carry position.

"I see no danger standing before me, the visitor's hut is at the end, next to the lake. A bed and wood is all we can offer, we are upon hard times but you are welcome."

Curry looked about and asked, "Might I ask your name sir?" Embarrassed the man brought his fist to his chest and bowed,

"Forgive my rudeness traveler, I am Martin, former Master Guard of the Rampart of Jerkin Castle, now the leader of the Sturgeon Village."

Curry presented himself as Curry only. "Not to be offensive but the people that I have seen seem afraid and bear the marks of hunger."

Martin felt that the village's problems belong to them and it had no concern to outsiders. There was something about this visitor, he couldn't quite put his finger on it. The look in his eyes or his sincerity, all he knew was that he could trust him and he needed to tell someone. Sometimes he had to unburden himself by telling of his troubles.

"Come and sit Curry, I will tell you how we came to be this way. We receive few travelers, so our problem remains here as our burden." Martin began, "Years back, I was the Master Guard of the Rampart for the Castle Jerkin, under me were twelve guards. My responsibility was to always insure that the ramparts were manned." Gathering his thoughts Martin continued on, "With peace continuing for six years the Lord felt the rampart guards were no longer needed. The Lord retained the other Master Guard who was in charge of the gate in case of trouble. The Lord Released me and my men. To honor our service to him he gave us a wine goblet each filled with silver coins."

"I mustered the men and we decided to use the coins to purchase settlement supplies. The men, wives, children and livestock traveled to start our own village. For two fourscores and one league we traveled. We came upon the lake above this one. Circling the lake we found the abandoned overgrown village. Things just didn't seem right. The dogs drank from

the lake and lived but we had a bad feeling about this place. Why abandon a village when there were stags and boars in the woods and fish in a lake. We found no old plantings of a garden. For as many years as this was abandoned the gardens may have gone to seed and the ground became sterile from over use. Continuing to circle we saw the lower lake. After a meeting of the former guards we all felt that the lower lake would suit us best."

"Finding an area containing the smallest saplings next to the lower lake, we began to clear for our village. Breaking the guard, I mean villagers, into groups we each had jobs. Some gathered stone for hut foundations, well walls and fireplaces. Others fell and limbed trees for a dock, hut rafters and boats for fishing. The children had a game of who could gather the most grass for the roof thatching. The women spun wool into thread then tied fishing nets. Things were going good for us. We fished and caught several sturgeon, hence the name of our Village. Most of the fish were bass and catfish and we salted these and took them to market. What we couldn't sell, we bartered for other things.

The things we needed most was salt, fruit, spices and vegetables."

"Vegetables, with all this land why not buy seeds and grow your own?" Curry asked.

Martin replied, "Odd as it is, we cannot grow anything here. True the forest is massive but nothing we plant comes up." With a frown, Martin said, "One night there was a great rumbling, at dawn we saw that the earthen dam above had cracked and was giving away. Taking our families and livestock we fled deep into the forest incase the entire lake came down upon us. Luck was with us, the upper lake did empty but the extra water only flowed over yonder bank into the next valley. We suffered no damage, even our boats were spared. That was when our problems began."

"Several of us went to the upper lake to pull what fish we could from the muck. Two men stayed at our village and set their boat out to finish our catch so we could go to market. Casting their net they immediately caught a massive fish. It must have been a sturgeon weighing 10 stones or more. "A stone," Martin told Curry, "was the weight of rock that was the size of a man's head. The thrashing was incredible. Suddenly their boat capsized and no heads returned to the surface. Launching another boat we found no sign of the men. Tying off the first boat they brought it back to the dock. That night we built a fire next to the lake and the Village sat up with the memories of those who had drowned and gone into the void."

"A moon later two children sat on the end of the dock dangling their feet in the water as I was mending my net. I looked and they were there, looked back again and they were gone. No thrashing, no waves, no cries…nothing. They were just gone. Boats were launched and pikes probed the bottom, no bodies were found. Grief filled the hearts of not only the parents but of us all. A moon later another man was lost in capsized boat. We stopped fishing, what fish we had we kept to eat. The upper lake was searched in earnest for clams or anything living. We even lowered a man into the hole in the center of the dry lake. All he found were bones of large animals. They looked like sticks in the mud."

"Living off what fish we had, stags and boars from the forest, we quickly depleted the silver coins we had left. We now have nothing left, the parents do without so the young ones will have something." Martin looked with anger at the lake, "Evil is there and nothing I can do as their leader can help my people. Shortly the people will begin to give up hope and leave, family by family. What we had was wonderful, now we have nothing, we can't grow anything so there is nothing left to live on."

Curry now knew that what ever the problem was lay in the bottom of the lake and to identify it he knew he had to enter the lake. Biding Martin good night, Curry went to the Visitor's Hut. He then waited for the lights to be extinguished in the other huts.

Quietly, Curry went into the woods to check on Ral. Curry didn't really need to check on Ral, he knew that of the two, Ral was better suited to survive than he. He was frightened, in the morning he would go where he had little experience and confront something that kills and kills without remorse. Curry was saying goodbye to Ral. Knowing he could not take him into the lake, and he may never return, he motioned him to go far and hunt then search for Curry's aura. Finding Curry would be great, not finding him would release him to wander on his own.

Returning to the Visitor's Hut he rested and waited for morning. At dawn he went to the dock and sat cross legged on the end, there he waited for the time to be right. Taking his cord he tied a rock to his belt. A rock weighing a stone would be enough to hold him on the bottom and give him better traction that to not have one. When the noon sun shined straight down into the water, Curry stood and walked two paces towards the Village. Stopping he scanned the village for any watching him. If he didn't return they would think he left on his journey. He saw no need to add to their grief.

Turning Curry ran quickly to the edge and enveloped himself in levitation. Floating he drifted out over the lake. When the wind stopped his movement he grasped the hand staff in the other hand and enveloped himself in slowing his metabolism. Blowing out his breath so he would sink, he slowly released the levitation so he would not make a warning splash to alert the village or what was under the water.

Sinking Curry was amazed at the clarity of the water. He could see from seven to ten paces in all directions. Looking around he saw what he felt he should, a small rotting log here, a branch there, algae and underwater ferns. Nothing out of place, he even saw fish of several species. Settling on the bottom, Curry began walking deeper into the lake. From what he saw at the upper lake, whatever was there lived in the center of the lake. The rock greatly assisted in moving about. As a caution Curry had tied the rock with a slip knot just in case he had to move in a hurry.

Deeper he trudged, soon he neared the center of the lake and silt was spread before him. Sensing movement he turned quickly to the right and was startled by a Sturgeon weighing six stones coming directly at him. Suddenly the Sturgeon turned and sped away.

Returning to his path Curry saw two large things coming towards him. They paused and sank to the lake bed. Lifting his hand staff Curry began to envelope the freezing of stone upon them. Quickly the two things waved what would be called hands and the silt billowed around them. Even the direct sun light could not penetrate the cloud of silt. Sending out a finding aura to locate the two, Curry was surprised from the rear. Two of the figures he had not seen came from behind and grasped his arms and spread them. His hand staff was useless if he could not motion with it. The first two approached and grasp his legs. The captured Curry was taken deeper into the lake.

Looking from side to side Curry examined his captors. Their skin was like that of a catfish, a grayish white in color. Thick tough skin without scales and large, wide webbed hands with eight fingers with hooked claws for positive gripping. The grasp on Curry was firm but the claws were not used. Their feet were identical to their hands since walking was not needed, so a foot like his own would be useless in the water. Their eyes were the size of a plum, solid black in the center and dark yellow around the rim. He could tell that they were predators because their eyes were located towards the top of their head so they could always be looking up for their prey. The pulsating gills were located just under their arm pits, so that the inside of their arms could protect them. They only had flesh tearing front teeth because they had no need to chew. They would just tear and swallow. Why they did not kill him he didn't know. Warlick give me patience. Since he could not break free from the four he relaxed and allowed them to take him to the depths.

Coming to a steep drop off, the escorts took Curry straight down into a crater. Curry saw many more of the creatures and the bones of their past kills. What he saw began to nauseated him. Bones of animals gleaned of flesh had no effect on him.

This he had seen many times before. It was the decaying corpses of the dead villagers that made Curry ill. No mark was seen on them, only the tiny bites of curios fish as the flesh decayed. In the center of the crater was a creature like the others only slightly larger, to this one he was taken.

Curry heard clicking and squeaking sounds coming from the large one. Curry opened his mouth and began snapping his teeth together. Startled, the large one became curious and swam closer to Curry. Taking Curry's head in his clawed hands he looked closer at him. The large one, the leader, was confused. Releasing Curry he returned to his former position and suspended himself by using an internal aid bladder that all fish have.

For a moment of time nothing, then Curry heard noises. Not from around him but from within. Inside his head he heard noises, then noises changed to sounds and sounds to words.

"Why do you not fight the water, land walker?" the large one mentaled. Curry felt that if he told the truth now, no matter how bad it made him look, the creatures would believe everything he would say. Anyway he couldn't be in anymore trouble than what he was in right now.

"I am Curry, a Searcher of Wizardry, I have the gift to go into water." The screams of a dozen entered his mind, he thought his head would explode.

"KILL! KILL! KILL!" they repeated over and over.

The larger one mentaled, "Hold fellow Watkils, death may come or it may not, that decision only I will make. First I will mental with this land walker." With that the Watkils became quite. They did draw closer in anticipation of inflicting a killing wound should the large one declare it.

Looking a Curry the large one began to mental, "I am Krill the Clan Leader of the Watkils. We are here because of a curse by a Wizard so no one of Wizardry is welcome here. Many generations ago my forefather was a land walker. Stories told to me by the prior Clan Leader revealed that the village, on the bank of the lake, had meat from the forest, plants from the soil and fish from the lake. One day one dressed as you, came and all changed. The land was killed from growing anything planted by land walkers forever. The villagers were forced into the water's edge by the Wizard of dark hair,"

Curry jerked upon hearing this, "Krill did the clan leader mention his eyes?" he mentaled.

"Yes," Krill answered, "large, dark and ones you never wish to look upon again." Continuing Krill said, "The villagers stood knee deep in the lake and the Wizard reached out his hands and a mist covered all of the villagers. The mist then turned into a cloud like the ones above us. Suddenly the people began to struggle for breath and suffocate. First one, then three, then all collapsed into the water dying. Then the changing happened and they all became as you see me now. Never again to breath the air above. Curses were heaped upon my people. The flesh of fish you will not eat, flesh of man you will not eat, only those lake edge drinkers will you eat."

Curry better understood the cause of the troubles. When the dam broke it washed the Watkils into the lower lake. The crater in the upper lake was filled with the bones of animals caught while drinking water at the lake's edge. The humans had been killed for two reasons. They were either splashing in the water that attracted the Watkils attention. After pulling them in thinking they were animals, they drown quickly and the bodies were left to decay. The other reason was that the fishermen caught the Watkils in their nets and it was only self preservation that they capsized the boats and killed the fishermen.

I don't know if I have the ability to change these Watkins back or not. I don't know if they would even want it. The skills of hunting and farming were lost to them generations ago. The land about this area could not support another village and the Watkils could not survive elsewhere. No, it would be best to leave them in their own domain.

Krill looked at Curry and mentaled into his mind, "Be you good or bad I do not know. The Watkils want your life, it is mine to give to them. A land walker is of no use to us, the knowledge you have of us could cause our end. We of the Watkils do have honor. I will give you a chance to live and leave here unharmed. You are to do but one thing, doing this and any boon, I will give to you and freedom you shall have. Fail in the task and your death, I promise will come quickly. Krill continued, "From only Clan leader to Clan Leader the answer to this task has been passed. The knowledge of it only I have, are you ready land walker?"

Curry was placed in a situation where his next action would either kill him or free him. At his young age he had many doubts. All he could do, was the best he could do. Olen, Master of all Wizards, look upon me. "I am ready Krill."

Krill made clicking noises and a half pace long log was brought and placed end first into the mud in the center of the crater. Another Watkil brought a rock and placed it upon the end of the log. Krill looked from the rock to Curry, "Land walker," Krill mentaled, "make this rock disappear."

Curry searched his mind. He had but one chance to solve this problem and one only. With a motion of his hand staff he could make it become invisible. He had never done that under water but felt that it would work. As Warlick told him it only makes the object so you cannot see it, it does not make it invisible or disappear. Krill could reach out and feel the rock even though he couldn't see it. His end would come quickly with that discovery. There was a trick within the question somewhere. Make the rock disappear, make the rock disappear.

Curry mentaled to Krill, "May I touch the rock?" Krill knew that even with his gifts, Curry could not avoid all of the Watkils, his escape was impossible. With some clicking noises Curry was released. Reaching his hands forward and waving them back quickly Curry moved through he water. Some of the Watkils laughed at his awkward land walker movements in the water. Krill silenced them. At the upright log Curry picked up the rock and turned it this way then that. A rock nothing more, hard and cold. Make it disappear, make it disappear. Then something told to him a long time ago by Warlick flashed into his mind. A small smile came upon his face. Curry set the rock down and waved himself back to where he was being held. Turning to face Krill and the rock, he lowered himself to the lake bed then began staring at the rock.

A moment passed, then another, Krill mentaled to Curry, "Land walker, either you make the rock disappear or you die."

Curry said, "I am making it disappear."

"I still see it land walker!" Krill mentaled,

"Be patient Clan Leader, it will disappear in time. Eons to come the lake water will soak into the rock making it soft. Unseen tiny flakes will drift away. Rays of sunlight and water motion will wear the rock away until it disappears. Be patient Clan leader, you must have patience." Warlick told him he had to be patient in Wizardry and he knew only patience would make the rock disappear.

Krill moved up and towards Curry. Hatred was in his eyes as he began flexing his clawed fingers. He lowered himself in front of him. Since he had no control over his life or death he lost his fear. He looked into Krill's eyes with confidence and didn't flinch. Relaxing his hands Krill mentaled, "Name your boon Wizard?" Loud clicking was heard from each Watkil. They were dumfounded, why hadn't Krill ordered his death? Then they realized that something that could not be done, was accomplished and by a land walker. Floating backwards the Watkils knew they were not in the presence of just any land walker.

Curry thought of the problem the Watkils had and those of the Sturgeon Village. A compromise somehow had to be made between the two, where they could exist together. Then a solution came to him.

"Krill," Curry mentaled, "my boon I ask is this, any land walker thrashing in the water and making the loud noise, Help!, a Watkil will raise up and move until his feet touch the land and he can stand."

"Done!" Krill mentaled.

"Any net dropped into the water the Watkils will herd the fish towards."

"Done!" Krill mentaled.

Krill didn't like to do something and gain nothing in return but he had to grant this boon.

"For doing this the land walkers will, when sunlight comes after the fullest of moons, bring meat of lake edge drinkers. It will be dropped from the land walkers wooden walkway into the water.

Krill now saw what the land walker was doing. Krill mentaled, "We do not trust land walkers, if they will honor your sayings then the Watkils will also. If they stop then we will stop and your boon is canceled." Krill didn't want him to ask anymore for his boon. "Land walker you are free, two of mine will take you to the wooden walkway. With that Curry was grasped and quickly taken to the dock of the Village. When he could stand the two Watkils swirled and were gone.

As Curry walked from the water two small girls screamed for it was forbidden to enter the water. The villagers poured into the common area to find out what was going on. Dripping Curry approached the village well. Martin approached carrying his pike and asked what had happened, he thought Curry had left that morning. Curry said, pitch your boats with pine rosin and make them ready, it is time to fish. He recanted what had happened at the bottom of the lake and asked if the village would honor the agreement he had made with the Watkils.

Martin burst into laughter, "Lad has your mind left you. Creatures in the deep who will help us fish if we give them a stag or a boar. You stupid, stupid child, off from our Village and leave us with our misery you simple minded fool."

Curry had worked very hard and risked his life for these people. Martin's comments brought him to anger quickly, even Krill of the Watkils would listen and consider. Maybe walking the parapets of the lord's castle had hardened his head. Either that or the heat caused his ignorance. Maybe a cooling would give Martin a better perspective.

Curry enveloped Martin in levitation a hands width above the ground. Reaching out Curry grabbed his leather vest and began moving him towards the dock then to its end. The villagers were stunned, this was a young lad and he had control of the best fighter of the guard. With a sudden shove Curry pushed Martin out over the water.

"Help me someone, I can't swim, help me," he begged. Curry let him hang a moment longer then removed the levitation and Martin dropped into the lake with a loud splash. Screaming for help Martin began slapping at the water. Under once he went, then a second time he went under, then Martin began to rise out of the water until his shoulders were exposed. No one could tell if the fear on his face was from drowning or from the unseen thing lifting him up. When Martin's feet touched the bottom and he could stand, there was a swirl behind him and the unseen thing or things were gone.

Martin looked at Curry then turned and looked at the water, then again at Curry. Calling out Martin said, "The boar kill from yesterday, bring it to the dock." All stood and looked, none moving. "Have you no ears, we have an obligation and friends to feed." At once two men ran for the cooling pit to get the butchered boar. The hunt for the boar took four leagues of time and they didn't want to give it up easily. Their trust in Martin was complete and they complied quickly.

Curry told Martin, "Cast a net from the dock, take the haul and feed your village, they are hungry. When the boats are ready, fish the lake with your nets and take what you catch to market. Barter some of your fish for seed and plant your gardens. What you plant will now begin to grow."

Martin said, "Casting a net from the dock is a stupid idea, no fish can be caught that way and the ground is dead." Smiling Martin then added, "and a drowning man can't be saved by some kind of fish person."

Martin stepped from the water, drained his boots, then walked to the drying racks and lifted a net. Returning he cast the net from the end of the dock, they all waited. Seeing a swirling action around the net, Martin then began pulling the net back in only to find out he could not pull it in alone. Hands reached out and helped him pull in the catch. One cast revealed fish that would feed them for two days. "Build fires and we will feast tonight friends," Martin said. "And soon our gardens will feed us."

Two men pulled the boar halves to the dock, Martin said, "I want this honor." Grabbing a boar half Martin threw it far from the dock over the water. The boar half hit with a splash and submerged. Then it shortly bobbed to the surface. A moment later something pulled it under the water. The same happened with the other boar half. Wiping his hands on his pants Martin turned and looked for Curry so he could thank him. He was no where to be found. A quick search of the village found no trace of him. Standing at the village well Martin said, "The Village of Sturgeon exists no more, from this day forward we will be called the Village of Curry."

When everyone's attention was on the two boar's halves being brought to the dock, Curry quietly walked past the village well, between two huts then melted into the forest. Stepping into the gloom he saw Ral approaching him. Kneeling Curry reached out and scratched behind Ral's ears.

Taking his hand staff in both hands he enveloped a searching for the death in the ground. Quickly he sensed the aura of the enveloping made by the dark wizard. Curry asked the aura to release from the ground. Looking around he saw a very faint mist rise from the ground. Soon the wind blew the mist away deep into the forest. He knew the mist would never harm anything again because it would have to be forced into the ground by Wizardry.

Turning Curry witnessed the search for him and later Martin's statement. Curry smiled, his pride swelled with this honor Martin had given him but he also remembered that an ego could be his downfall. He had been adopted by a Providence Castle and now a village, and a village bearing his name no less. Homes they would all be but a birth home evaded him. How he could not know where he was born and to whom, he didn't know. In Wizardry there is an answer for every question. Hopefully, one day, this question would be answered, in time.

CHAPTER 7
The Globe

Once again Ary's message became clear, 'you will disappear the depths of despair.' By making the rock in the depths of the lake disappear it also made the despair in the village disappear. Skirting the wood line, so as to stay out of view of the village, Curry came across a well worn deer trail.

Looking at Ral, Curry asked, "Any objections if we follow the deer trail Ral?" Ral cocked his head upon hearing his voice and began panting. Smiling Curry said, "I thought not." He then began to lead the way down the trail. Since, at presence, he was not on a journey given to him in a message from Ary, he decided to wander. A visit at a village or castle was not regulated by time and the days came and went. The weather was comfortable and there was a coolness in the morning, then warmed to a comfortable level by the afternoon. Ral fed when he grew hungry or just explored the thickets and woods as Curry walked the roads at a leisurely pace.

Sighting a castle in the distance Curry thought he would stop for a visit, he motioned Ral into the woods to hide and wait. The castle was slightly smaller than the others he had seen. The huts surrounding the castle were well maintained and the harrowed fields were full of growing crops. The parapets held two guards, one at each corner. As a whole all looked quite and peaceful. People were entering and leaving across the moat on a drawbridge. As they entered all were stopped by a guard and questioned, none were being searched, which was a good sign. He had learned a valuable lesson about being searched.

From the looks of the guard, he appeared to be the Master Guard of the Gate. Knowing now, with his present skills, he could escape unless surprised from behind, he approached the gate with caution. Glancing around for any threat from behind and seeing none, he walked and stood before the Master Guard.

Standing more than a pace and a forearm high, the guard posed a formidable figure. Dressed in half armor with a brown tunic, the guard looked down at Curry. Staring for just long enough to make Curry feel uncomfortable the guard spoke.

"Traveler, are you a liar, or not." Curry was confused, never had be been questioned like this before.

Standing as high as he could, he looked the guard directly in his eyes and said, "I don't lie." The guard's brow furrowed a moment then broke out into a roaring laugh. Those nearby who had witnessed the conversation also broke out in laughter. It was as if they all held a secret between themselves that Curry was unaware of.

"Young traveler," the guard said, "My Lord, Lord Harper, the Keeper of the Tanslow Providence asks to meet all new travelers who enter his castle, especially those who do not lie." Smiling he added, "Please allow my men to escort you before my lord, even now he is holding court in the great hall greeting all new visitors." Curry had heard this before and was cautious after what had happened in the past. Relaxing his mind he sensed the auras about him and felt no deception or anger.

"At your pleasure sir," Curry replied.

Motioning at two guards standing next to the drawbridge winch, they moved towards and in front of Curry.

"Please follow us." Saying that they strode across the

courtyard. Each held his scabbard to his side sword and constantly scanned the people in the courtyard. Should anything develop they would be ready.

Curry looked about him as he followed the escorts. Against the wall of the castle were two large roasting pits. Four pigs were spitted there, by the looks of them they were about ready. The cooks were playfully swatting at the children with hand towels as the children snuck in to snatch a piece of crisp pig skin to eat. With the pigs almost done the women were stripping silk from the ears of corn then dipping the ears in water before wrapping the husks back around the corn. This would allow the steam to help cook the ears of sweet corn. As the corn was cleaned others took them and began dropping the ears on the hot coals to roast.

The breeze changed and Curry froze in his tracks. Jerking his head around he searched for the aroma that drew his attention. Sensing the absence of their guest, the guards turned and looked at Curry.

"Something wrong?" one guard asked.

"No, no I just smelled fresh bread from your bakery," Curry replied. "Would you know if they are known for their pastries?" he further asked.

The guard said, "Lord Harper would not allow them here if they weren't, please traveler, this way."

Curry was taken before a great double wooden door leading to the great hall and one of the guards whispered to the door keeper. The guards left Curry in the door keepers care and returned to the drawbridge. Making sure they were not going to try and sneak up behind him, he entered the great hall.

Inside Curry saw tables laden with different foods and chairs lining the walls. Two areas were left open for the pigs and roasted corn. At the end of the hall sat a simple throne and before it a smaller identical throne. The simple throne told Curry that the lord of the castle was the controller of the Providence and he didn't need an elaborate throne to prove it. He ruled by ability and not ornaments. He could see no waste of the tithes the lord charged the villagers. The door keeper escorted Curry to a bench where another sat.

Looking around confused, Curry heard Lord Harper announce,

"Bring forth one who does not lie." With that the Lord pounded his scepter on the arm of his throne.

The one sitting next to Curry stood and walked to the smaller throne and sat. Above the head of the person was the word, "LIAR" carved into the head piece of the smaller throne. "Begin," the Lord commanded with a scowl.

"My gracious Lord Harper, for a traveler I have been and sights before my eyes were remarkable. The story I am to tell is true for my lips have never had a taste of a lie upon them."

Two who had been sitting in chairs around the wall instantly stood, pointed their finger at the speaker and yelled, "Liar!!!" The two then looked towards the Lord.

"No, not enough, not enough," The Lord said. The two returned to their seats.

Curry then got an idea of what was happening. The test is to tell a false story and make everyone believe it or at least put doubt in their minds that it might be true. Another came and sat down next to Curry.

"I have been here before stranger, on this day every week the Lord holds a Providence banquet. All in the Providence are invited to come and eat their fill for free. As you can see the finest of food is prepared and served. For entertainment, the Lord holds a challenge, anyone surviving the Liar's throne is granted a boon. Don't get your hopes up friend, it is rare that anyone can survive the Liar's throne. Our Lord has a very discerning ear.

The current speaker on the throne began his story, "My Lord, as I traveled the Forest of Demons with but a dagger in my belt for protection, I viewed a massive male dragon twenty paces long." One stood from his chair at the wall, thought better of it and lowered himself. Curry knew this was a lie because there was only one dragon living and it was a female, he held his tongue. "Slowly," the story teller continued, "I circled the great beast and hid behind a tree. Carefully I climbed the tree and then launched myself upon the great beast's back and...

"LIAR...LIAR...LIAR," the whole crowd screamed at once. Lord Harper had a look of one with a heart that had just been crushed.

"How could you be my guest, eat my food then tell a falsehood before my Court." Pointing his scepter at him, the Lord said, "LIAR!" Upon hearing the Lord declaring him a liar, all those who were standing, threw pieces of bread at the Liar. The Lord said, "Guard, take him and feed him to the lions." A guard came forward, drew his dagger and took the man away. Out of ear shot the guard leaned closer and whispered to the man,

"What the Lord meant to say was take him and feed the liar." With a wink he lead him to a chair near the feast table then returned to his post.

Curry thought this was an odd game but everyone seemed to enjoy it. He did feel it was a waste to throw the bread.

Feeling a nudge in his ribs, the one sitting next to him said, "The bread and all food left over after everyone has had their fill, is fed to the pigs to fatten them for our weekly feasts. Oh, by the way there are no lions in this country."

The Lord said, "Bring forth one who does not lie." He pounded his scepter on his arm rest. Curry was pushed to his feet by the stranger sitting next to him and stepped to the Liar's throne.

Taking a seat at the Liar's throne, Curry said, "My most benevolent and merciful Lord whose realm is an example for lesser Lords to emulate, I have traveled but for a short time in my limited years and the things I have seen would only bore and disappoint this respected audience."

The Lord smiled, he knew something good was about to happen. "The Court will determine that, continue," he ordered.

"I have but one simple tale my Lord. While traveling I chanced upon a shady opening in a forest. Going there to rest from my long journey, my ears picked out the sounds of sawing. Thinking a axe man was at work, I ventured closer. Before me I saw a gnome standing on the antlers of two stags that had been locked in combat and could not untangle themselves."

Three stood and yelled "LIAR" then looked hopefully at the Lord. All in the audience gathered a piece of bread and prepared to launch them.

The Lord looked at Curry and frowned then said, "Careful stranger, your feet may not be able to carry you the full journey, continue."

Curry bowed and continued, "The gnome was sawing the antler of the smallest to release the stags. After the antler was freed the stags fled into the forest. As the gnome watched them run, I walked up behind the gnome and jerked him around. Locking eyes with him, I knew he had to grant me a boon or I would not release him." Several in the audience grabbed their heads and began to moan louder and louder.

With a wave of his scepter the Lord silenced them. "And what boon did you ask of this gnome stranger?" the Lord asked, "and be very, very careful with your answer."

Thinking for a moment Curry said, "The boon my Lord was this, I ordered the gnome to grant me the boon that the benevolent Lord Harper would be able to see the truth in my story."

The hall went completely silent, mouths with food became still, then the hall erupted in laughter and the pounding of arm rests and stomping of feet. After a few moments things became quite and Lord Harper told Curry to stand.

Wiping tears from his eyes, Lord Harper said, "The lions will go hunger today. You have provided this court with a tale few have been able to get away with. Tell me truthfully traveler, was there such a gnome?"

"Gnome? I have no knowledge of any gnomes my Lord."
Again the court erupted in laughter.

"Ask your boon traveler and it is yours, that is something
within reason."

Curry smiled and said, "Does the Lord of this Castle, the
Keeper of the Providence, the feeder of lions have any sugar
pastries within his domain?" Again laughter erupted in the hall.
Many had expected him to ask for money.

Calling for silence Lord Harper said, "A stiff boon you ask for
but one I feel I can grant." He called for a guard. "Take this teller
of truth to the bakery and allow him all he can carry." Looking
at Curry he said, "Thank you traveler, smiles you have given us
all."

Curry was escorted into the courtyard and to the bakery. The
guard told the baker of the boon and Curry made a pouch from
the hem of his cape and filled it with the promised pastries.
Looking at the sky he saw that dusk was upon him and knew he
had to leave. Hurrying, he crossed the drawbridge and followed
the road to where he left Ral. In a thicket of brush Ral hid and
waited. Sniffing the air he knew Curry was approaching alone
and stepped onto the road. Ral also knew that Curry carried
something special in his cape. Tail wagging Ral waited for the
sweet treat.

Retreating from the road for privacy, Curry and Ral found a
secluded spot and laid on some soft grass. Sharing his boon,
Curry began thinking. So far in his travels Ary had given him
messages. These messages were all cloaked in mystery. Half he
understood and the other was lost to all meaning. Always in the
end the puzzle came together. Curry came across this castle
without a message from Ary and found that these people were
healthy, happy and had a purpose. Either they had been like this
always or had been visited by a Wizard who helped them right
some wrong.

One question Curry had pondered was that if the Providence
he was in had a Wizard, why was he assigned to solve the

problem that was the responsibility of that Wizard. Curry thought for a moment and said to himself, I'm not very good but I'm slow. All in the Wizardry, except for maybe Olen were mortal. Being mortal they would enter the void one day. Someone must replace them and that person must be able to think through any difficulty. The Wizard of each Providence knew what would be best to test the Searcher's skills and assist in his maturity. The messages from Ary come from different Providence

Wizards. This is why a Searcher travels the whole Country in his training to become a Wizard. Grasping the meaning of something not understood before, gave Curry great satisfaction.

As darkness fell Curry enveloped a small companion fire. Leaning against a tree he locked his hands behind his head and closed his eyes. If the situation presents itself he wanted to ask Warlick about his life before his thirteenth birthday. So many questions to ask. Curry thought. Hearing a buzzing sound like a hummingbird, Curry opened his eyes and saw Ary approaching.

"Welcome Ary," he called as she approached. Coming to a hover in front of his eyes he saw from the firelight that this was not Ary. This Mintz had hair of black and her skirt was a rose petal wrapped around her waist. Like Ary, she had a horsehair belt with a dagger. Her presence perked Curry curiosity.

Moving to his ear the Mintz said, "My Searcher needs help!", she returned to the front of his face and hovered a pace away.

Curry said, "Ral, let's go!" With that Curry jumped to his feet and removed the companion fire. He and Ral began following the Mintz's glow. This was the first message that did not come from a Wizard. Curry thought that some Searcher had gotten into trouble and he was the closest one of Wizardry who might be able to help.

Continuing to follow her glow against the night sky the three made good time. Curry feeling an urgent need, had set a pace that began to tire him. He knew Ral could outdistance him but at some point even he would have to rest. After four lengths of time Curry called out to the Mintz, "Mintz, I'm sorry but I have to rest, I can't go on." Dropping to his hands and knees he rolled onto his back, his chest heaving. The Mintz quickly returned and entered Curry's ear.

"My name is Amber, we must leave now!"

"I can't Amber, I want to but I'm exhausted."

Amber left his ear and hovered over his panting face, drawing her dagger she placed her hand around the blade and held the hilt out towards Curry's face. The hilt began to glow a bright orange then the glow flew straight at his face and for an instant his whole face glowed a bright orange. Taking a deep breath the glow entered his mouth and disappeared into his lungs. Curry's eyes grew wide then he relaxed. Sitting up, then standing, Curry said, "Hurry Amber." He was filled with energy he had never felt before. He was alert and anxious to get to their destination.

At daybreak Curry saw Ral begin to tire. Tail drooping and panting he knew Ral could not last much longer.

"Ral," Curry called and Ral stopped. Reaching out with his hand staff he enveloped Ral in levitation. Reaching down he picked up the cave wolf weighing fourteen stones and carried him like a loaf of bread. Ral trusted Curry with his life and knew he would come to no harm. Relaxing under Curry's arm, Ral soon drifted off to sleep.

Fortunately they met no travelers along the road. A sight of a Mintz and a caped figure carrying a full grown cave wolf would have caused a great deal of attention. After two lengths of time Ral awoke and Curry released the levitation. Ral began following along at their fast pace. The threat of possible discovery by travelers ended shortly thereafter. Amber left the road and began to cross an open field. With the brightness of the day Amber had to remain closer to be seen.

Curry had a first hand experience of what a Mintz could do. He wondered what all they did possess in powers. Only Olen knew that. Traveling took them across fields and through thick forests. Deeper and deeper into the forest they went. Soon dusk came and was followed soon by night. No moon was in the sky that night due to it's phase. Curry continued to follow the tiny speck of light.

Breaking into a open field, that was circled by towering hills, Amber disappeared. Ral went quickly about sniffing the air. Curry looked around and could see no sign of Amber or another Searcher. He could not sense anyone around. Knowing that wandering the wooded area could prove to be dangerous he decided to sit and wait for daylight.

To the West, Curry saw lightning arc across the sky and several came to Earth. The time between the flashes and the sound of thunder grew quicker. The storm was coming their way and coming fast. The tree they were standing under would give some protection from the rain but would also attract the lightning. Smelling the rain coming Curry called Ral to his side and walked into the open field. Enveloping levitation for four lengths of time the pair lifted from the ground about a half a pace. He then enveloped themselves in a shield. With a rain deflector above them and being off of the ground they would be able to stay dry and rest up for whatever tomorrow morning would bring. The green glow given to Curry by Amber had dissipated and he again grew tired. Sleep would help but most of all he needed to rest and recover. The rain began to fall and fall heavily. Lightning began hitting the surrounding hills and the pair waited for the nearby tree to be hit. Ral, a full grown cave wolf, tucked his tail and tried to crawl under Curry at each lightning strike. Curry reached down and comforted his friend. Both waited out the night and the storm.

From the time they had entered the clearing, a pair of eyes full of hate had watched them from the tree top of the tree they had just stood under.

As the Sun crested the East hill the pair began looking about. To the South was a tall hill that gleamed white in the sun light. It appeared to be made completely of ice. The other hills were covered with trees and brush. Looking about Curry saw no sign of Amber's Searcher. Looking down at Ral he noticed that he was looking up as if to begin a wolf howl. Following Ral's nose, Curry looked up and said, "There you are."

Suspended about four paces above the ground was the Searcher. He was encased in a clear globe that appeared to be made of ice and was about one and a half paces in diameter. The Searcher was standing with his hood pulled over his head and his arms hanging straight down. About a forearm length in front of him was his hand staff, also frozen in the globe. Curry felt that there was no need to rush now, of course that was only his opinion, the suspended Searcher may have had another. Had the Searcher been dead, there would not have been such elaborate measures to display his remains. He was alive, the question was how to get him down, then how to free him from his frozen prison.

Thinking of what to do next he felt the breeze begin to blow at is back. Looking up at the suspended Searcher he saw that the globe began to float away, being pushed by the breeze.

Looking at the direction he was floating, Curry saw that he was headed towards the hill of ice.

"Come Ral," Curry said and they began running towards the frozen hill.

At the foot of the hill Curry ran up the side. First his left foot slipped out from under him then his right. Falling face first onto the ice hill, Curry slide down the side becoming soaked with water. Getting to his hands and knees he motioned Ral to climb. With his claws digging in Ral climbed about a pace then all four legs went out from under him. Landing on his chest he too slid down the side getting his coat of fur soaked with water.

Standing, Ral slowly crept to the side of the hill and began sniffing. Curry stood and walked to where the hill began from the field. Reaching out he felt the ice but there was no feeling of cold. The hill was made of a clear material, as clear as a brook stream and was covered with standing water. The water did not flow down the side as water should, it was suspended on the clear rock face. A dagger might gouge a hole in the rock face allowing him to climb to the Searcher, who was now bumping against the top of the hill but Curry had never had a need for a dagger.

He thought of levitating but he could only go up or down and not sideways. True the wind would blow him towards the globe but the wind would also blow the globe away from him at the same time. Wizardry had made a barrier to stop the globe and to prevent anyone from reaching the globe.

Suddenly the globe stilled and began floating back into the field. Curry and Ral followed the globe remaining underneath it. As it came near the tall oak in the field it again stopped.

"Well Ral what do we do now? Ral hearing his voice turned and looked at him, then sat and began panting. "Excellent advice." Curry also sat and then laid back on the ground and looked at the globe. Placing his hands behind his head he began going through his list of skills.

At first glance nothing reasonable seemed logical at the time. Invisibility, no that would only hinder finding the Searcher within the globe. Sending out a blast of fire, no the globe may be of the same material as the hill and would have no effect. Levitation, no he could only move it up and allow gravity to lower it. Since some Wizard had suspended the globe, his levitation would be repelled by his enveloping. Suddenly it came to him, sitting up Curry looked at Ral and said, "If I can't levitate the globe, then I will levitate myself to the globe. If the wind stays calm it should work."

Walking to the oak tree Curry pulled the long length of cord from his cape and tied it to the cord he kept in his belt. Tying a bowline knot to a stout limb, he played the cord out until he was standing under the globe. Judging the length of cord left, he knew there was enough to reach the globe.

Ral growing tired of sitting, laid on the ground and placed his head between his front paws. Curry took his hand staff and enveloped himself in levitation and began to rise to the globe. When he had reached a height of about two paces he heard a loud screech as a red tail hawk launched himself at him from the oak tree. Glancing over his shoulder he saw the hawk was almost upon him, seeing the talons spread ready for attack he immediately enveloped a shield to protect himself. All would have been perfect except that Curry had forgotten that he could only envelope one thing using one hand. When he enveloped the shield it removed the levitation. Curry fell and hit the ground like a rock. Knocking the breath from him he laid there dazed. The red tail hawk circled and dove at Curry. As the hawk was in mid-flight Ral sprung and covered Curry's body with his own. Bearing his teeth he released a growl that turned the hawk. The hawk climbed and circled looking for an opening to make his attack.

Regaining his breath, Curry sat up and reached for his hand staff. Motioning with his hand staff he sent his aura to the hawk. The hawk sensed Curry's aura and knew this caped figure and the wolf meant no harm to him or the Searcher. He winged over to the oak and perched on a limb. The hawk sat and watched the pair below him in case the aura sent to him was false.

Ral moved from the protective position over Curry. Curry then stood and brushed the loose grass from his cape. Stretching his arms he realized he had come to no harm from the fall. Looking at Ral, Curry said, "Looks like the Searcher above has a friend also." Again he placed himself below the globe and enveloped levitation. Raising upward he kept an eye on the hawk. It remained on its perch and only watched.

Reaching the bottom of the globe Curry reached out and felt the side. This was not a rock like the hill. It was cold, very cold. Curry levitated upward until he was half way up the globe.

Reaching into his belt he removed the two prong fork, swinging the fork by a length of cord he threw it over the top of the globe. The cord slipped and fell from the globe. Pulling the cord to himself with one hand he again tossed it. This time it passed over the center of the globe and hung from the other side. Lowering himself he took more cord and whipped it towards the fork. The line caught on one of the fork tines and he pulled tight. He released some of the levitation and lowered himself to the ground. Taking a firm grip he began pulling the globe to the ground or tried anyway. Pulling with all his might all he managed to do was pull himself from the ground. Rubbing his face with his hand then placing his hands on his hips he pondered his next move. At least the globe would remain where it was by being tethered to the oak tree.

Again Curry sat and tried to work through the problem. Had the globe not been effected by some Wizard he could make it rise, then gravity would lower it. Make it rise, make it rise, "That's it," he shouted. Ral jumped and his hackles raised. Looking at Ral, Curry said, "Rest easy Ral." Hearing his calm voice, Ral relaxed and sat watching his friend.

Curry thought to himself, If I can ask something to rise then possibly I can ask something to lower. Taking his hand staff Curry enveloped the globe with heaviness. The globe almost seemed to bob a small amount. Curry then took the hand staff in both hands and strongly enveloped heaviness towards the globe. Slowly it began to sink towards the field. Hand width by hand width it descended. When it was a forearm length from the ground Curry reached out and carefully gripped the cord with two fingers that circled the globe. Making sure he maintained both hands on the hand staff he began walking to the large oak tree. Looking up he found a strong limb the size of his thigh. This limb forked about two paces from the trunk. Placing the globe beneath the fork he released the globe and then released the hand staff. The globe hesitated the began to rise. It lifted itself until it became wedged in the fork of the limb.

Curry stood back and saw that it was not going to move any furtherer. Looking into the tree top he saw the hawk perched watching intently.

"Feel better now my feathery friend?" he asked. The hawk looked at Curry then began preening himself.

Curry circled the globe looking here and touching there, even Ral circled it sniffing the ice globe. Once more Curry sat and looked at the globe. The Searcher within was immobile as was his hand staff. The warm Sun had no effect on the frozen ice. It didn't even have any moistures on the outside. This would require more heat than the Sun's warming rays. Curry enveloped a heating fire around the globe. The flames circled the globe and then covered it completely. Thirty heart beats later he removed the heating fire and inspected his work. Nothing, not even a drop of water dripped from the globe. Curry had learned from experience that if something didn't work the first time it wouldn't work the second time either.

Looking around he saw some small pebbles, levitating them he forced them at the globe. So far that was about the largest item he could force by levitation. The pebbles bounced off the globe with no effect. Since heat was the enemy of ice he again returned to fire but in a different way. This time instead of heating the outside he would try an internal heating fire. Closing his eyes Curry enveloped a heating fire and directed it within the globe. Opening his eyes he saw a yellow glow within the globe. Thirty heartbeats then thirty more he waited. Removing the enveloping he watched, nothing. The globe was as cold as before.

Leaning forward he placed his chin in the palm of his hand and propped his elbow on his knee. Gazing at the grass he began to think. If you take cold away from something it becomes hot, if that is true then if you take heat away from something it becomes cold. If you take heat away it becomes cold...if you take heat away it becomes cold...if you take..., Curry lifted his chin from his palm and looked at the globe. I have been doing it all wrong. This was done through Wizardry. I have been forcing heat onto the outside of cold, the heat has to be pulled within the cold where it was once was.

Curry took his hand staff and enveloped the aura of the cold globe of ice. He then asked, with respect, that the ice recall the heat it had released to become cold. The grass surrounding him began to bend and lean towards the globe as hot air was drawn to the cold ice. For twenty heartbeats the hot wind was drawn to the globe then it stopped. The globe began to shimmer and suddenly it collapsed straight to the ground in a torrid of water. Startled, Curry turned and dove away from the oncoming water, covering his face he waited for the water to settle. When all was quiet he sat and turned towards the remains of the globe.

The caped figure, from the now dissolved globe, slowly stood. Reaching out his arms he slung the water from his hands and cape sleeves. Looking at Curry he said, "Took you long enough!"

Curry was assaulted with many emotions. He responded to a strange Mintz's plea for help. He had traveled as fast as he could to reach here, was attacked by a red tailed hawk, fell two paces to the ground then released this Searcher from his ice prison and all he could say was, 'Took you long enough!'

Anger filled Curry's breast, dripping with sarcasm Curry said, "If you didn't like the way I was doing it why didn't you say something?"

"Brilliant!," the wet Searcher said laughing, "Finally I have found someone with a wit of humor." Walking forward he pulled his right sleeve up above his forearm with his left hand and extended it to Curry. Confused, Curry did the same and they grasped forearms. "Searcher, I'm called Wayne, and your name?"

Curry answered, "Curry and the cave wolf is Ral, my friend."

Releasing his grip, Wayne pulled his left sleeve up exposing a leather guard laced to his forearm. Raising his right hand above his head, he shook his hand twice then lowering it, he patted the leather guard twice. At once the red tail hawk flew to his arm.

"This is Sparrow, I wouldn't make jest of his name, he is very sensitive."

Bringing his fist to his chest, Curry bowed. Wayne turned and called his hand staff, from a puddle of water the hand staff flew to his hand.

"Bless me how I ached to feel this in my hand while I was frozen. Come let us sit and I will tell you of my little episode, my bones still feel the cold and I need to warm myself."

Moving beneath the oak tree Wayne sent the hawk to a perch. Sitting on the ground, Wayne enveloped a warming fire, encircling himself.

"Bless me that feels good," as he held his hands to the fire. "First, how did you happen upon me?"

"Amber sought me out and brought me here."

"She is a prize, she is, let me begin. Amber gave me a message to come here and remove the evil. When I arrived I found the field and hills as you see them now. Except the clear rock hill was as the others. Sitting against this oak I waited to see what problem would develop so I could see about solving it. I had just sent Sparrow off to hunt when a caped figure started to cross the field towards me. His hood was pulled low over his head, I thought it was Warlick coming to explain what I needed to do. At two paces he pulled his hood back and I saw a head of black hair and black beard. The eyes, I tell you, I never want to see again. Such evil was in them that the bile began to rise in my throat. Pulling my hand staff from my belt, I started to envelope a shield. The hand staff was snatch from my hand, by an unseen force, and flew to the stranger's feet."

"Worried about losing your hand staff child," he said. "I will insure it is always within your reach."

He then raised his hands over his head and then lowered them in my direction. The hand staff flew to me but stopped an arms length from me, before I could reach for it I was encased in the ice globe. True to his word my hand staff was always within my reach, only I couldn't move my arms to reach it. He then changed that hill into a clear rock. He knew the globe would float there and he didn't want anyone climbing it to rescue me."

"Curry I thank you, if ever you need me for anything, at anytime, I will be there. On that I give you my oath and my bond."

Curry nodded his head and said nothing. Both knew the oath went both ways.

"I have failed in my journey," Wayne said.

"No you haven't Wayne," Curry interjected. "Your journey has only been delayed for a bit. I suspect that you will finish what you started out to do but at another time and another place."

"Amazing, one with wit and wisdom," Wayne said, "What shall we do now?"

"The clear rock hill possess no threat or harm, I say leave it as is. As for us, tell me of your adventures and I will share mine, hopefully we may learn skills from each other."

Wayne began, "When I woke, I saw that Warlick was gone, confused, I called Amber and…"

The adventures of their journeys were swapped one for one. They talked from dusk of one day to the dusk of another. Ral and Sparrow feeling hunger that their companions didn't, left to hunt, then returned to wait for the two to finish their stories.

On the morning after the second dusk, the two Searchers stood. Bringing their fists to their chests, both bowed to each other.

"Time to wander," Curry said.

"Yes, time to wander," Wayne replied.

Turning, Curry and Ral headed East and Wayne and Sparrow headed West. They may meet again, they may not. They would know in time.

CHAPTER 8

The Serpents

Walking through the woods, Curry and Ral came upon a small pond. Feeling gritty from travel Curry decided to rinse off in the pond. Not wishing to be embarrassed by Ary again, Curry kept his breeches on. He could envelope dryness when he finished to dry them. Knee deep in the pond, Curry rinsed out his tunic and cape. Pulling his extra cord from the cape he rinsed it also. Ral was laying on the edge of the pond watching Curry. Looking at Ral, he began to smile, an idea had come to him.

Calling his hand staff to him, he approached Ral. Curry enveloped Ral in levitation to a height of one hand width above the ground. Ral began to rise, surprise filled Ral's eyes. He had been levitated before but usually there was a reason. Reaching out Curry grabbed Ral by the back of his neck and his rump. Pushing him rump first out onto the pond he watched as Ral levitated about ten paces out. Slowly Ral finally came to a stop.

Curry then released a little of the levitation so Ral's paws sank about a hand width into the water.

Curry then began clapping his hands together and said, "Come Ral, come on boy." Ral tried to walk to Curry and noticed that he moved a little as he pawed through the water.

Suddenly Ral began to run. True he couldn't walk on water but he could propel himself along by pushing against the water. His feet became a blur as he paddled towards Curry. It was hilarious to watch Ral running on water, he was running at full speed but only going the speed of a fast walk.

As he came closer be built up speed. Curry smiled at his antics, then giggled and finally burst into laughter. Curry misjudged Ral's speed and Ral collided with him. Knocking his hand staff from his hand he and Ral both went under. Curry came up sputtering and coughing between the laughter. Ral paddled to the shore and got out. Shaking vigorously, he flung the water from his coat. He then walked to the water's edge and looked at Curry and began to whine. Curry thought to himself, I may have started something that I can't control.

Curry repeated the game again. Ral returned but this time Curry was ready for him. He stepped to the side and grabbed Ral as he went by, spun him around and sent him back into the pond.

This time Ral circled the pond then returned to the shore. Stepping out, he shook the water off then walked to a shady area and laid down exhausted. Smiling Curry finished his laundry and bath. Dressing, Curry enveloped dryness of his clothes then went and laid next to where Ral was sleeping.

Looking closely at Ral, Curry saw why almost everything except maybe a she bear feared him. His shoulders had muscles that rippled and seem to go on forever. The strong jaws were filled with teeth that could crush a thigh bone and in three bites pull the leg free from the body. The pads on his paws were the size of his palm, the long black claws came second to his teeth in the ability to tear flesh. With all his strength he did have one weakness, that one little itchy spot at the tip of his sternum on his chest. Scratching it rapidly makes his leg kick and his eyes roll back in his head. That is the only time he had mastery over this cave wolf. "Bless me I am thankful to have a friend such as you," Curry said.

Looking up, he relaxed and began looking for figures in the shape of the clouds. About a length of time later Curry woke Ral and they stood, stretched and continued on with their wandering.

Curry and Ral traveled all day, then into the night. Coming upon a road they turned left and set off down the road.

The moonlight gave them plenty of light to remain between the ruts of the hundreds of wagons that had passed before them. The night air was cool and the night had many benefits that day travel did not have. The main benefit was that you didn't worry about passing another traveler. The one downside was that you might cross the path of a bandit. Curry smiled at the thought of a bandit coming face to face with Ral, a full grown cave wolf, the largest of the wolf breeds.

The two traveled for three lengths when they happened upon a small bridge. Curry sat on the railing in the center of the bridge as he watched Ral thread his way through the vines and weeds to get a drink of water. Listening to Ral slurp the water, Curry didn't hear the buzzing sound coming at him.

Startled, Curry cried out when Ary landed in his ear. "Searcher always be aware," she warned, then began the message. "To the Village of Malon you journey, from the roost a male you shall give birth." Ary then left and hovered in front of Curry. He then brought his fist to his lips and Ary landed lightly and kissed his nose. Before he could ask who sent the question, she was gone into the night.

Ary's messages bear the same patterns. The first part was simple to understand, it was the second that he always wanted to ask Ary about. Curry didn't think that Ary would have the answer. She was just a messenger but a very special messenger.

Calling Ral, Curry took his hand staff and enveloped the finding for the Village of Malon. The reeds along the bank of the creek that followed the road leaned towards the East. Curry headed in that direction.

The weather was comfortable now but he knew the North

winds would be coming soon and with it, the cold. He just didn't like the cold. His feet got cold, his head got cold, everything got cold. The enveloping to speed his metabolism will be tested this Winter. There was one good thing about the coming of Winter, flavored snow. The thought of honey mixed with blueberries or sugar water mixed with horehound, began to make his mouth water. Even though he didn't need to eat, he could and he did it only for pleasure. Flavored snow would indeed be a pleasure, one that he would savor, over and over again.

The view had slowly changed. On Curry's right the creek had moved to the South and the land turned into a thick forest filled with oak and saplings of birch. Also it was overgrown with ten beat vines. Ten beat vines were the ones that when you try to walk through them they get tangled around your feet or pack and it takes about the time of ten heart beats to untangle yourself. On the left was a large pasture, crossed and divided with fences built of stone, split rails and thorny bushes.

Split rails were made by placing wooden wedges every half pace along a long log, then pounding them with a large wooden maul. After the log is split, the procedure is repeated on the two halves making the rails for a fence.

Looking up the road, Curry saw a boy with some sheep next to the road. Sending Ral into the forest to hide, he approached the boy. Standing next to a section of collapsed split rail fence, stood a boy of about eleven years old. His face was streaked with drying tears. In the ditch next to the fence was a ewe wedged tightly in the ditch.

Looking at the boy, Curry asked, "I see what has happened, my question is how did it happen?"

With slight sobs the boy told his story. "Sir, my father sent me to bring in the sheep to begin shearing for their wool. I was leading the head matron, the one with a bell around her neck, to the area for shearing. Two of the younger ones began chasing each other and bumped into her causing her to fall against the fence and it collapsed. Struggling to gain her footing she rolled over and fell into the ditch." Ending the story he said, "She is too heavy for me to lift and if I go for my father the others will get loose." Curry remembered Warlick's words that a Wizard cannot pass anyone in need.

Walking from the front of the ewe to the rear Curry said, "Where I am from this happens several times a day. All the children developed a special strength and leverage to lift trapped sheep so they would not have to go for help. May I help you?"

"Yes please sir, I can't go home without the matron ewe."

Curry carefully edged his way down the ditch to the side of the ewe. Reaching out with his left hand he grabbed the wool at the ewe's neck, with his right, holding his hand staff, he grabbed some wool at the ewe's rump. Enveloping levitation, he acted as if he were staining and slowly lifted the ewe from the ditch. Stepping over the ditch he walked up and placed the ewe on the other side of the collapsed fence and let her go. Quickly she trotted to where the rest of the sheep were grazing.

Curry picked up a rail from the top of the fence and wedged it under the collapsed section of the fence where the two sections of rails came together. Placing the end of the rail on his shoulder he levered the fence back to its original position. Setting the rail back on top in its original position he stepped back and admired his handiwork.

"That will hold them, just check your rails from time to time."

The boy brought his fist to his chest and bowed thanking Curry.

Curry asked, "Do you know of a village named Malon near here?"

"No sir, none by that name within two leagues of here, that I have ever heard of." Curry thanked him and set off down the road.

Moving down the road he saw that it moved away from the pasture for a ways then turned to the left back towards the village. He motioned at the woods where he had left Ral to remain hidden. He knew Ral would be watching. Approaching the village, Curry saw the boy leading the matron ewe and about five other sheep into a fenced in area for shearing. A man wearing an apron and holding a pair of shears was standing there waiting. The boy said something to the man, and pointed at Curry. The man brought his fist to his chest and bowed his head. Curry returned the bow and continued into the village.

For the past length, Curry had noticed a hot spot developing on the ball of his foot. A hot spot was where your boots or gloves had a thin area and provided less protection than the rest. As your foot began rubbing against the thin area, first it became hot then developed into a blister. Walking tenderly to a bench next to a hut, he sat and pulled his boot off. Placing his hand into the boot he located a thinning spot on the sole that was splitting. The tip of his little finger could be poked through the split. Nothing in Wizardry had prepared him for this, sure he could call a dragon or battle a Kligget but fix his own boot, no, that was beyond his skills.

Leaning out the window the owner of the hut asked, "Having a problem traveler?

Turning Curry said, "That I do sir, sometime during the night a thief stole part of my boot an left a hole as you can see."

Roaring with laughter the owner said, "Bless me that was a good one traveler, yes, mighty good. Look there, see that slanted bench two huts down on the far side."

Curry looked and said, "Yes."

"That's our village cobbler, he will see to your needs." Curry thanked him, pulled on his worn boot and moved towards the cobbler. As he walked he overheard,

"A thief stole a part of my boot." Then another roar of laughter.

Looking in the cobbler's door, Curry saw a large man at a cobbler's bench building a boot. Rolls of tanned leather, boot patterns and stacks of rawhide were stacked behind him. The floor was littered with scraps of leather and old worn out boots and slippers. An unpleasant odor came from the rear of the shop. Being polite he wasn't going to say anything about the odor when he spoke to the cobbler.

Setting his clay smoking pipe to the side, the cobbler looked Curry up and down and said, "Name's John, can I help you lad?" Curry pulled a three legged milk stool in front of John and pulled his boot off. Handing him the boot, John glanced at it and said, "Two coppers will fix it right."

Curry didn't have a ring, silver or even a copper. "I don't have a copper to my name sir."

Tossing his boot back to him, John said, "The door's there lad, have a good journey." Curry was perplexed, he couldn't travel with his boot this way and he had no money.

Curry looked at John and asked, "Barter?"

Dropping his sewing awl into a box of sinew cord, he looked at Curry and said, "Barter you say, will you work here for three lengths for your boot repair?"

Quickly, Curry said, "Done." What kind of hard work could there be in a cobbler's shop? He thought.

John asked, "What name do you go by, lad?"

Curry replied, "Curry, sir."

As he began cutting a patch for Curry's boot, John said, "I'll be making a Winter vest soon, go in back where the shepherd dropped off two salted wools, they need fleshing, braining and wringing."

Curry stepped back and said with eyes wide, "John, I heard words come out of your mouth but I have no idea what they meant."

Laughing, John stood and went to the rear of the shop. "Here," John said, "these are two hides that the shepherd removed yesterday and rubbed salt into the moist side so it would not rot or grow maggots until I could get to them. Take them and go sit in front of the hut. There is an angled bench, called a fleshing board, it has no sharp edges on it to cause the hide to be punctured when you clean it. There you will flesh the hides. Fleshing means to remove all of the fat and loose membranes with a curved metal fleshing blade. Braining is to take the brains of the sheep and boil them, then grind them up in the same water. Once it cools you will soak the hides in this mixture and wring it out, three different times. That's all there is to it Curry."

"Done," said Curry, but not with as much enthusiasm as the first time.

"Mind you," said John, "if you have to relieve yourself, use that bucket there." Looking over at the wooden bucket in the corner of the back of the hut, he saw where the odor came from. Old stagnate urine filled the bucket.

"You want me to dump it John?"

"Dump it!, bless me no lad. It's used in my trade." Now Curry was completely bewildered and becoming a little nervous. "A hide with hair comes in and the hair needs to be removed. I mix water and ground up charcoal from my fire then add some stale urine. I soak it for about three days and the hair slips away easily. The older the urine the better. I also use it to make a white hide from a brown one." Curry took the first wool hide and went to the fleshing board to begin, thankful to be outside away from the smell of the urine bucket.

Curry tried to think of any way to invoke Wizardry but none would come to mind. Removing his cape and rolling up his sleeves of his tunic he began his work. Fleshing and braining were messy jobs and had he had a tendency to scrap his hands. Curry was almost grateful when he began wringing the hides. After the third soaking and wringing he was finished. Washing his hands in a bucket of clean water he started drying them on a piece of scrape white chamois hide. Remembering what John had said about turning a brown hide to white, he dropped the hide and finished drying his hands on his breeches. He then rolled down his sleeves and went to John.

"Finished John, want to check my work?"

"No," John said, "I kept my eye on you. A hard worker you are, you in a mind to take on a trade."

Curry said, "I thank you John but I have a journey to finish first." John nodded and tossed him a pair of boots.

Catching them Curry looked closely at them. They were calf length boots with boot straps on each side of the top to assist pulling the boots on with. By the smell they had been placed in a smoke hut to waterproof them then stained black with dissolved inky cap mushrooms.

"John these are not my boots, this is a pair of new blackened boots."

"That they are, you earned them lad. Make note that the leather boot straps that you use to pull the boots on with have a small hidden pocket on each side."

Finding the hidden pockets, Curry also found that a copper was placed in each pocket. "John, I can't accept this, I feel I would have cheated you."

"Rest easy Curry, the boots are from me, the coppers are from my brother. He said something about you saving his favorite matron ewe." Curry's eyes began to well up, quickly he sat and pulled on the new blackened boots and hastily left. John thought to himself that the sight of Curry's face was payment enough for the boots. Helping someone in need did give you good feelings. John picked up his clay pipe and began packing it with rabbit tobacco.

Curry moved quickly from the village. The boots had a snug comfortable feel and he could tell that the soles were made thick for traveling. They matched his hooded cape in color and made traveling a lot easier, not to mention the hidden treasure in the boot straps. The swinging of the weighted boot straps reminded Curry that he was a man of means now, proprietor of immense wealth, for him anyway.

'A Wizard cannot pass anyone in need,' these were the words of Warlick. Curry was repaid many times over for his help with the ewe.

Sending out his aura to the winds he waited for Ral. Moments later Ral loped into view and they continued their journey. Three leagues and four lengths passed when they topped a small hill. In the distance Curry was surprised to see dragons circling a field.

"Dragons…, no that's impossible," Curry told Ral, "There is only one dragon living and that's Kiliac, these are not dragons, they must be Serpents.

As they watched, three dove and whipped the calf with their tails then taloned it. Sinking their talons deep into the calf they took to wing and flew up and over into the thickest part of the forest.

A few villagers could be seen. Some were hurling stones with slings at the Serpents and some were using long bows. The sight of that many longbows concerned Curry. Rarely will a village have more than one longbow and it would belong to the village hunter. This must be the Village of Malon. Curry knew there was trouble and he had a good idea what it was.

Sending Ral to the woods, Curry entered the village and approached a man holding a longbow. Being direct always drew suspicion of strangers so Curry asked him, "Sir I have been traveling for many leagues, could you tell me where the visitor's hut might be?"

With anger the bowman said, "It might be in the talon's of those Serpents yonder!" Three heartbeats later his face softened and said, "Sorry stranger, We have been cursed with serpents and can't rid ourselves of them, the visitors hut is at the end of the village next to the lake."

"Have you a tavern or a place for food?" Curry asked. He had no need for food but people assembled around a table usually spun stories.

The bowman said, "The hut with a double door, the table is laid at dark."

"Thank you sir," Curry said. The evening meal was not for another length so he decided to check the traveler's hut and the lake.

The Traveler's hut was similar to others he had seen. Coin box on the door, a small fireplace, cattails for fire starter, wood, candles and the beds were covered with cypress limbs. Simple enough Curry thought. It was dry and clean, ideal for a night or two but not enough to live in, that was its purpose. Written with a piece of charcoal on the wall were these words; *Wine, Brew, Mutton and Beef, Double Door at Dark, One Copper.*

Walking down to the lake Curry saw seven boats and their nets drying on a special rack. The lake was about eight hundred paces long and about a hundred and sixty paces wide. In the edge of the water, he watched minnows jumping from the water avoiding the attack of yearling bass and once he saw a shape the size of his forearm moving along the shallows, probably a catfish, he thought. Looking at the ripples on the lake made by the blowing breeze, he saw a massive sturgeon surface then sound going deep. Plenty of fish to eat, Curry thought.

Walking to where the Serpents were attacking the cattle herd, he looked around the ground for anything that may help him solve what appeared to be the villager's problem. It just looked like any other grass pasture every village had.

Curry thought back to what he had learned about Serpents. Females are about twice the size of Ral and the few males that exist are four times the size of the females. All had barbed whipping tales used to defend themselves or attack. Covered in scales the size of your hand and had finger long teeth made for tearing. They all flew and fortunately they did not belch fire. Darkness was almost upon him so Curry headed for the hut with a double door.

Entering the hut Curry saw long benches ringing the room, numerous men and a couple of women sat at these, each with a goblet in hand. There was fireplace large enough to warm the room in the coldest of times and a long table with stools was in the center of the room. This was used for those eating the evening meal. On the side near the kitchen was a table laid with plates, beef, mutton, boiled potatoes and bread. In the corner was a table with two pitchers on it, behind this table were two large oak casks. Apparently one had wine and one had brew. Standing empty handed drew attention so he walked to where the two pitchers sat. He pull a copper from his boot and handed it to the mistress of the hut.

"Brew or Wine?" she asked.

Brew was a fermented drink made with yeast, hops sugar and malt barley. You could smell this brewing five hundred paces away. The only thing worst than the smell was the taste, at least to him it was. How anyone could drink brew was beyond his comprehension.

Wine was made from crushing grapes by stomping on them with your feet. They had tried wooden presses but found out that the presses crushed the seeds and left a bitter taste in the wine. Sugar, yeast and dandelion petals were added to the juice and then let it sit. Curry could handle wine a little better than brew but only just a little.

"Wine," he replied

Pouring a goblet of wine she motioned to the table near the kitchen and said, "Yours for the taking young sir."

Curry carried the goblet to the table and filled a plate with some mutton and bread. Taking a stool at the eating table he began to slowly eat. Around him things were quite then slowly normal conversation resumed. Weather, rotating crops, fishing and redness on baby's bottoms. Normal subjects, nothing of interest to Curry. A patron continued the story that was interrupted by Curry's entrance.

"Feeling his net snagged by a sturgeon, Brum pulled with all his might, just as the fifteen stone sturgeon surfaced, he put his hand in the loop of his gaff, lifted it high over his head and WHACK! he pierced it's side. Apparently the sturgeon didn't like this because he sounded and sounded deep. Since the gaff was attached to the loop and the loop was attached to Brum, Brum went with the sturgeon. Twenty heartbeats later Brum came sputtering to the surface minus a gaff. To this day he never carries a gaff in his boat." The room erupted in laughter.

"Bless me," said Mame the hut mistress, "That sturgeon gets bigger each time I hear the story, if it gets any bigger you will have to have two people to tell the story, it will be so heavy." Again the hut exploded in laughter.

"Those sturgeons have always caused us problems," Mame said, "tearing the nets plus they can't be cooked because of their numerous bones and oily taste. Too many people have choked on the bones." Suddenly the door burst open and in walked the bowman.

"Jake, mind your manners, this is still my home!" Mame said.

"Sorry Mame, today got the best of me," he turned and closed the door. He went to get a community clay pipe from the fireplace, breaking the tip off of the mouth piece so he would mouth a fresh end, he packed it with rabbit tobacco and put a flame to it from the fireplace. Puffing deeply he turned and dropped a copper on the table as he picked up the goblet of brew. He went to the sitting benches where he sat near two other men and took a long drink. "Blast those Serpents!" he said. "Slowly the village's calves are being taken and all we can do is watch. Without the calves the herd will eventually die out."

Breaking in, Curry said, "As I came in today I saw several men with long bows, that seemed unusual for a village to have."

Looking at Curry, Jake recognized him, "Oh yes, the young traveler, yes lad most villages have one long bow for the village hunter. When the Providence Lord came through on his annual inspection, we told him of our plight and he ordered his armory to give us four bows with forty shafts. Little good it did."

"I am not from here Jake, what is your plight?" Curry asked.

Looking intently at Curry, Jake began, "About four months ago a herder was checking the beef stock. Looking to the South he saw flying shapes coming in his directions. As they approached he saw that they were Serpents. They circled the pasture several times then flew into the deep forest. A few days later a calf came up missing. Searching the pasture for the missing calf no signs of a feeding were found. No bones or

blood stains were found that a pack of wolves or wolverines would leave. A week later two herders saw the Serpents wing over the forest tree tops, circle the herd and attack a calf. Whipping their tails they killed a calf then sinking their talons deep, they lifted the calf and disappeared back into the deep forest. Since then they have returned about once a week to claim another calf."

Taking a breath Jake continued, "We tried building fires, erecting sharpened poles pointing upward, arrows and stones thrown with slings. Nothing affected them, they still continued to claim their prizes.

"Have you gone into the forest to find them?" Curry asked.

"I have asked but these people are herders and fishermen not guards, they lack skills in fighting and are all afraid. I am the village hunter and the only one with some killing skills." Jake said motioning to his unstrung bow and quiver of shafts.

"Has anything worked?"

"Absolutely nothing."

"If you go, I will stand beside you," Curry said.

Jake broke out into uncontrollable laughter, "Lad, you lack the size, strength and skills needed to outwit a cow, let alone a Serpent." Wiping his eyes of tears, Jake looked at Curry's face, especially his eyes. Any thought of further laughter died in his throat. There was something behind those eyes, deep within his soul, something a lad his age shouldn't have. He had the eyes of a Master Guard, one who has seen death and fought to the death.

"Have any others offered?" Curry asked.

"No they haven't lad," thinking a moment Jake knew something had to be done and done now or the village would begin to die. "Done lad, I'll meet you at first light at the visitor's hut."

Curry stood and gripped Jake's forearm then left leaving his unfinished meal.

Curry went to the visitor's hut, took a three legged stool and set it outside and sat waiting for the village's lights to extinguish for the night. A half a length of time after the last light was extinguished Curry walked between the lake and the huts towards the pasture of beef.

Sending out his aura to Ral he waited. Glancing about he saw a beige form loping towards him. When Ral came and sat at his feet, Curry knelt and scratched behind the ears of his massive head. It amused Curry to watch Ral close his eyes as he scratched him. Curry told Ral "Serpents are about Ral, at morning I will travel to the Serpents and try to help the villagers get rid of them. Travel with care Ral, Serpents have no mercy in their hearts." Curry then motioned Ral into the woods to wait for him and Jake to pass then follow them. He didn't want to handle this problem without Ral nearby.

With the scratching finished, Ral turned and trotted into the darkness and was gone.

Curry returned to the traveler's hut, bolting the door for safety, he laid down on the bed and enveloped himself in intense sleep.

Just past dawn, Jake approached and found Curry sitting on a stool in front of the hut.

"Morning lad, Jake said, "you can still return to your hut and none think the less of you."

"No Jake, I would know, I am ready."

With that the two headed to the edge of the deep forest. At the edge Jake pulled his bow and inspected the sinew bow string, then strung his bow. Last he removed his quiver and checked each shaft for fletchings, broad heads and nocks. Seeing all were ready he slung his quiver and stepped into the woods followed by Curry.

"How far from here do you make them Jake?" Curry asked.

"Near as any can tell, about a length of time at a normal pace but the thickness of these woods will make a normal pace impossible.

The traveling was difficult. The area between the oaks and birches were choked with saplings, brush and ten beat vines.

Most of the time was spent untangling themselves from the ten beat vines.

After traveling about a length of time Jake froze. Silently, as he was trained by his father, who was trained by his father, he pulled and nocked a shaft without looking at his bow. Making a half draw he eyed his target. Curry peered around Jake's shoulder and saw a small bear cub of about five stones in weight. The cub stood in the middle of the trail facing Jake. Standing on his hind legs he sniffed the wind. Bears, Jake knew had bad eyesight but their nose could smell a stag carcass a length away. Jake was crosswind and knew his scent was safe for now.

Curry whispered, "NO! don't shoot the cub."

Jake whispered, "No lad, a bear cub is not my target. No cub walks without its sow and that is what I am looking for. I want to find her before she finds us. I would rather fight a pack of cave wolves with a feather that cross a she bear with a cub. A low growl that turned into a snarl drew their attention. To the left and on higher ground stood the she bear. She had scented them from the crosswind. Dropping to the ground she charged to protect her cub. Saplings the size of Curry's wrist were snapped off at the ground as she charged to kill the man things threatening her cub. Curry instantly pulled his hand staff as Jake came to full draw.

Enveloping levitation on the she bear, she began to travel through the air rising higher and higher at a high speed. A blur of beige bumped against Jake then launched and hit the side of the she bear causing her to spin as she levitated past the two. Bumping Jake caused his shaft to fly wide. The cub watched his sow moving through the air across the steep hill. He quickly dropped to all fours and followed along on the ground. Releasing the levitation, the she bear fell into a laurel thicket unharmed. The cub caught up to his sow and both disappeared into the woods.

Jake pulled another shaft and was preparing to nock it to shoot the beige cave wolf when Curry said, "Hold hunter, there is no danger here." Jake looked from the cave wolf to Curry then back to the cave wolf. The cave wolf only sat in the middle of the trail panting.

"What happened here lad?" Jake asked.

"I am a Searcher of Wizardry and this is my friend Ral, neither he, nor I will cause you any harm."

Stepping to the side so neither was to his back Jake looked from one to the other. "Why are you here Lad, I mean Searcher?" Jake asked.

"I was sent to help your village with their problem. My journey will continue into the deep woods with you or without, to be honest I prefer you to be with me."

Jake taking a deep breath, returned his shaft to the quiver and slowly said, "Bless me Searcher, from what I have just seen, I would rather have you with me than against me. Your journey and your cave wolf's is mine, no matter how it ends." Bringing his fist to his chest he bowed his head, Curry returned the bow.

Another length of time and the woods began to thin out. Stepping carefully by placing their toe first then lowering the foot along the outside edge of their sole to the heel, then slowly lowering the arch to the ground so as better feel the ground and not to break any twigs, they stalked closer. Ahead they could hear what sounded like the crunching of bones. Then they heard the flapping of large wings. They had finally located the Serpents. Jake pulled and nocked a shaft.

Curry touched his shoulder and whispered, "Your shaft will do no good here, return it to the quiver." Jake knew Curry's statement was true. Of all the shafts released at the Serpents over the pasture none killed or even injured the Serpents. Looking at his shaft then at Curry he realized the best weapon he had was standing before him, he then placed the shaft back in the quiver and stood to the side of the trail.

Curry quietly stepped around Jake and began to lead the way. Kneeling, Curry gently pulled a leafy branch to the side and saw a clearing. All the vegetation was gone or dying from being torn from the ground. Bones of cattle and sheep of their kills littered the area. Scattered about were large broken egg shells, some resting in small bunches of branches pushed together and some in the open. They had located the nest.

Curry noticed that the shells had been crushed instead of being broken from within as would happen during a hatching. The trees were denuded of all leaves leaving limbs that the Serpents roosted upon. Two Serpents were on the ground chewing the bones until they crushed them so they could reach the nourishing marrow.

In the broadest tree sat one Serpent alone. This one was three times the size of the others almost nine paces long from nose to the end of the tail. Its face bore red from his yellow and black eyes down the side of its head. Twin short horns on the crown of his head pointed backwards. This was used to pierce flesh when he would whip his head from side to side. A greenish blue ran down the bridge of the snout and the brown scales, half a palm wide, covered the body. The tail was four paces long ending in a single barb that had seen much use. The leathery stretched translucent skin covered it wings that were folded along his sides. On the end of each leg was a four finger gripping talon. It was the same that a hawk would have, only bigger. Each ending with ivory talons two hands long. Curry sensed that this was the dominate male.

Looking to each of the seven other Serpents, Curry saw no other Serpent with the same markings. This was not only the dominate male, this was the only male. Never had Curry ever heard of a flock, group, herd, school or anything that only had one male. The females were in constant movement, always they kept their distance from the male. They seemed to keep in groups as if for self protection.

Curry motioned Ral to stay and protect Jake, to Jake he said, "Remain here, if the worse happens Ral will watch you until you get back to the village." Curry grasped his hand staff, pulled his hood over his head, then stood and walked into the clearing. At once three females screeched and launched themselves at Curry, raising their tails for a death blow they came in a rush. Raising his hand staff he enveloped freezing of stone. The three fell to the ground frozen but unharmed. Three others prepared to attack when Curry mentaled to them, "I have not brought harm with me, let there be no fear or anger." Curry released the three frozen females. Standing and shaking their heads they spread their wings and returned to their roost.

From the largest of the females, Curry was mentaled, "Behind you lies one that sends flying sticks at us."

"He and the wolf with him are sworn to my command and orders, neither will cause harm, you have my word and bond on it," Curry mentaled.

"Why invade our nest, one who can mental?" the dominate female mentaled.

"I am a Searcher of Wizardry, I am sworn by oath to Kiliac the dragon of Sulferic Caverns. The nest of those near here next to the big water are in fear of you. You take their food and they begin to grow hungry." This was not quite true but if the killings continued the people would indeed begin to starve, for meat anyway.

"We are dying, what care have we of you?" she mentaled. "As for Kiliac, she would be welcome to come and end this misery.

"Dying, from what are you dying, all here seem to be strong from feeding?" he mentaled.

"The male," she mentaled, "he tasted of milkweed and is slowly dying and vows to have the nest die with him."

Milkweed was a common plant in the country. It has a green

stalk of about two thumbs across and up to a pace high. The leaves were broad with thick veins. Breaking the stalk or brushing against the leaves causes a milky white fluid to begin leaking out. The leaves can be eaten if they are boiled several times to leach out the biter sap.

"Serpents who taste of the plant die, if they land on the plant, then talon a prey, the milk enters the prey from the talons and they begin to die after eating. This kills slowly and painfully. The male is dieing slowly and is killing us so as to have the whole nest die with him. Our nest is without eggs, the male crushes all we lay as you can see. Without offspring, the nest is without a future of Serpents. If one of the shes is alone and unaware, he attacks and kills. What care we of you, we are dying."

Curry saw their problem and the problem of the villagers. He felt a deep sorrow for the Serpents. The male was dying and he would kill the last female before he became to weak, then he would die alone. He didn't know if the village's herd could survive until the Serpents died out. In a desperate act the dominate male might begin attacking the people of the village. The question was how to help the village and insure the survival of the Serpents. Looking at the dominate female, Curry mentaled, "Can you eat things other than meat?"

"Meat of the empty area at the nest next to the big water is the easiest to find and kill. We can also live on those that do not walk and do not fly of the big water."

"If I can make it so you have eggs, offspring and a future for Serpents will you take only the largest of those of the big water?"

The dominate female mentaled the remaining females, their thoughts passed back and forth then she replied, "If we survive and hatch young, yes we will take only the largest of the big water and leave the meat of the empty area. What of those who send flying sticks at us?"

"None of the nest at the big water will harm you, your offspring or your eggs."

"Enough!" the dominate male screeched. "This is my nest and my rule, the shes are mine and will obey me or die now if I wish." With a grand display of dominance the male spread his leathery wings to their fullest in an intimating manner. With another screech he launched himself from the roost and flew straight at Curry.

Curry had seen many animals in the forest. All of the males he had ever seen would posture like the male Serpent but only as a bluff. Never had he seen them attack unless attacked first or during breeding season.

The male arched his tail for a final death blow as he descended quickly towards Curry. Behind him he heard Jake snatching a shaft from his quiver and the running feet of Ral. He knew that Ral was going to launch himself at the male Serpent in defense of his friend. Curry instantly enveloped intense sleep on the male serpent and he fell to the ground in the center of the nest among the bones and crushed egg shells. Ral instantly halted his charge and took a protective stance in front of Curry.

Jake nocked a shaft and came to a full draw. If my bones lie here, he said to himself, bless me so will a Serpent!

It seemed that even the wind stopped, not a sound, not even a breath was passed. The female Serpents looked from the dominate male to the dominate female, then back to the male. Then the attack came. From the roosts came the killing screeches of all the females, then the beating of leathery wings as they left their roost. Forward and downward they came with their talons spread and tails raised. Curry lifted his hand staff in both hands and began an enveloping to raise a shield of a heating fire, he hesitated, then lowered his hand staff. Before them was a carnage that even made the village hunter's stomach want to relieve itself.

The females attacked with tails and tearing teeth, their prey, the sleeping dominate male. Scales were torn from flesh, flesh ripped from bone, bone pulled from muscle and muscle chewed from sinew. After their hatred was cooled in the male's blood they turned and returned to their roost. The dominate female looked down on Curry and mentaled.

"Searcher, no male have we to sire our eggs, we are still dying. Our death now will come slowly and lonely. We will have no bond with the nest next to the big water."

Curry closed his eyes, reached out and sensed each of the female's auras.

"First She," he mentaled, "within two of you are males waiting, the eggs when they come will be safe. When they are of age the dominate one will declare his nest and chase the weaker one off. With the weaker will go a pair of females to start his own nest. My bond is the same as before, will you give and honor your bond of your future nest?"

"I see truth before me Searcher," she mentaled, "I, we and our offspring will honor our bond to you as does Kiliac to you. Only large of the big water we will take, from the nest at the big water we will not take of any meat from the empty area."

Bringing his fist to his chest and bowing to the dominate female, Curry backed away. Ral also turned and followed Curry keeping the Serpents between him and his friend.

Jake was still at full draw, his eyes widened and asked, "What do I do now Searcher?"

"Quiver your shaft Jake, its finished," Curry said.

"Good or bad? Jake asked.

"Come, I will tell you as we return to the village, I don't like being in the forest when it turns dark, it scares me."

Jake stared at Curry, "You fought off a charging she bear with a cub and a nest of Serpents and you are afraid of the..." then it hit him, Curry's sense of humor. Jake laughed until tears rolled down his cheeks. "And Brum thinks he had a good story to tell."

As they walked Curry told Jake of what was mentaled between him and the Serpents. Jake wondered why he only stood there looking at the Serpents without talking. He had never heard of mentaling. Curry told him that the large sturgeons, that had been fouling their nets would be taken by the Serpents and no more calves would be taken. In return no villager would not try to harm the Serpents as they took the sturgeons or flew over the village. No Serpent of any size or its egg must be harmed.

"This only applies to this nest, should different Serpents come, take milkweed and tie it to the backs of the cattle. No Serpents will touch them.

Breaking through the wood line into the pasture, Curry sent Ral away and walked with Jake to the double door hut.

As they approached, Curry asked Jake, "Do you think Mame would have any pastries sprinkled with sugar?"

"If not I will bake them myself Searcher," Jake smiled.

"First let me introduce you properly, as a Searcher should be introduced. Afterwards you can spin your tale to those in the hut. Make sure Mame hears your story, if she hears it then the whole village and beyond will know of it. She can't keep a secret." Laughing, Curry and Jake entered the double doors.

After two lengths of time telling and retelling the story Curry begged his leave. Mame came around the wine and brew table and gave Curry a hug then kissed him on his cheek. Slipping her hand into his she left two coppers. "You will never be able to buy anything in this village ever again Searcher." She then kissed his other cheek.

Meeting Curry at the front door, Jake handed him a cloth bundle saying,

"For later." Jake then stood there awkwardly shuffling from one foot to the other. Wiping his eyes, Jake said, "Best you be off now to rest, for I know you journey tomorrow. Remember you will always have friends here and a bed will always be empty for you in the visitor's hut." With that Jake turned and walked into the night towards his hut.

Curry waved goodnight to those in the hut turned and walked to the traveler's hut. Sitting on the stool outside the hut in the dark, he enveloped his aura to the wind so Ral could find him. Several moments later Ral came around the hut from the lake side like a shadow. Walking up to Curry, Ral pushed his nose into the bundle that Jake had given him and sniffed. Opening the bundle, he found pastries and from the feel, they were coated with sugar. Ral laid at his feet and Curry tossed him a pastry. As they snacked on the pastries Curry thought back on this experience. A valuable lesson he had learned was that sometimes reasoning out of a problem by talking accomplished more that violence. The dominate male brought about his own death by his violent treatment of the females.

Ary had said, 'From the roost a male you shall give birth.' Again what was a senseless statement became perfectly clear in the end. Fortunately Curry and Ral were able to walk away after the end. With his help, the Serpents on the roost would now be able to give birth to a male so they could survive and prosper. Raising their young to feed only on sturgeon may also prevent problems at other villages. When the nest divides and sends the second male away with his pair of females, hopefully they will only eat sturgeons.

Tossing Ral another pastry Curry said, "We have met many nice people along our travels Ral and a few bad ones." Hearing his name he looked up expecting another pastry, smiling Curry tossed him another. Many places would make a good home but it would never be my home. Something would always be missing. Come and sleep now Ral, we need to be off before the village wakes tomorrow, I have had enough goodbyes." Ral then curled into a ball and slowly closed his eyes, Curry did what he always did and recited his auras. For the rest of the night they would relax, for tomorrow who knows how they would be tested.

CHAPTER 9
The Butchering Vines

Curry was beginning to gain confidence in the skills that he was acquiring. So far he had been lucky and his choices had been correct. What was wrong had been made right. No matter how well he masters his skills he knows that he will always be challenged on his next journey. Quickly he has found that he was given a box of skills. Warlick reached into the box and showed him a few, which he had mastered. Then from time to time he had to reach into the box and find a skill he didn't know he had. He knew that there was a limit to what he could do as a Searcher.

He also knew that to earn the rank of a Wizard someday he must not only have the knowledge of a Searcher but master all of the Searcher's skills. Pity there was no list showing what skills only a Searcher had. All of these skills he had to learn on his own. So far wisdom and good judgment had been the edge that had saved him and Ral from serious injury and possible death. They had been very lucky so far.

Curry and Ral had been wandering for eighteen leagues passing several villages. Journeys always had a purpose and a destination. Ary's absence left the two on their own and this was when they would wander. A night here at a visitor's hut learning of the problems of the local people, seeing they needed no help he moved on. At times he would meet and walk with another traveler for a short period of time. Many a strange tale would be passed around a campfire at night with others. Sometimes Curry could detect Wizardry occurring in their stories sometimes not.

As the two were walking, Ral suddenly froze, then bolted into the short brush. Rushing out the other side was a large swap rabbit, three times the size of its cousin that lives near most huts. Seeing that Ral would be awhile hunting and having dinner, Curry paused and looked around. On the other side of the road was a small stand of pine trees. Many had been cut years ago and the stumps had been decaying. Glancing back at Ral to see if he was still busy, Curry walked to the decaying pine stumps.

Approaching a likely stump, Curry kicked at the bark and saw it explode from rot. Kicking away the rest of the dead wood he reached over and picked up a stick. Placing it in the hole he began stirring the rotten wood inside. Pulling the stick out he carefully looked inside the hole. Curry never did like spiders or snakes. Seeing none were present he stuck his hand into the hole.

Feeling around the center of the hole he found a very hard piece of wood. Twisting, pushing and prying he finally got it out. In his hand he held a piece of wood about two hand lengths long and about three fingers wide. Walking over to one of the standing pines he began striking the piece of wood against the tree trunk. After all the dirt and rotten wood was knocked off, Curry examined his prize.

Lighter knot, Curry said to himself, just a sliver shaved from the side of it and it will start any fire, plus it is not effected by water. Since Curry didn't need any help starting a fire he knew that the lighter knot would be an excellent form of barter. Many a visitor's hut would trade a night's lodging for a piece of this. Tucking the lighter knot in his belt he returned to the road.

Curry saw Ral returning from the brush. At the edge of the road Ral dropped his head and chest to the ground and kept his rump high in the air. He then began rubbing one side of his snout on the grass then the other. Repeating this several times he then stood and shook himself.

Curry looked at him and said, "I am glad you have begun to care about your personal hygiene. Bless me I would have been embarrassed to let my Mother see..." Curry then realized he had no Mother and no knowledge of ever having a Mother. It was as if his memory had been removed. Thinking back it seems that his memories began when he met Warlick. Still he did remember some things but they were never related to a Mother, Father or a home that he was raised in. Searching his memory he did recall glimpses of certain faces an the wearing of certain types of clothing but as soon as they appeared they were gone. Maybe one day he would get the answers.

The Curry and Ral moved on seeing new things at every bend or turn. About midday they came upon a village. There seem to be a great deal of commotion at the edge of the village. Curry sent Ral into the woods and motioned him to guard. Curry knew that he would not have to worry about anyone approaching him from the rear and harming him.

Continuing towards the village Curry saw that the people were gathered at the center of a dike that was about thirty paces long. They were working franticly at a hole that was pouring water into the village. Speeding into a trot Curry hurried to see if he could help. When he arrived he saw that the adults were placing rocks and dirt into the hole and the children were grabbing snakes and throwing them back into the small pond. Curry didn't like snakes in the first place and seeing children tossing them about amazed him. The amazing part was that none were being bitten.

The adults were fighting a loosing battle. As soon as they placed a rock or a bucket of dirt in the hole it would wash away. Standing there he watched a man with the forearms the size of

Curry's thighs pick up rocks weighing eight stones apiece and place them in the hole. These quickly washed away also.

Turning, the man eyed Curry and said, "Lad be a solution to the problem or be gone! This is not for the amusement of travelers."

Curry said, "I don't like snakes."

"Snakes! Bless me lad those are eels, now give a hand before they all wash away and die."

Curry glanced about, his mind racing, rock and dirt was not working. Something had to slow the water until the rock and dirt could take hold. As a Wizard, Curry was told he would be able to control water, he didn't think the villagers could wait until them. Eyeing a serving table a pace wide and three paces long weighing at least twenty stones, Curry approached it.

Taking his cape and placing it on a stool he pushed the table over on its side. Taking his hand staff he stood so the legs of the table were away from him and he levitated the table. Grabbing the table to look as if he was actually lifting it he trotted towards the hole in the dike.

"Yield! Yield!" he cried. The people tripped over themselves to get out of his way. The man with the massive forearms stood with his mouth agape. Curry quickly gained the top of the dike. Taking the serving table he quickly and with force pushed it straight down into the water. The force of the water trying to move through the tiny opening forced the table against the hole all but stopping the water. Curry stood and turned to face the man with large forearms. Slinging water from his hands he said, "You there, be a solution to the problem or be gone! This is not for the amusement of villagers."

The man with forearms and the villagers roared with laughter then they all jumped to the task. Within a length of time the hole was patched and reinforced. Four men then jumped into the water and dragged the serving table over the top of the mound with the greatest of difficulty. Taking a bucket they poured water on the table to clean it then returned it to its original position. All the time they were eyeing this stranger who had lifted it over his head.

"My name's Gott, thanks for the help lad." Gott offered his forearm to Curry. All Curry could do was lay his hand flat against the man's forearm. It was too large to grip.

Curry introduced himself, "I'm called Curry."

"Those hereby sometimes witness my strength but you put me to shame. How do you account for your strength Curry?" Gott asked with a suspicious stare.

Curry knew one day he would have to answer this question. Many feared Wizardry so he came up with what he thought was a plausible answer, that is if you were gullible enough. "Where I come from we raise cattle. The land is filled with hundreds of small sink holes. As the cattle feed sometimes the calves fall into the sinkholes. They are not deep but the calves can't get out. At a very young age we are taught to lift them out. Its not really strength that we use, but leverage."

Gott looked Curry straight in the eye and said, "Yes, it was obvious to me and everyone that you were using leverage to lift a twenty stone table."

Changing the subject Curry asked, "What is the purpose of this pond, its obvious that the village build it?"

Gott said, "A small stream ran beside the village, we decided to build a pond to raise a delicacy in this area. After the dike was built it filled quickly. Several trips of three leagues away and we had captured enough of our prizes from another pond to begin breeding. Today we sell the eels live, fried, boiled, raw, roasted, you name it and we will fix it. Come let me fill a plate for you, how do you like your eels Curry?"

Curry looked at Gott and said, "In the pond." The villagers broke out into another round of laughter.

Gott said, "You saved five years of work and the village's livelihood, how can we repay you?"

"Use of your traveler's hut for a night will cancel our debt," Curry said.

"Done," said Gott.

As the excitement of the day passed the villagers began to return to their huts. All took one last look at the repair for any sign of leakage. Seeing all was right, they left to prepare their evening meal. Curry passed several huts until he found one with a coin box attached to the door.

This must be the traveler's hut, Curry said to himself. Pushing the door open he found the standard set up for a traveler's hut. Taking a stool outside Curry sat and listened to the night sounds of the village. He was drawn to the sounds of children playing inside of the huts and the laughter of the villagers. He could live here for the rest of his life but this would not be enough for him. His destiny was elsewhere and that was the road he must follow.

Watching the candle lights through the open doors of the huts, Curry didn't notice a light coming at him. Suddenly Ary swooped in front of his face then circled to enter his ear. Perching in his ear canal she said, "To the Castle of Varton, in the Providence of Shinning, you will weed the garden of butchers."

Winging to his mouth Ary waited for his fist. When it didn't come she hovered in front of his eyes. In his eyes were a far away look, then he focused on her.

"Sorry Ary, when you said the Providence of Shinning, I had a faint vision of a table having a crock of butter on it and flour on a table. I apologize, thank you for the message." With that he brought his fist to his lips, Ary landed lightly and kissed his nose. Looking to the left then the right, Ary flew to the right and into the woods where Ral was waiting.

Ary flew straight to Ral as if she had been following a map. Seeing her light coming Ral sat up. Ary came to a stop and hovered in front of his nose for about thirty heartbeats. No sounds or motions passed between them. Quick as she came she was gone. Ral laid back down looking towards the village, remaining downwind so he could always scent Curry. What had passed between Ral and Ary, only they would know.

At daybreak Curry walked to the road and enveloped his aura to the wind for Ral to come to him. He then enveloped a finding for the Castle of Varton in the providence of Shinning. The grass beside the road began to immediately lay flat showing the path to follow. He began to walk following the signs of the findings and immediately came across a large beige cave wolf laying in the grass. If a wolf could smile, he would be doing it now.

"Morning my lord," Curry said, then made an elaborate bow. "Unless you have other plans would you care to join me?" Ral cocked his head to the side then stood and began following the faint trail to their next challenge. A puzzled look came upon Curry's face. He wondered why was Ral looking at him like that.So far Curry had not heard of any of the destinations that Ary had sent him to. They could take anywhere from a length of time to thirty or more leagues of time to arrive. Unless some other traveler, that he would meet on the road, or a villager tells him the location all he can do is follow the finding signs until they stop. Then he knows he has arrived.

Looking about to make sure he was unseen, Curry began playing kick the rock.

It was a child's game, where you would kick a small rock down the road then walk over and kick it again. The game part was to never have to change your stride as you were walking. True it was not too challenging but it did help the leagues to pass quickly. In Curry's case he didn't kick the rocks. He would levitate them then hurl them down the road. Practicing this skill Curry had slowly began to be able to move items away from himself. So far he could levitate something but only straight up or down. With small items he was developing the skill of casting them where he wanted them. The largest stones he had mastered were about the size of an egg. He had the ability to hurl a stone that size with great force but at nothing of blood. He could not directly injure anything of blood. He knew that in time and with lots of practice there would be no limit to what he could move, within reason of course.

For twelve leagues and nights they traveled only stopping for Ral to sleep and for Curry to let his body rest. Eating was no problem. Ral would enter a field or a wood line and find his supper. Finishing he would later catch up to Curry.

Cresting a hill top, the finding signs disappeared. The Castle of Varton was revealed below. Curry had learned early through trial an error to observe closely before he makes any decisions or take any action. He observed the distant castle closely.

A peninsula two thousand paces long by five hundred paces wide jutted out into a sea. High waves and large rocks encircles the land mass. Where the peninsula began was only twenty five paces wide. Seventy five paces, from the start of the peninsula, there was a high wall all the way across the peninsula with a small gate allowing one cart at a time to enter. A perfect defense for the castle where a few guards could hold back an attack until reinforcements could arrive. Pounding waves prevented any attack from the sea. The placement of the castle was well thought out. The Village of Varton, just outside the castle never had to worry about a surprise attack.

From his vantage point the vegetation where the peninsula began had an odd look about it. Seeing no travelers in either direction along the road, Curry motioned Ral to stay with him.

The pair traveled down the hill to the turn off for the Castle. Following the turn off it lead to an area that had no life.

Stopping, Curry looked intently at the decaying area. Having no life was an understatement, everything was dead and decaying. Nowhere was there anything of green and all growth had ceased. It was as if a sword was drawn across the ground. On one side everything grew and was green, on the other everything was dead. Seeing parts of the first wall ahead through the dead branches of the oaks, Curry started forward. The guards may be able to explain the reason why this area was the way it was. Possibly this was some type of castle defense, after all the forest decayed away, there would be nothing for an attacking army to use as protection from the castle's archers.

A pace into the area Ral froze. The hair from his neck to rump stood on end and a defensive growl began deep in his chest. Curry stopped and took his hand staff from his belt. Looking about the bare area he could see nothing threatening, no one was there. In fact nothing, no bird, animal nor insect was there. Sending out a sensing aura, Curry could not sense anything of blood in front of or around him except for Ral.

Being very careful, because of Ral's warning, he took another pace. Ral immediately leaped in front of Curry and blocked the road with his body. Curry looked at Ral then looked down the road. Ral's action had saved his life. High in a tree came an object flying straight at the two, the speed was incredible. Ral lunged at Curry knocking him backwards to the ground. Between Curry's feet the object hit the ground leaving a gash in the dirt a hand's width deep. The object that came flying at them was a vine. Quickly Curry crawled back into the green area. He watched as the vine withdrew and climbed up a tree. After climbing the tree it became motionless, and waited. Patting Ral's side, Curry said, "Thanks Ral, I think we have found the problem here."

Curry walked to the center of the road and sat. Considering all of the traffic that he had seen so far he didn't feel he would obstruct many carts. First he began by looking at the decaying forest as a whole. All he saw was a dying forest, nothing remarkable or out of place. Then he singled out the largest oaks. The limbs were bare of all leaves and the smallest of the branches were beginning to fall to the ground from rot. He then looked at the smaller trees and saplings, again the same conditions. Last he examined the ground. Dead leaves and branches were the only things on the ground. No life, nothing of any color existed.

Ral knew his friend was aware of the danger so he stood and

crossed the road to a small creek. After drinking his fill he entered the adjacent field and began to hunt.

Gray or black was all that could be seen by Curry in the forest. As he looked to the left near the water line he saw a butterfly crossing the water towards the area of vines. Suddenly a vine, no longer than his forearm whipped out and slashed the butterfly in half. Standing quickly, he hurried to the tiny vine, making sure he remained in the green area. Sitting down he had a safe and close up view of one of the vines. The vine, after it killed the butterfly, reached out with the tip of its tentacle and snared one part of its kill and pulled it to where it grew from the ground. It repeated the same actions with the other part. Looking closely Curry saw that the dismembered butterfly began to slowly darken and decay before his eyes. It was as if the ground itself was draining nourishment from the butterfly. Taking a stick, he reached out slowly to the vine, nothing happened. Dropping the stick he very carefully reached out to the vine. Instantly the vine whipped out and lashed at Curry's hand. Jerking his hand back he saw a small cut on his thumb that began to seep blood. The vine only attacked something living, only things that gave it nourishment.

The vine had a row of sharp thorns along the length of its body, similar to a saw blade, only sharper. With this it could grip a tree or lash out cutting its prey in half. About a tenth of the way down from its tip was a small growth like a bulb. Curry had no idea what the purpose of this growth was used for.

At a glance no one would notice this or any of the other vines as he could attest to. There was only a very slight color difference between the tree and the vine. Looking into the forest he could make out a vine here and another there because now he knew what to look for.

Curry sent out a searching to examine their auras. They had none, this was definitely Wizardry. Thinking of all the envelopings he possessed, he decided on the ones that might rid the Castle of their problem.

Curry tried levitating the vine, the roots held it firm in the ground and its grip never released from the sapling. He then enveloped a heating fire, the sapling darkened and began to burn. Removing the fire it appeared that it had no effect on the vine. Then Curry had it and began to smile. Raising his hand staff he enveloped the freezing of stone. The vine remained immobile. Reaching out with his hand to examine the frozen vine closer, the vine attacked his hand. The speed of its attack had been reduced to a quarter of its regular speed but it still attacked. His smile quickly faded. He remembered what Warlick had told him about the freezing of stone. Things of blood were all effected the same way. Things not of blood were effected in different degrees of freezing or not at all. These vines only became slower. Placing his chin in the palms of his hands he sat and stared at the vine. The butterfly had turned into pile of dust.

Ral, having eaten, returned to where Curry sat at the edge of the dead forest near the water. Standing beside him, he sniffed the air, then laid at Curry's side. Curry reached over and absentmindedly began scratching behind his ears. Heartbeats became moments, which stretched into a length of time. Arching his back to stretch he vigorously started scratching his hair, he turned to Ral and said, "This is making an old man out of me. I wish that I had more..." then his head snapped up. "That's it Ral!, or maybe that's it." Curry remembered enveloping aging on a set of chains and they dissolved. The worse that could happen would be nothing.

Curry gripped his hand staff and removed the freezing of stone from the vine. He then enveloped aging on the tiny vine. Immediately it began to grow slowly. Terror filled his heart, what had he done now! If it kept growing what would he do. Sliding back further into the green area he watched as it grew. When it had increased its length by one third it released from the sapling began to sway then fell to the ground. The color changed to a dark black and it was dead. Fear turned into exaltation. The problem was solved and only in about a length of time, he thought to himself. He stood and began brushing the grass from his cape. Taking a last look at the dead vine before he walked away, he saw a tiny puff of dark dust rise from the bulb near the end of the vine. Kneeling and looking closely, Curry saw that the small bulb on the vine had been filled with seeds or spores of some type. When it died, it sent the seeds into the air to begin growing. If it had allowed the seeds to drop earlier it would have to compete against its own offspring for food. This way the species would continue.

Curry could kill the vines but the solution would only cause a greater problem. If this tiny vine spewed forth that many seeds he could only imagine how many a mature vine would cast. If the wind should catch these seeds and blow them the wrong way there would be no stopping their spread until everything living had been killed. Fortunately none of the vines had died yet so the problem with the seeds hasn't occurred. This problem needed action now before it cannot be controlled. He stood and began walking the length of the dead area making sure he stayed in the green area.

Every time he had a solution he was thrown another bigger problem. Finding several small vines near the green area, he cautiously approached them. First he made sure a larger vine on a tree nearby could not reach him. He then sat and examined the vines. Same as the first he had killed, only slightly larger.

Curry knew what would happen if he enveloped aging. Now he had to start applying different options with the aging and see what would happen. Picking a small vine he aged and froze it.

This would age the vine and make it move slowly. As it began to fall Curry crushed it with a stick, seeds exploded from the bulb. The second one he aged and crushed just before it released from the sapling, seeds exploded. In frustration he aged one and then tried snatching it from the ground but only succeeded in shearing it at ground level and cutting his hand. He held it and waited and waited, nothing happened. The seed bulb did not explode. He continued watching the vine in his hand and waited for the bulb to explode with seeds. He knew it was coming, his luck hadn't been that good lately. Reaching down he felt the bulb. It was growing softer and softer, then it began to ooze a yellowish liquid that had a foul odor. The vine was dead and so was its bulb. Wiping his cut hand on his breeches he enveloped rapid healing. The blood flow stopped almost instantly and began to scab over.

Thinking about what had just happened, Curry reasoned that the vines must be killed before they can die of the ageing. This would prevent the spreading of the seeds. The killing requires that the vine be severed at the base just after the enveloping of aging.

Curry again stretched and said to himself, "Now what?"Ones that were small and away from the larger vines he could handle. The others would not be so easy, they may be even impossible. He didn't have the strength to sever the large vines. As he attacked one, his back would be exposed to another, which was not a good option. Ral with his strength would be of no help either. If he aged the whole forest he could not be able to sever the bases before they died, resulting in seeds being spread. Curry needed some help. Looking about he observed the first wall and saw guard standing there in the gate.

Ral became nervous because Curry hadn't moved in several moments. Hearing the whining, Curry looked down and said, "I'm going for help." He then motioned Ral to guard and pointed at the forest. Ral would not allow anyone to enter the forest from his side, not that anyone would try and pass a cave wolf standing in the middle of the road.

Curry walked to the center of the road and looked into the forest. Reaching down he gathered up the hem of his cape and tucked it into his belt. For what he was about to do he needed speed and didn't want his feet getting tangled in his cape. He also didn't want the vines to have anything extra to grab onto.

Turning he looked at Ral one last time and motioned for him to stay.

Facing the forest he began running, holding his hand staff in both hands he enveloped the strongest of freezing of stone that he could. Ral howled from frustration as Curry began running into the forest. He knew the terrible danger that his friend was running into and there was nothing he could do to help. The howl of a cave wolf, especially in the middle of the day attracted the attention of the guards at the first wall. Staring in disbelief they shook their heads out of pity, someone was being chased into the butchering vines by a cave wolf, at least it would be a quick death for him.

Curry ran straight down the center of the road. Looking to the front and either side he watched as the vines began to release and approach him. True they had been slowed in their speed but there were so many of them. Ducking, diving and jumping he managed to avoid the slashing of their saw edges. Ten paces from the safety of the other side Curry felt a pain at his ankle and he was snatched to the ground. Turning he saw a vine had grabbed him and had stopped his progress. The thorns were slowly cutting into him and dragging him back into the forest. In desperation he pulled his fork from his belt and began savagely stabbing at the vine with one of the fork's tines. The vine held tight then began to loosen slightly, just enough for Curry to jerk his bloodied ankle free and lunge for the safety of the green of the other side.

Standing, Curry began pulling his cape out from under his belt. Shaking his cape free he returned the fork inside his belt. Curry was glad that the hard part was over, now to get help from the castle. Turning he was confronted by four guards standing in the gate of the first wall. They were all holding pikes at the on guard position, this was where the pike was held diagonally across the chest. He had seen many guards in his travels and knew that these were trained by a professional and they acted as professionals. They all moved as one and none had a lapse of concentration.

"Hold there!" a guard shouted at Curry. "Turn, and about you go or face our pikes."

Curry was confused, it seemed that anyone passing thought the forest would be welcomed. Now he was being challenged, to either return back through the forest or face their pikes and die. Either way he would probably die.

"I have come to help, I have found how to kill the vines."

The guards looked from one to the other, then one said, "Hold there," stepping backwards he turned and shouted, "Master of the Guard! Master of the Guard!" His shout was repeated by all of the villagers who could hear and relayed to the castle.

From the Castle was heard the hoof beats of a running horse. Across the drawbridge came the Master Guard at full speed. Racing to the first wall he observed his guards had a blacked caped figure under the on guard position. Reining his horse to a halt, he slide from the saddle pulling his pike from its saddle scabbard. The two guards in the center stepped backwards and to either side to allow the Master Guard to pass. The other outside guards never took their eyes off of Curry.

Spinning his pike he went from the on guard position to the lunge position, where the pike was held in a horizontal position aimed at the foe's chest. Curry locked eyes with him and knew any movement on his part and his life would be ended.

There was violent hatred in the Master Guard's eyes. Curry was looking at the face of death and didn't know why he was being threatened this way. Slowly the Master Guard's face began to soften and seeing that this was not the one that had burned hate into his heart. He relaxed and spun his pike to the carry position, where the pike was held at a forty five degree angle over his right shoulder. Turning he tossed his pike to a guard and ordered him to scabbard it. The guard raced to the Master Guard's horse and placed the pike back into it's scabbard. These men, Curry noticed, obeyed their orders instantly and without question. This would come in handy if Curry's plan was to be carried out.

"Young sir, may I be of assistance to you?" the Master Guard asked in a no nonsense tone.

"My name is Curry and I think I can help you rid yourself of your problem." He turned and motioned towards the forest. He then turned to the Master Guard looking for some signs of gratitude. None were forth coming.

"How, may I ask will you perform this task, sir?" The sir was almost spit out as an insult by the Master Guard.

"Master Guard, may I speak to you alone?" The Master Guard was suspicious about this traveler's conduct. He did owe Lord Varton a full report of anyone passing through the forest to the first wall. He was going to be sure that he kept this visitor at a disadvantage.

"Follow me." Curry was taken a short distance to the side of the gate but still on the forest side of the first wall. As the Master Guard turned to face Curry he reached behind his back and pulled a dagger partly from its scabbard. He didn't become a Master Guard by being careless.

"Master Guard, I am a Searcher of Wizardry, I was sent here to give what help I could. I have found a way to rid you of these vines but it will require the help of you and your guards. I can begin to make them die but they must be severed from the ground before they die or they will spread their seeds and more will grow."

"Searcher, we suffered these butchering vines because of a Wizard, now you want us to trust another Wizard to stop it?

"I don't understand?" Curry said.

"Some time back, one dressed in a cape as you with dark hair came to the first wall and was turned away. There was something about his eyes, something a person never wanted to look upon twice. The person just smiled, turned and walked away. Stopping he reached down and pulled some drying grass from the ground. Rubbing it between the palms of his hands he turned and blew the dust at the guards. Laughing he walked away."

"About a week later the ground began to die in the little forest. All of the rabbits, moles and vermin disappeared. Later the village dogs began to come up missing. Before we knew what had caused the disappearances the vines had taken control. Nothing living could pass the forest road without being butchered and dismembered. We send boats out to bring in supplies but for every ten boats we launch nine would sink. You are the first to make the trip on this road and live." Pushing his dagger back into its scabbard, the Master Guard brought his hand in front of him and hooked his thumbs in his belt. Tell me more of your plan and I will present it to Lord Varton."

Curry Explained in detail to the Master Guard of how he planned to attack the vines using the castle's guards. After asking a few questions the Master Guard turned and walked to his horse, placing his foot in the stirrup he swung up and mounted his horse.

Looking at Curry, he said, "Remain where you stand." He then looked at the four guards and knew he didn't have to give them orders to guard him closely. Spurring his horse's flanks, he galloped to the Castle.

A length of time later Curry heard hoof beats. Looking up Curry saw two riders. One was the Master Guard and the second who rode before him was a man in a long green tunic bearing a crest and a belted side sword. As they came to a halt Curry brought his fist to his chest and bowed his head. He held this position until he was addressed by the Lord.

"Searcher, the Master Guard has explained your plan, I am responsible for my people and I will not endanger any of their lives on the spoken word of a stranger. Convince me of who you are and we will talk of action, if not, you will! return on the road from which you came and you have my word and bond on that."

Curry knew this was a no nonsense Lord. Thinking for a moment he thought of a way to convince the Lord. To the astonishment of the Lord and his guards Curry disappeared. The Master Guard pulled his side sword and moved his horse between Lord Varton and where Curry had been standing. The four guards with pikes also advanced to protect their Lord. Curry moved and stood next to Lord Varton and removed the invisibility. "Convinced, my Lord.?" He asked Lord Varton.

Astonished Lord Varton shouted, "Done!" Turning to the Master Guard he said, "Turn out the full complement of guards for orders." With that he turned and returned to the castle.

The Master Guard turned to the four frightened first wall guards and said, "Turn to!" Instantly the four went to the carry position with their pikes and began trotting to the castle. "Come Curry we have much to prepare." He made sure he kept a sword's blade distance from this Searcher. He didn't know what he could or would do next and wanted to be prepared.

When the full complement was assembled the Master Guard held inspection. "Stand to," he ordered. All came to ridged attention. "Present side swords." All the guard pulled their swords and held them by the hilts with the blades straight down. The Master Guard went from man to man looking at each blade, here he looked at the tarnish or there he tested an edge with his thumb. After finishing the last line he ordered, "Secure side swords." As one they all returned their swords to their scabbards. After looking at each man in each rank he said, "At daylight we go to war," several in the ranks turned their heads and looked at the Master Guard, a stern look and they returned to their position of attention. "Your life depends on your edge, the villager's lives depend on your edge, if you are satisfied with its sharpness then sleep well, Dismissed."

Curry asked the Master Guard, "That's it, you are not going to order them to sharpen their swords?"

"Curry, in the morning you will not be able to find any blade that you couldn't shave with, well that I couldn't shave with.

From the looks of it you haven't a need of a sharp blade yet. Come and tell me of your plan again, I don't want any surprises tomorrow."

The night was filled sounds of grinding wheels and wet rocks as the guards prepared for battle. Each sword, dagger and pike was inspected, sharpened and then stropped. First the blade was put to a grinding wheel where a new edge was cut into the metal. Then it was used on a wet rock. A wet rock was a flat stone that had just the barest of roughness. The blade was passed back and forth while water was poured on it to rinse away the blade filings and loose stone particles. This removed all the metal burrs and refined the edge. Last of all the blade was rubbed against a large leather strap until a shaving edge was made. Their arms freshly oiled were ready but were the guards, the next morning would tell.

At daybreak Lord Varton, the Master Guard and Curry stood before the two lines of guards.

Curry began his instructions, "Rear line of guards pass your swords to the front." Without question they obeyed. "Belt these on so you have a sword on each side." After his was accomplished he said, "First line pass your daggers back to the rear line so they can belt them on." The second line did as instructed. "Second line take up a pike." When all was ready Curry gave the assault instructions.

"First line of guards as we approach the dead area I will cause the vines to slow down and grow older, they will begin to grow longer and become weaker. Before they fall to the forest floor you must cut the base of the vine completely into. If you fail to do exactly as I have instructed they will spread their seeds and you will have a worse problem that before. Second line will use their pikes to protect the first line as they approach the base of the vine. Deflect or pin the vines until the first line has done their job. They will be slower and weaker but don't let your guard down, remember that a tiny one can trip you and make you a victim for a larger one."

"Questions?" Master Guard asked the lines of guards. "Ask now if you have any questions or any doubts before we move out. Last chance…bless me I will have your eyes for buttons if any man says to me, I thought he meant something else." All stood silent and ready. The Master Guard looked at Curry.

"With your permission," Curry said looking at Lord Varton who nodded his approval. Looking towards the guards Curry said, "we are off."

The men broke into teams of two, a pike behind each sword. Spreading out so that a pike blade could touch a pike blade to either side of him they came abreast of the dead line. Each team had a responsibility of about four paces wide to their front.

Advancing to the front, Curry said, "All must be killed before they fall, allow none to die of age." Turning back he enveloped aging for about the distance of a pace. Then the slaughter began. Never had Curry seen such mastery of arms. These men were experts with swords and pikes they didn't just hack at the vines. The pikes shot out like vipers protecting the backs of the swordsmen. Deflecting here, pinning there and at times severing the tips. The swordsmen wasted not a blow, vertical slash here finishing with backhanded diagonal slash. The word mercy was left in the village, even though they were just vines they were butchering vines, a dangerous foe.

Slowly Curry expanded the aging. The attack continued for two lengths of time. When Curry saw the men begin to tire he stopped the aging and pulled the men back. Villagers brought water and sweets to the guards. The sweets were not a reward but to give them a surge of energy for the second attack. Rested, the guard began the battle again. Each tree and sapling was circled to insure no vine was left in hiding. As they approached the end a shout was sounded.

"Wolf my Lord," shouted a guard. Two with pikes advanced to attack the wolf.

A wolf standing in the middle of the day on the road was a

most unusual sight, so was the sight of Curry. The Master Guard felt these were linked somehow.

"Hold!, what were your orders." At once the two pike men turned and returned to protect their partners. Neither wanted their eyes used as buttons.

When all had reached the green of the other side Curry called out, "Ground your weapons and draw your daggers." The pike men placed their pikes on the ground and drew both daggers. The swordsmen placed both swords on the ground and took one of the daggers.

"Touch hand to hand and return to the first wall." The guards raised their arms to their sides at chest level. When they each touched a guard's hand to his left and right they began to advance. Any vine no matter how small was to be severed at it's base. The Master Guard in his tactful manner encouraged the men.

"Bless me if I find but one vine without a blade mark I will have your future children in my coin pouch!" All the men as one felt their loins tighten. Stopping without being ordered to, they all returned to the green area and began again, this time no branch or leaf was left undisturbed in a search for the butchering vines. Just at dusk the line had returned to the first wall. It had taken a full league of time to battle the vines.

"Have them stand down, rest and eat. Tomorrow we repeat with rakes and daggers to be sure." the Master Guard ordered. Too tired to ask questions they all left except for the Master Guard and Lord Varton.

Curry said, "The ground has been leached of its very life, in the morning all of the trees, branches and leaves will be gone, have the men rake the ground and be positive that all vines are gone." Lord Varton felt it was best not to ask how they would disappear. Nodding he turned and spurred his mount back to the castle.

The Master Guard dismounted his horse and removed the belt holding his side sword and dagger. Draping it across the saddle he approached the Searcher. Curry was astonished by his actions. A Master Guard approaching without arms and defenseless was the highest honor he could bestow on anyone. This honor was never given to anyone except the Lord of the castle.

"Searcher I have a tingling at the back of my neck that tells me this will be the last I see of you. He then rendered a Regal Salute. Bringing his fist to his chest he bowed his head and went to one knee. "I thank you for my Lord, my guards, the village and myself." Curry was shocked. This courtesy was reserved only for the ruler of a country. Honored by this salute Curry's eyes began to tear and fall from his cheeks. Turning his back out of embarrassment, he stood there a cried silently.

The Master Guard was not offended by Curry turning his back on his Regal Salute. Curry's tears acknowledged the salute. Quietly the Master Guard stood and went to his horse. Taking his belt from the saddle the threw it over his shoulder and mounted. Hearing him mount, Curry wiped his eyes and turned to look at the Master Guard. They made brief eye contact then both turned and walked their different ways. Master Guard to the castle and Curry to Ral and their future.

Curry passed through the dead forest towards Ral. Sitting in the center of the road, Ral had waited patiently. Turning he looked one last time at the forest. Raising his hand staff he enveloped a warming fire for eight lengths of time. The forest from the green at his feet to the first wall and from water to water burst into flames and rose to a height of three paces. These flames would burn hot and continuously until the enveloping ended. Everything within the fire would become dust by morning. From the dust blown from the hands of some evil Wizard to dust it will return.

Looking down at Ral, Curry said, "Ary said you will weed the garden of butchers. This involved a little more than just pulling some weeds. Fortunately the guards were excellent gardeners. Smiling they turned and melted into the night.

The night of fire would be written in the chronicles of the Providence of Shinning. Every villager in the country side would see the glow of the fire that night. The next morning the people from all over the Providence would come to investigate the huge blaze. Once again they would be able to safely travel the road to the castle. What would not be written in the chronicles is that a black caped lad had made it possible.

The true story of how the castle was saved would be remembered by the Master Guard who had knelt before a mere child.

CHAPTER 10
The Calling

Curry and Ral traveled for several lengths of time then moved off of the road into the security of the forest. When it became too dark to walk safely, he had enveloped a companion fire and levitated it in front of them as they traveled. Coming upon a small clearing, Curry stopped and sat with his back against a log. Ral scented upwind for any intruders then listened for strange noises downwind of his nose. Finding nothing out of place he laid on the opposite side of the fire from Curry.

The small no heat companion fire gave Curry comfort. Even thought there was no heat, the glow provided a sense of security to keep the wild animals away. Smiling Curry knew no animal could or would approach with cave wolf sitting next to a Searcher. Still it gave him psychological comfort and it was nice to look at the ever changing yellow, red and orange flames as they danced in front of him.

He settled back and began to recite his list of auras as he had done everyday. Finishing his list, he dimmed the fire's radiance slightly and laid back and sought out the star that didn't move. Finding it he mentally located East where the morning Sun would rise. He felt that he should always know where North was located. That way he could find any direction. It would be embarrassing, if not disastrous, to walk North for three lengths to find out you have been walking South. Since he was being given assignments to help people, he knew he had to know his directions.

There were several ways he could directions. If he saw a crescent moon he could mentally draw a line from one tip through the second tip straight to the Earth. Where the line touched the Earth it was South. Another was on a cloudy day where he couldn't see the Sun, he would find a fire ant mound built next to a tree, rock or fence post. By lining himself up with the ant mound and then the object he would be facing North. They build the ant hill to allow the last of the southerly Sun rays to warm the hill for the night. The unmoving star was always North.

Curry laid back and closed his eyes relaxing in the calm of the night.

"By what are you called?" came a voice. Jumping to his feet and gripping his hand staff, Curry was amazed that anyone could have come this close without Ral giving a warning. Peering into the darkness Curry enlarge and brightened the companion fire to reach into the darkness illuminating their uninvited guest. Again the voice called out, "By what are you called?"

Then it struck Curry like a thunder bolt, he was being mentaled. Turning around in a full circle Curry peered not only on the ground but in the branches of the trees. Some creature was close and trying to reach him. Eyes scanning, Curry knelt and encircled Ral's neck with his arm hoping he might aid him in finding their visitor and protect him if the need arose. Together they waited for the creature to expose himself. Touching Ral always gave Curry strength and confidence to do what he felt he couldn't do.

Pulling away from Curry, Ral turned and sat staring into his eyes. "I asked, by what are you called?"

Curry stared for a moment, stood, then stepping backwards to sit on the log, tripped and fell over the log into the leaves. Regaining his feet, he stepped over the log and sat heavily facing Ral.

Regaining his composure Curry said, "I knew of mentaling but I never thought to try it with you." Ral only stared at Curry. Slapping his forehead with the palm of his hand, Curry mentaled. "I knew of mentaling but never thought to try it with you."

Ral mentaled, "Sometimes things are too close for you to see."

Nodding in understanding, Curry brought his fist to his chest and bowed, "I am Curry, a Searcher of Wizardry who responds to the messages of a Mintz named Ary, I have been calling you Ral."

Ral mentaled, "With your permission I will call you Searcher, the man sound you make when you call me, I do not find displeasing, you may call me that." Curry mentaled to Ral what had happened from the time of his waking in the woods with Warlick until he met the wounded Ral. Ral told him of being wounded by the guards who were hunting him.

Curry mentaled, "At Lady Currant's Castle I was attacked by Lord Marko. I am not offended by your actions, I was just wondering why you didn't come to my aid?"

"I knew the man weapons, where I stood, would cause greater harm than what he was doing to you. Had you really needed help I would have come to your aid. I had decided that if he touched any weapon I would have sent him to the void. Before he touched one, he tripped over me and sent himself to the void."

Curry mentaled, "How far is it possible for us to mental each other?"

"We must be in sight of each other, even if we are unseen."

"I don't understand?"

"If we are on a straight road and I alone walk away, we can

mental until you just lose sight of me. That is the distance we can mental. If you are on one side of Lady Currant's den of stone and I am on the other, we can mental. If it is like now, with darkness, we can mental for the distance as when we have lightness. Never farther than sight. We do not have to see each other to mental."

"Could anyone, man or creature, hear us?" Curry asked.

"Mentaling is special. Man cannot mental man. You can mental towards one or several who are of fin, fur and feather, only they can hear. You can mental them but they may choose not to answer or acknowledge that you even mentaled them. I have mentaled you for your actions of saving my life in the past."

"Can you mental those of fin, fur and feather?"

"Only those who are like me, other Rals only."

"Can you choose to mental another man?"

"I can choose only one man to mental to in my lifetime, no others can I mental. I can answer them but cannot start a mentaling. I have chosen you to mental to as my lifetime choice."

In a brief period of time he has been given a supreme honor of a Regal Salute by a Master Guard and now Ral has chosen him as his lifetime mental partner. Being overwhelmed is an understatement. He needed to sit and think for awhile and be alone with his thoughts. There are so many things in Wizardry and he felt that he has only just started to scratch the surface. With the powers and skills he has now he could only imagine what he would have as a Wizard if he were chosen. It was clear to him why the Cosmos chose only certain ones to have this power and to only use it for good. It would be so easy to turn to evil ways to gain riches and fame. That is why Olen and Warlick are so careful about who is chosen as a Searcher.

Curry mentaled, "Rest and sleep now, I will watch over you tonight. I know you don't need me to do this but it gives me a good feeling to be able to protect you from time to time. Even if it is just to watch you sleep."

"Guard me Searcher, then I will guard you." Ral laid down and slowly closed his eyes. Shortly his quivering legs showed he had been taken by sleep.

Curry had Wizardry forced upon him by Warlick. Tonight he accepted and embraced the responsibility and the awesome power of Wizardry. So much good could be accomplished, he knew he had made the right choice. Come morning he would walk the path of Wizardry willingly with Ral as his friend.

Just at daybreak Ral woke and guarded Curry as he had his intense sleep. After a few moments the pair walked to the road and began to wander. Up until now, Curry only had himself to talk to as they journeyed. The problem is that you sometimes become bored with who you are talking to. Now he had a friend to talk with. They could answer each others questions, give advice or just plain talk to pass the time as they walked. The most important thing for Curry was that he could better learn of the animal world.

They were into their fourth league of wandering and Ral had asked of the man ways. Curry had been explaining the ways of humans. Marriage, mating for life, naming of children and the word called ego. Curry also gave Ral the correct terminology of the language he was using.

Curry mentaled, "Lady Currant's stone den is called a castle. The sticks with daggers are called pikes and the metal thing I keep in my belt is called a…"

"Listen, a young female is calling for help," Ral mentaled.

Both began to run in the direction that Ral had been looking. A short distance away they turned a small curve and Curry saw four lads standing around a young girl. Each had a blue scarf tied around his forehead and a dagger was tucked in the back of their belts. The blue scarf was apparently a sign of their association with each other. They were pushing her back and forth from one to another. One reached out and kicked the basket she had been carrying and spilt the blackberries she had just picked.

"Go to the right through the woods and come up behind them quietly. I will approach them from the road," Curry mentaled. Ral ran into the woods.

Curry ran towards the tormented girl. When he approached he went to the side of the road away from Ral. He wanted to distract them long enough to give Ral a chance to get ready.

"What have we here, a hero come to save this girl?" the tallest of the four asked.

"I want no trouble from you, I heard her cries and came to see if I could help." The girl was laying in the dirt of the road crying.

"We run the village North of here and we own the people. Be off with you now! No, wait. Dennis mark this lad with your blade as a reminder not to interfere with us again."

Dennis said, "Right you are Jason." Dennis then pulled a dagger from the small of his back and slowly advanced on Curry.

"I must warn you I have a stick," Curry said as he lifted his hand staff in his right hand for them to see. They all began to laugh.

"Mark him and be quick about it Dennis." Dennis came closer.

"You wish to mark me, here let me help you." Curry pulled his left sleeve back to his elbow and offered it out for Dennis to cut. Curry envelope the freezing of stone on his left arm. Dennis slashed out and cut Curry's arm, or tried to. The blade sounded as if it had hit a rock and left no mark.

The four were shocked. They saw he had a bare arm yet he was unharmed.

"I suggest you sit on the road for a moment, while I speak with the girl," Curry told them.

"I don't take orders boy, I give them," Jason said.

Curry mentaled Ral, "Make yourself know and frighten them."

Ral had stalked to within three paces of the four as Curry had distracted them. Raising up he advanced to within a pace and released a snarling growl. As one they all turned and saw the huge cave wolf. Dennis the youngest of the four wet himself in fear.

"Daggers," Jason yelled. They all pulled their daggers and prepared for the attack.

Curry enveloped deep sleep on the four of them and watched as they dropped like stones. Turning, he stepped towards the crying girl.

"No please don't kill me," she begged.

Curry sat on the ground in front of the girl.

"You have nothing to fear from me, I came to help you."

"You killed them and the wolf, make him go away please."

"He is my friend and the four are not dead only sleeping. No harm will come to you. You are safe now, are you hurt?"

"No, I'm fine. I have gotten use to it as has everyone in the village."

"Who are you?" Curry asked.

"I'm Heather."

Heather was sixteen years old and very, very pretty. It made him uncomfortable just to have her looking at him. As he listened to her he was constantly brushing dust off his cape, pulling at it here and tugging at it there to make it neater. Never had he been self conscience about his looks before.

She had red hair the color of strawberries and very pale green eyes. She had just a few freckles across the bridge of her nose and was wearing a short sleeve white blouse with ribbons on the sleeves. Her blue skirt fell to just below her knees and was finished off with a pair of leather slippers. Her face was smooth and without blemishes and when she smiled it would cause a scholar to begin to babble. Curry only hoped that he could make full sentences when he spoke to her. To be safe he choose to use small words and speak slowly.

"You may be able to help, could I tell you about them

208

please?" Thinking, Curry realized what he had said, this was going to be harder than he thought.

"What I meant to say was, I may be able to help, would you tell me about them please?"

Heather frowned at him and said, "They are the village bullies. Now we will be punished for what you just did."

Looking at this stranger who couldn't be cut and who had a cave wolf as a friend, she wondered if he just might be able to do what the villagers couldn't.

"Jason's parents died last Winter of the fever. He was old enough to work, learn a trade and had many offers from the villagers to learn their trades. He refused them all. He was big and lazy, the two conditions don't go together. He became the village bully. It wasn't a great problem then and many overlooked his conduct because he was an orphan. When the other boys were kicked out of their villages and came here the trouble started. It was as if bad was attracted to bad. The three newcomers moved into Jason's hut."

"For food they would just walk into someone's hut and take the food they wanted. With four daggers none of us could stop them. Whenever a traveler left they would steal the coppers from the coin box on the traveler's hut door. Widow Martha would clean and maintain the traveler's hut for the few coins she collected from the coin box. With the money she bought what she had to have to exist. Whatever they wanted they took. It started with just pushing people around, now if they are crossed they will beat the person or mark them with a blade. Several have had bones broken."

"I jar jelly when the blueberries, blackberries and strawberries are fresh and abundant. I boil the berries with water and honey. When it thickens, I pour it into small clay jars and then pour melted bee hive wax over the top to make it last. In the Winter when all the berries are gone, I sell the jellies to travelers to help make money for our family. My Father is the village axe man, he cuts firewood for the village and my Mother is the village seamstress. I also watch the village children and get paid a few coppers for the service."

"I was out picking blackberries when they came by to make sport of me. Like I said they will get revenge on us when you leave. We don't have enough strength to fight them off or to make them leave." She leaned over slightly and lifted the hem of her skirt to clean her face of dust and tears. This innocent action exposed her leg just above her knee. Curry's heart began to race. He was terribly confused about how he was reacting in front of this girl.

Standing, Curry turned his back so he could regain his composure. Taking a deep breath he turned and helped Heather to her feet.

"These four will trouble you no more Heather." He didn't have to say her name but he couldn't help himself.

"No, please don't. No matter how bad someone is they shouldn't be killed. Punish them yes, but don't kill them."

Curry thought for a moment then a moment longer. He then said, "These four will not be harmed, they will go away and never again harm another person again. In return I will ask that you and your village do something for me."

"Yes, if you can make them go away we will do anything within our power," Heather said. Her voice was having a strange effect on him. He needed to deal with this quickly and have her be off.

"I know of four gentlemen needing a place to sleep and a means of making money for food. Would you give up the watching of the children and allow them to do it?"

"If these four bullies are gone, then the men you talk of could have their hut. Giving up the few coppers I get for watching the children would be little sacrifice to rid us of them."

"One last question, is there a pond or creek near here?"

"Yes, yonder through the woods." She had pointed in the direction where Ral had been hidden.

Taking her basket, Curry walked into the blackberry bushes

and enveloped levitation and pulling. The blackberries pulled from their stems and came to Curry. When her basket was full he turned and took it to her. He had duties to perform and she did not need to be around when he did it.

"Here Heather, take your basket and return to your village, leave your problems with me and remember your promise."

"Thank you," she said and turned and began to walk away.

Stopping she placed her basket on the ground, turned and returned to Curry. Wrapping her arms around his neck she gave him a lingering kiss on his lips.

"What is she doing Searcher, do you need help?" Ral mentaled.

"Not now Ral," he mentaled back.

Breaking the kiss she looked Curry in the eyes then turned, grabbing her basket, ran for the village.

Never had Curry been kissed like that. As a matter of fact he had never been kissed before by a girl. His body was reacting the same way when he fought with Lord Marko. He was shaking, sweating, breathing heavily and his heart was racing. It was an excited reaction not one of fear. Looking at the four sleeping figures he began to calm down.

"Time to deal with these four," he mentaled Ral.

"How are you going to make them go away Searcher?"

"I'm not."

"I don't understand."

"Come with me I will need your help Ral."

Curry levitated the four and grabbing their collars he pulled them into the woods towards the water. About sixty paces away he came upon a small pond. Looking about he saw it was a secluded area. Curry didn't want any witnesses for what he was about to do.

"Are you going to send them to the void by using water?" Ral mentaled.

"As a Searcher I can't injure anything of blood but they don't know that. When they awake I want you to put your face close to theirs and give your most vicious snarl. I will deal with them after that."

"Tell me when Searcher," Ral mentaled.

Curry lowered the four and placed them with their heads touching as they laid on the ground. He reached down and removed the blue scarves from their heads. They no longer needed a symbol of unity. Straightening their legs and putting their arms to their sides he looked at Ral.

"Get ready for when they wake."

Ral went and stood at their heads. Curry grasped the hand staff and enveloped them from the neck down with immobility. They could talk, breath and their hearts would beat but that was all. He released the hand staff that he had enveloped them with sleep and they all woke at once. Ral emitted a snarl that even frightened Curry. In an instant all four began screaming. A huge cave wolf's hot breath was in their faces and the sound they heard was the sound that they knew would send them to the void.

"Help us, help us, somebody please help us," they screamed.

Curry mentaled Ral to step back. Curry pulled his hood over his head for effect, then went and stood over the four. "Do I have your attention?"

"Yes, yes just save us from the wolf," they screamed.

"Screaming irritates my friend, you might consider not raising your voices again. I may not be able to stop him next time. They immediately became quite. They kept turning their eyes to the left and right, as mush as they could, to see if the wolf was coming at them again.

"Nothing upsets me and my wolf more than someone who takes advantage of someone else, like the four of you have done."

"We are sorry," Jason said on behalf of the four, "We will never do it again, only please let us live."

"Why is it that I knew you were going to say that, the only

problem is that I know you are lying. As soon as I leave, you will begin your terror of the village again.

"No, no my lord, we swear that we will never harm another person again as long as we live, if you let us live," Jason pleaded and the other three echoed his plea.

"No, the only way to stop your ways is to send you into the void," he then stood and very casually said, "prepare to die." With that, Curry turned and walked out of their eye sight.

"No, no anything you want we will do, just tell us. We will go away, far away and never return. Please spare us," they pleaded again.

Curry grasped his hand staff and levitated their feet. Their feet began to rise turning them upside down. When their heads were about a half pace above the ground he mentaled Ral. "Go and sniff their faces one by one." Ral walked over to them and did as he was asked.

"What is he doing?" Dennis asked.

"Picking the throat he will tear out for his supper. That is unless one of you volunteers to be his supper, otherwise he will have to chose his own." They were dead quite, none wanted to volunteer to die in such a gruesome manner or watch it happen to another.

"Ral, pick one and begin snarling only in his face," he mentaled. Ral went to the second in line and brought his face very close to this one. Slowly he revealed his tearing teeth and emitted a terrifying snarl. The bully he had chosen could only scream and beg for mercy. The other three closed their eyes for they knew what was coming next.

"Hold my friend," Curry motioned Ral back, "I feel compassion today," he said. "I will not allow him to kill any of you today."

"Thank you my Lord, we will not return to our bad ways. We will not harm another person again, ever," Jason said.

"This time I believe you, I know you will never harm another person again because in my mercy I will permit you to drown in yonder pond."

Curry sent to them his aura of truth. When the aura of truth is received by someone it tells their conscience and sub-conscience that what they are about to hear is the truth. In Wizardry, the aura of truth must be spoken with a true statement or the person will know it is a lie. Curry knew to use this he had to pick his words very, very carefully.

"You are going to die," he said. Someday, maybe forty years from now they would die so he was not telling a lie. They interpreted his statement their own way.

Curry levitated them higher and walked over and pushed them towards the pond. They floated about four paces out then stopped. He changed the levitation from their feet to their heads. Instantly they inverted until their feet were pointed at the water. Slowly he began lowering them into the water. Feet, knees, waist then chest, he stopped them at this point. Knowing the wolf couldn't reach them they again began screaming for their lives. Curry hesitated briefly then lowered them to their necks then their chins. Curry could see the fear of death in their eyes. Just a bit more and he could finish with his plan. He lowered them until the water was at their bottom lip. They began begging again, this caused the water to enter their mouths. This caused them to sputter and choke on the water. Holding them briefly there, he raised them up to their chins.

Their pleas became more and more urgent.

Curry sat cross legged on the shore and just stared at them. Ral came and laid down beside him and watched their antics. After a period of time the four became tired and just looked at Curry.

He removed his aura of truth. "Do you acknowledge that I have the power of life and death over you four?" Curry asked.

"Yes my Lord," they all said, completely in submission.

"I have command over all creatures that that fly, walk and crawl, they will summons me back if my commands are not obeyed by you, do you understand." Fortunately the Wizardry allowed Curry to lie when he felt there was a need.

"Yes my Lord, we will obey anything," Jason said. He had a glimmer of hope that they would be spared.

"You will return to the village and ask for Heather, tell her that a traveler in a black cape has sent you to live in an abandoned hut. Ask her if the four of you may watch the children for the coppers she was being paid. These coppers you will use to buy food and food only. You will eat no meat, fish or fowl. These are my messengers and the ones you don't kill will come and tell me what you have done. If I have to return you will pray to the Cosmos that I should have allowed you to drown today instead of what I will do to each of you." They all saw a glimmer of hope in their future and their spirits were lifted.

As the spokesman Jason said, "This we will do my lord."

"You will not return in your present form, for it will frighten the villagers and you might return to your old ways. You will return in a new form. Do you understand?"

"Yes my lord."

"Last and most important, If you speak of what has happened today or what I have done, to anyone, even among yourselves, my messengers will come and tell me. Your death throws will last three leagues of time before you enter the void." Looking from one to the other Curry knew they would obey, he then asked them. "Can you all swim?"

All answered "Yes my lord."

Pointing towards the woods Curry told them, "Go and each of you cut a staff one pace long then sit and wait for me." With that he removed the levitation and immobility. They all sank and came up swimming for shore. Without a glance at Curry or Ral they ran to the woods and using their daggers each cut a walking staff. Trimming the small limbs from it, they went and sat next to each other and waited for Curry. Today these four learned what the word fear meant. When the woods became quite from their cutting and trimming Curry went to them.

"After I have left for a length of time you will walk to the village and do as I have instructed, do you understand?"

"Completely my Lord, and thank you."

"Don't thank me, you will be punished for what you have done and it will last a long time." Curry raised his hand staff and enveloped aging upon the four bullies. They all began to grow taller, stop then began to shorten a small amount. The color of their hair began to lighten then gray and most fell out to land on their shoulders and the ground. Their smooth hands, wrinkled, developed age spots and gnarled almost into claws from the joint disease of old age. All their joints stiffened and grew painful. Their faces began to wrinkle and develop age spots until their looks had changed completely. At this point Curry stopped the aging.

"Leave your daggers and wait one length of time," Curry said, a reply was not needed. He knew they would obey. He and Ral walked through the woods to the road turned towards the village.

"What were the long sticks for?" Ral mentaled.

"Old men with painful joints need a walking staff to be able to walk. They will never be able to harm another person again, I made sure of that. I did not age their hearts, lungs or any organs, that way they will live a long time remembering how they treated the villagers."

Passing the empty blackberry bush, Ral mentaled, "Why did that She taste your mouth?"

"Sometimes a She, called a female, shows gratitude by touching her mouth against the mouth of a male. This doesn't always happen, I was surprised that she did it."

"Is that why we are going to the village, so she can touch your mouth again?"

Curry only blushed and quickened his pace. He had thought of a second kiss but decided against it. He had acted too foolish the first time to risk it again, and what if she wouldn't kiss him. No he didn't need that kind of pressure right now, maybe later.

They would travel through the village this time and not stop, someday he may return and buy a jar of jelly from the red haired girl.

Late one night, three leagues later, the pair were laying next to a companion fire in silence. They were just enjoying the waving cool flames of orange, red and yellow. They were both rested and eager for something more that just wandering. Suddenly Ral sat up and looked into the darkness.

"Listen," he mentaled to Curry. Looking in the direction Ral was staring, Curry saw a tiny glow.

"Its Ary," Curry mentaled.

Ary flew straight to Curry and circled his head once then landed in his ear, "The Calling, Now!"

"Thank you Ary," Curry whispered. Bringing his fist to his lips Ary landed and kissed his nose. Ary then flew backwards from Curry's face, about a forearms length away, and hovered staring at him. Curry began to mental to Ral what the message was when suddenly Ary pulled her dagger and flew at Curry's leg and pricked his thigh. Crying out Curry grabbed his thigh and backed away.

Mentaling to Ral, "Now means now." Enveloping the finding of the Calling, Curry levitated the companion fire and moved it towards the road to guide their way.

After a few steps Ral mentaled, "Searcher return." Curry turned and saw Ary hovering in front of Ral. Returning he was surprised to see the leafs and saplings moving not towards the road as it had always done but deeper into the woods. The finding went straight and never deviated a finger's width. All the other findings would follow a road or a trail. Curry set off on the new trail. Ary hesitated a moment to insure the Searcher was on the right path, then hovered in front of Ral's face for ten heartbeats. Suddenly she flew into the night and Ral turned and followed Curry.

Curry followed the finding trail. At times he crossed creeks and streams. The crawling under and over dead falls proved to be a little more challenging but so far nothing too difficult. Several hills and flat pastures passed during the past three lengths.

"Searcher, I must sleep and rest, I cannot go on." Curry stopped and looked at his friend, Ary's message seemed urgent. Taking his hand staff Curry enveloped Ral in a deep sleep and levitated him a half pace above the ground. Taking the cord from his belt he tied the end around Ral's chest and continued along the finding, pulling Ral behind him.

Curry continued on until he felt Ral had rested enough. Releasing the deep sleep and levitation, Ral stretched, wagged his tale then began following behind Curry. As they walked Ral and Curry mentaled their lives to each other. Curry mentaled what had happened on his adventures when he had to send Ral into the woods to hide. Traveling the lengths turned into leagues and the leagues into weeks. Two weeks and three lengths after receiving the message from Ary then Curry broke through a wood line into a wide pasture.

Looking to his right he saw a hooded caped figure with a walking staff moving in the same direction as he. To his left he saw two other figures, walking in the same direction but on different paths. Rubbing his thigh, Curry remembered Ary's recommendation to hurry, he again set off still following the finding path. Two lengths later Curry saw more and more caped figures. All separated but headed towards one direction. It was like a wagon wheel, each had his own spoke and traveled towards the hub.

Cresting a hill Curry saw a large basin below about two hundred paces across. At the far edge of the basin was a small elevated rock mound. The basin was surrounded by a ring of large mature oak trees. They all appeared to have been planted on the same day as they were all the same size. The basin was bare of all shrubs and saplings and only short grass was present. Looking around Curry noticed the finding trail was gone. This was Curry's destination, he told Ral to stay close.

Mentaling to Ral, Curry said "I apologize, mentaling to you is new, I will try to remember. Stay close to me."

Making his way down the hill into the basin Curry came upon level ground. All the caped figures seemed to be heading towards the rock mound so he joined them. Curry noticed that almost all of the Searchers and Wizards had companions. Hawks, ravens and ospreys were mounted on shoulders or arm guards. Red Foxes, timber and gray wolves, lynxes and others followed their companions. It looked as if Ral was the only cave wolf here. If that had an significance it escaped him for the moment.

Closer and closer they all gathered at the rock mound. This was a calling of the Wizardry of the Country of Carlin. For this to happen the Mintzs had to been sent at different times so all the travelers would arrive at once. Only Warlick the Wizard Master of the country could do this. This explained why Ary was so insistent I leave at once. If he had delayed he would not have arrived with the others. Rubbing his leg he reminded himself to obey Ary's messages immediately if she ever hovered in front of his face again.

Coming closer Curry saw that they all stood in order of rank. Warlick the Wizard Master with his leather cap stood half way up the stone mound. Warlick was responsible for the country of Carlin. There were twelve Wizard Masters in all, one for each country of the World. In front of him were twenty four Wizards in a circle with their walking staffs. One Wizard for each Providence plus one Guardian Wizard to serve at the Cavern's of Sulferic honoring the oath of Olen with Kiliac's foremother. Behind them stood the forty six Searchers with their hand staffs, there were two per Providence. Counting again he could only come up with forty five. One Searcher was missing.

The Searchers looked one to the other and nodded at each other. Not knowing what to do or why they were there they all fell silent. Looking up at the rock mound he saw another figure. This one stood at the top of the mound. Pulling his hood back the

Wizard revealed white shoulder length hair and a white beard. Looking around quickly Curry noticed no facial on anyone, this must be Olen The Master of all Wizards, he thought.

Looking about Olen made a small motion with his hand. The companion birds took to flight and perched in the nearby oak trees. The four footed companions, including Ral, loped off to lie under the shade of the trees.

Raising his hand to the East horizon he passed his arm over his head until his hand was pointing at the West horizon. At once the Sun lost its light, no moon, no stars, nothing. What Curry saw, or didn't see, was black within black. The blackness was so intense that it seemed to pull your aura from you. He now knew what it felt like to look through the eyes of a blind man.

All of a sudden everyone attention was drawn to a speck of light high in the darkness. More and more lights appeared until they numbered seventy one. A Mintz for each of the Wizardry in the country, except for Olen. They slowly winged their way around the calling. The Wizards in the circle formed into a single line revealing a levitated hooded caped figure by the light of the Mintzs. In front of the figure was a levitated hand staff.

Raising his hand slightly Olen watched as the Mintzs came to the suspended figure. Each gripping the figure, they flew him up and over the Calling. Releasing him, half of the Mintzs began flying left to right around him and the others flew right to left. Faster and faster they flew. The specks of light became lines of light, the lines of light blended in with the others until the entire figure seems to glow as a cocoon of light. A humming sound like that of seventy one hummingbirds came to everyone's ears then the glow brightened and exploded into nothingness.

Each Mintz flew in her own direction up and through the darkness to disappear. Moments later a light haze developed, this into brightness, then into Sun light. Things were as they were before. The suspended figure was gone. Only his hand staff remained above the Calling. Olen motioned with his hand

and the hand staff flew to the Guardian Wizard. Taking the hand staff the he tucked it into his belt.

Olen looked at the Wizards and spoke. "When will a new Searcher be ready?" One Wizard said two days. Olen replied "You cannot reach him in time, release him and allow him to learn his father's trade."

A second Wizard said, "A week and a league of time."

Olen said "Leave now." The Wizard immediately turned and left. He would prepare the way for a new Searcher and wait for Warlick to appear to begin the training.

Curry knew that if a boy with the mark was not needed to begin as a Searcher he was released to live as a normal child on his thirteenth birthday morning.

Olen began to speak, "Those of Wizardry we have lost a Searcher. At the Falls of Foam the Searcher Warren slipped and fell striking his head on the travel stones that crossed the pond at the base of the falls. Being unconscious Warren could

not use his skills to slow his metabolism or levitate himself. Sinking to the bottom of the pool Warren's aura left him and entered the void. The Mintzs have taken his form and returned it to the Cosmos from which we have all come. You are all mortal and all are in training for the next level. Now we are short one Searcher and your work may intensify until the new Searcher gains his skills and confidence." Pausing for a moment Olen said, "Wizards form a gauntlet."

The Wizards formed two lines facing each other a full pace from each other. Warlick went to the end of the gauntlet and told a Searcher to enter the end and pass through to the other, then gather farther away in the basin. One by one each Searcher passed through the gauntlet. As each passed through, the Wizards would sense his aura and skill level. Lowering his walking staff as he passed through meant that the Wizard felt he was ready to advance to the Wizard's level.

Passing the gauntlet did not make you a Wizard, it was only a sensing of their opinions that Olen wanted from the other

Wizards. Olen alone would pick the next Wizard. To advance to a Wizard's level there had to be a position to fill, there were none at the present time. Keeping the staff erect meant he felt the Searcher was not ready. Olen watched with interest at the judging.

Curry watched as the Searchers passed one by one. Some staffs were lowered, most remained erect. Two Searchers had no staffs lowered at all. Olen showed no emotions when these two passed. Curry thought they may have been new Searchers and have not acquired their skills yet. Curry's time came and he entered the gauntlet. He felt the Wizards reach into him and sense the aura of his sprit and his mind's ability. Unknown to Curry as he passed, each Wizard had lowered his staff. Olen closed his eyes and raised his hand slightly to sense Curry's aura himself, then he frowned. The frown was not from disappointment but in a journey he would be forced to give this young Searcher. Possibly his last journey.

When all of the Searchers passed through the gauntlet and gathered in the basin they turned and looked at the Warlick, Olen and the Wizards. They seem to be discussing something. The Wizards bowed to Olen and Warlick and slowly walked away to be joined by their companions. As quick as the meeting began it ended. The air filled with a buzzing sound and lights appeared. The Mintzs came and sought out their Searchers. One by one then in small groups the Searchers began to leave the basin. The companions both in the branches and on the ground raced to their Searchers. That is, all but three wolves. They all remained under the trees.

Ary found Curry and landed in his ear. Ary said, "The calling you shall remain, Sit and remain." Bringing his fist to his lips, Ary kissed his nose and left. Immediately Curry sat on the ground. Any message from Ary would be obeyed at once and to the letter from now on. Ral was one of the three companions that remained under the trees. Curry watched as the Wizards and Searchers left the Basin. Looking behind him he saw two

Searchers also sitting on the ground. He nodded his head towards them and they returned the nod. Curry returned his gaze to the rock mound. Olen and Warlick were standing there talking.

A length of time passed then another, just after dusk the glow of a companion fire appeared and levitated towards, then past him. It lowered itself near the three Searchers. All three then stood and walked over and sat at the companion fire. The sound of loping was heard in the darkness and the three companions appeared at the glow of the fire. A gray wolf, timber wolf and the cave wolf came and laid near their own Searchers. The cave wolf stood three hands taller at the shoulder than the timber wolf and five taller than the gray.

Suddenly Olen and Warlick were standing there looking upon the three. They then sat facing the three Searchers.

Olen addressed them, "Searchers, the Mintzs will carry this message tomorrow but I wanted to inform you personally. Wizard Shane has asked to be charged as the Guardian Wizard of the Caverns of Sulferic to guard over Kiliac the Dragon and her egg.

His skills and ability as a Wizard are of the supreme level. He informed us that his body cannot keep up with his skills and asked that this be his final assignment. Regrettably Shane's time grows near and a Searcher will be called forward to replace him. You three have been looked upon favorably by the gauntlet. I remind you that I, Olen, make the decision of advancement. You all will be considered as will the other forty two Searchers when the time comes. Now for why you three are here."

"Each of you, Dale, Curry and Kelly, have been challenged with overcoming the Wizardry of a Wizard having Dark hair and a dark beard. The three looked at each other then back at Olen. In the beginning the Cosmos picked two for Wizardry, myself and one called Kane. Both with the same skills, ability and knowledge. I was chosen to be the Master of all Wizards and Kane was chosen to be the first Master Wizard. Kane's ego would not allow him to be just a Master Wizard, he wanted the title of Master of all Wizards given to him. In an outrage he blamed me and vowed forever to gain his revenge against me for doing this to him. Kane turned from the Wizardry of good and began to follow his own path of evil.

Kane became a Turned Wizard. By turning he was cursed by the Cosmos that created him and restricted him in some of his abilities. He could never train another Searcher or Wizard to assist him nor could be harm me either directly or indirectly. He causes me pain by his actions to others. Alone he travels bearing dark hair, beard and the evil in his eyes. He cannot cause injury to one of blood but he uses his skills to cause death and misery around him. The evil inside of him used up his aura quickly and he has to transfer to another body to continue his quest for revenge. Should his host become injured, too old or is dying Kane sends his aura in the form of a mist to another and absorbs their body. Their form is changed to the original form of Kane with dark hair and a dark beard."

"Searcher Warren's death was caused by Kane."

The three Searchers looked shocked. It is one thing to tell them they might die on their journeys but to actually know that a Searcher was killed by Kane put reality in his statement. The one that were going after had killed a Searcher. The thought of one with Olen's abilities on the side of evil frightened them.

"Warren was fleeing from Kane when his vision was taken from him causing him to misstep and fall on the travel stones striking his head."

"Tia, Warren's Mintz came to Warlick and told him what she had witnessed and where his body could be found, for his aura was gone. Warlick ordered her to grieve for Warren. She flew to the Cavern's of Sulferic where she would be guarded over and kept safe under the constant eye of the Guardian Wizard. Tia entered the Guardian Wizard's private cave, within the Sulferic

Cavern. There she landed in a small opening in the wall that the Guardian Wizard had prepared.

The Guardian Wizard's cave was about two paces wide and a pace and a half high. It was dug to a depth of about eight paces into the lime stone mountain by gnomes. At the back of the cave rested Kiliac's incubating egg on a she bear rug. The egg was about one pace around and a pace long. The texture was similar to that of a snake's egg, leathery and slightly rough to the touch. Moving closer to the front of the cave was a stone chair, carved from solid rock when the cave was made, this was for the Guardian Wizard to sit on. On the wall next to the chair were tiny openings, one of which Tia was in. Next to these openings were two others. Both about two spread hands high and wide. One was a little over two hands deep and the other was a pace deep. In the shorter hole laid eleven Searcher hand staffs and in the other laid seven Wizard staffs. These were the staffs of those who had died along their journeys. There were no windows or openings in the cave. Light was provided by tiny companion fires along the edge of the ceiling. Anything trying to get to the egg or a Mintz would have to confront Kiliac the Dragon first then the Guardian Wizard. Over the mouth of the cave was a boulder twice the height and width of the opening. This was suspended by levitation. Should the Wizard have to leave or in the case of an emergency, he would lower the boulder to protect its contents.

Setting her dagger at her feet, Tia, then removed the horse hair belt and dropped it and the flower petal skirt to the cave floor. Picking up the dagger and holding it to her breast she began spinning. A cocoon began to form around her. Tears of grief over her dead Searcher were flowing down her cheeks as she spun the cocoon. Finishing it she finally cried herself into a hibernation of sleep.

Sleeping she will remain until a new Searcher is chosen. Using her dagger, she then will burst from her cocoon and go to this Searcher to be named. One blessing she will have is that she will have no memories of her past Searcher. When she memorizes the history of Wizardry at the blue moss trees, from the other Mintzs, the name Searcher Warren will be just a name."

"As I said you three will challenge Wizard Kane."

They have just begun their journey into Wizardry and are being asked, no, ordered to challenge a Wizard having the skills of Olen.Each were asking themselves why them, why not three full Wizards or call together three Master Wizards from around the World. Any of these would have a better chance of succeeding that them. They kept asking themselves, why us.

"Being of blood you cannot injure him directly but using the skills you have acquired you must try and capture Kane. The memories of your challenges against Kane's evil actions, I will place in each of the other's Searcher's minds. You will need your combined knowledge, wisdom and skills for you to succeed at this challenge. Kane will expect Wizards or Master Wizards to confront him, let's hope he will allow you three novice Searchers to get close enough to act before he realizes what has happened." Olen ended by asking, "Do any of you have any questions about anything that I can answer?"

Kelly asked three questions and Dale asked two. Olen answered these completely and then looked at Curry. "And you young Searcher?" Curry knew the correct answers to those questions asked by the other two.

Curry thought for a moment and asked, "If I have to have the power of my hand staff for me to envelope auras, then why does it come to me when I call, when it and not I has the power?" Olen thought to himself, yes this one is close, very close. Looking deeply into Curry's eyes he said, "In time young Searcher, in time." Again Curry had been given an answer requiring patience. Olen knew from sensing Curry's mind that Curry had been answering his own questions along his journeys.

This question Olen would answer should Curry be chosen to become a Wizard, unless he finds the answer himself. That all depends on if he survives his encounter with Kane. Standing, Olen and Warlick looked at the three and their companions and

Olen said, "To the Falls of Foam you go." With that the two turned and walked into the darkness leaving the three Searchers alone at the companion fire.

The Searchers decided to sit the night away learning of each other strengths and weaknesses. This allowed their companions to sleep and rest. Comparing skills they found that what one lacked the other had. At dawn Dale enveloped the finding for the Falls of Foam and the six travelers began their journey.

CHAPTER 11

The Falls of Foam

The three young Searchers and their companions ate up the distance towards their next objective. As with all messages given either by their Mintzs or by Olen it never gave a distance nor a time frame of arrival. Curry reasoned that if they knew the location they would not be alert to danger along the road until they arrived there. This ignorance kept them ever alert to any possible problems that may arise.

The three had worked out a system of travel so that when one Searcher tired one of the others would levitate him and tie Curry' cord to his waist. This would allow him to be towed. In this manner the third could rest or envelope himself in intense sleep. This allowed all to remain fresh and protective of each other.

The three wolves quickly acknowledged each others standing within the group. After some preliminary sniffing and triple marking of a bush they recognized the order of dominance. Ral the cave wolf, the timber and then the gray in that order. Initially the three roamed close to the Searchers but soon they became bored and ventured farther. This lasted for about three lengths. Calling the wolves in, the three Searchers assigned them duties. Each was sent to certain areas to travel and alert the group should they come across something. The gray to the left, the timber to the right and Ral in front. All stayed about forty paces from the Searchers. Most of the time all six walked and only levitated when it was absolutely necessary.

The sky began to darken in front of them and they noticed the wind was blowing in their faces. A storm was coming and it was headed straight for them. When the initial drops of rain began to strike their capes, Dale enveloped a shield to deflect the rain away from himself. The day being warm the other Searchers didn't feel a need to cover themselves. After the rain stops they could envelope dryness upon themselves.

The sky became pitch black and bolts of lightning tracked across the clouds and then began to come to Earth. The flash of the lightning caused the Searchers to flinch and duck. The wind picked up and leaves and small branches began to blow towards them. Enveloping their auras the three sent them out for the wolves to return. Quickly the three bounded in and leaned their sides against their companion's leg. Looking ahead Curry saw the tree tops begin to sway back and forth, then they began to lean in one direction from the winds force. Harder the wind blew, pelting them with rain and debris. Then suddenly the wind stopped and a deathly quietness surrounded them.

Looking about quickly, Curry saw a shallow gully about ten paces away. "RUN!" Curry shouted. The other two didn't question his order, in a swirl of capes the Searchers and companions ran for the gully. When someone tells you to do something, most people will ask why. Standing in the waist high gully the answer to the why came to them.

With the howl of a thousand wolves, a black cloud the shape of a whirlpool descended from the clouds and reached down to touch the Earth. The width where it touched the Earth was almost two hundred paces wide and it was coming straight at them.

Mentaling to Ral, Curry screamed in his mind, "DOWN,

NOW!!!!" Ral immediately dropped and Curry dropped on top of him. Pulling his hand staff Curry enveloped a shield over them. When the rain covered the shield, Curry grabbed the hand staff with the other hand and enveloped the freezing of stone. The rain on the shield immediately became as hard as a rock. Covering Ral's head and body Curry closed his eyes and waited. If the Cosmos had decided to try and take his aura this way then he was going to fight it all the way.

Around the black whirlpool of a spinning cloud were massive oak trees and thousands of shrubs. They were ripped from the ground and lifted two hundred paces above the ground. Some were instantly released at that height to fall to the Earth and others were carried along beyond their sight to land in another Providence. The sound grew to a painful intensity. Curry, holding his hand staff in both hands, squeezed his forearms against Ral's sensitive ears.

For as quickly as it started, it was over. Waiting a few moments Curry mentaled Ral. "Are you hurt?"

Ral mentaled, "Just a heavy pressure on my side and head." Curry was puzzled for a moment, then smiled. Removing both hands from the hand staff the shield and freezing of stone disappeared. He then got off of Ral's side and head. Ral stood and shook himself. Curry looked behind him and saw the black whirlpool cloud release its grip from the Earth and escape back into the clouds. Glancing in the other direction, Curry stood slack jaw at the amount of destruction that had occurred. Trees and brush were not just knocked down, everything was gone. Only torn up dirt remained.

Closing his eyes Curry thought to himself, Please don't let this be the work of Kane.

Standing in ankle deep rain water Curry looked to his two travelers. Dale stood and began slinging the muddy water from his sleeves. His timber wolf shook himself soaking Dale in more muddy water. Kelly laid in the deepening water, unmoving. Dale and Curry moved to his side and began to seek out his aura.

He was alive but unconscious. Using their hands just above him, they sensed him for injuries. His head, neck, chest and arms were fine. Checking his legs they found them broken and broken badly. It appeared that a large tree limb had entered the gully, struck his legs and flew away. He didn't have the time or didn't think to envelope himself with protection in time. Below both of his knees a darkness began to spread. Gently pulling the breeches up his legs, Dale and Curry saw pieces of bone sticking out of both legs just below his knees. Dale became dizzy from the sight and had to sit before he fell. Curry first enveloped Kelly into an intense sleep for two leagues and two nights. That way only one of Wizardry could wake him. Curry then enveloped him with absence of pain for five leagues and five nights of time. The extra time was incase help was delayed in coming.

Moving his legs would cause more damage so Curry enveloped them in freezing of stone for the same time as the absence of pain. Last he enveloped him to slow his metabolism for five leagues of time and five nights. This would stop the bleeding, spreading of infection and prevent swelling of his legs. Dale's dizziness passed and he stood shakily and went to Curry's side. Curry had done what he could for Kelly. Anything else that had to be done would be in someone else's hands now.

Curry asked Dale if he knew the name of Kelly's Mintz. Dale shook his head no. Closing his eyes Curry called for Ary. Seeing that they had done the best they could for Kelly, they moved him out of the ditch and sat and waited. Suddenly it came to them that Kelly's companion, the gray wolf was missing.

Dale said, "Looks like he tried to outrun the storm." Both tried to sense his aura but to no avail. Either he was too far away or his aura had gone into the void.

Ary knew the journey that Curry and the others were on and the dangers it held so she and the other Searcher's Mintzs remained close to them. In a hundred heartbeats from the time she heard his call she and the other two Mintzs arrived. Any time they were called they knew anything could be wrong.

When they arrived all smiled. Though one was injured all had strong auras and this pleased them. Ary entered Curry's ear and asked, "How can I help Searcher?"

Curry replied, "Kelly's legs are badly broken and needs help we cannot give. I didn't know Kelly's Mintz's name so I called you. Would you ask his Mintz to seek help for him?" Bringing his fist to his mouth, Ary landed and kissed his nose and flew to Kelly's Mintz. A few seconds later Ary left as fast as she could fly heading North.

Kelly's Mintz flew to Curry's ear and said, "I am Jae, Searcher Kelly's Mintz, I know of your journey. Ary has gone for Warlick so you may leave now, I will watch over my Searcher."

Curry said, "You may not be able to protect him if someone large comes along with intent to harm him."

In a stern voice Jae said, "Searcher, you do not know the powers we Mintzs have, no harm will befall him from anyone or anything!" She then flew to the front of his face and he presented his fist. Landing she kissed his nose then flew and landed on Kelly's chest. Sitting on his chest she drew her dagger and waited for Ary to bring help. Curry learned not to cross a Mintz, so he and Dale stood and left with their companions. Kelly's safety was in competent and trustworthy hands.

Curry thought to himself that the journey had just begun and already a third of their strength was gone. Feeling that safety was more important than speed right now, they decided to camp for the night. Finding a secluded spot, Curry and Dale enveloped dryness on themselves and their companions. Enveloping a small warming fire, the two Searchers sat and watched the flames. The two wolves laid near the fire and soaked up the warmth. As the night progressed the conversation slowly ended.

A brief period later Ral mentaled Curry, "Do you want to mental the timber and have him teach mentaling to his Searcher?"

Curry thought for a moment and said, "No, I think not, when

the time is right, either the timber or the Searcher will initiate it, let them learn in their own way as we did." Ral looked at Curry, then laid his head between his paws and dozed off. Curry told Dale to envelope a three length sleep so his body could rest completely. He would watch over the three until then. As the three became quite, Curry sat and pondered his cloudy future.

After being relieved by Dale, Curry took his turn at sleep for three lengths and woke refreshed and rested. Dale had canceled the fire and the wolves were out marking their bushes. Curry walked up to Dale and they talked shortly of the storm of yesterday. Both worried about Kelly but knew he was in secure hands, both Jae's and Warlick's.

The sky was clearing quickly, showing blue in the distance. The Searchers took to the road again. The road soaked up the rain from yesterday and no mud caked their boots. The finding gave faint directions towards their goal, somewhere West of here. A league and a night passed, they had levitated their companions so they could travel all night.

In the morning they saw signs of a village ahead. Fields were planted in wheat, hops and on the terraced hillside were arbors of purple grapes. In the distance the village came into view. The Searchers motioned their companions to skirt the village and meet them on the other side.

Walking into the village the two saw busy and smiling faces. Towards the end of the village they came upon a long hut that was fenced in the front containing a long bench and a number of three legged milk stools. Out of curiosity they entered the gate and approached what they thought was the owner. Seeing two caped figures in black the owner became wary. A small gust of wind blew Curry's cape to the side and the owner got a small glimpse of his hand staff.

Smiling, the owner stepped forward and greeted the two. Shoving his hand and forearm out to them he said, "Welcome, welcome my friends, I am Hugo, the owner, please come and sit for I serve the finest of the grape here." Taken aback, the two were not accustomed to this type of courteous treatment. In fact seldom are they welcomed anywhere.

"Woman!" he screamed, "Bring cheese, bread and our finest before I take a stick to you." Shocked at the way he talked to his wife, Curry and Dale waited for a cowering, frail woman to bring the platter of food. To their astonishment a woman the width of the door came out. Her height was more than a hand width over Hugo's and her weight four stones greater that he.

Walking up to Hugo, she glared and asked, "What were your going to go with a stick?"

"Hush woman, before I make you squeal like a little girl."

He then leaned over and kissed her on the cheek. Smiling she laid a platter of sharp cheese, half a loaf of bread and two goblets on the table.

"I have to keep reminding him who really is in charge." She whispered with a smile. A boy of about fifteen brought a pitcher of wine from inside.

Curry said, "Please sir, we don't even have a copper between us, there is no way we could pay you."

Leaning forward Hugo whispered, "No one of Wizardry pays here." He then called his son, Jules to the table. Come show them your arm.

Jules said, "Please father, not again."

"Come…Come," Hugo said. Pulling Jules to the table, Hugo pulled his sleeve up showing a bare arm. "See, do you see?" Hugo asked.

Curry and Dale looked at Jules's arm then at each other. "We see nothing Sir," Dale said.

"Exactly," Hugo shouted. "Two years ago, on the eve of his thirteenth birthday, Jules went to sleep with a mark on his forearm, a purple crescent with a dot between the tips. When he awoke the mark was gone, I was told he had been released. For giving me more time with my son and teaching him my trade, I welcome all of Wizardry." To honor Hugo's kindness, Curry and Dale took a pinch of cheese and a piece of bread and downed it with a sip of wine.

Dale asked Hugo, "Do you know of a place called the Falls of Foam?"

Hugo scratched his head and said, "No...No not that I can think of, sorry." Telling Hugo of the lateness and distance they had to travel the two bowed and left.

Hugo called after them saying, "There will always be a stool at my table for you."

Both waved as they walked away, Curry told Dale, "Remember this Dale, keep it as a good memory for those times when things don't go so well."

Dale said, "It does help bury some of the rudeness of those we have met." Leaving the village behind they continued following the finding signs toward the Falls of Foam.

With darkness upon them they enveloped a small companion fire and moved it before them to better see the road. About a hundred paces down the road they crossed a small wooden bridge over a stream.

Just after passing the bridge they sensed that something was wrong. Curry felt something push against his right leg and he dove to the left to get away from it. At the same instant Dale felt something against his left leg and he dove to his right. Both Searchers ran into each other. It looked as if two large bats were fighting each other with their black capes flapping. The companion fire went out and the two were left sitting in complete darkness. Freezing in their tangled positions on the ground they listened for the footsteps of their attacker. All they could hear was the panting of two wolves. Falling back on the dusty road they both began to laugh.

When Curry stopped laughing he said, "Ral has a habit of surprising me like that. One day he may frighten me to the void."

Dale said, "I hope we will be more alert when we meet Kane, than we were just then."

"I agree completely."

Both Searchers were very nervous. They were going up against one who had almost all the power of Olen and now they were missing a third of their strength. Curry knew that to have any chance they would have to surprise Kane. The trick was how do you surprise someone with the skills of Olen.

The destination they were given was to go to the Falls of Foam. Hugo having no knowledge of the Falls meant that they had a good distance to go to find it. Three leagues and three nights passed. None along the road had heard of the Falls of Foam. The pair continued following the findings signs.

One day the four sat under an oak tree resting when Curry heard something in the woods walking around. Reaching for their hand staffs both prepared for the worse. Closer the noise came and it was apparent that it was something large. They glimpsed something large and black in the openings of the thicket. Standing the two Searchers separated and waited for Kane to step from the wood line. They heard dried leaves being stepped on, then a twig snapped, then nothing. Slowly moving towards the thicket they tried their best to peer into the dense brush but it was futile.

Suddenly Kane burst from the woods, well almost, it was a wild black horse. Swallowing their hearts they pushed their hand staffs back into their belts. The black of his coat made them think it was Kane. The horse was not alone, two others followed the first from the woods. Looking one to the other Curry and Dale decided to try something.

Each walked up to a different horse. Taking their hand staffs in hand they sent their auras to the horses. Sensing that these two man things meant them no harm they allowed them to approach. After petting them they again looked at each other and nodded. Grabbing the horse's mane near the its withers, Dale and Curry mounted the horses. Both horses stood still and the Searchers felt the muscles of the horses quivering. Then the horses slowly relaxed.

The horses allowed the Searchers to guide them around the field by using their knee pressure to make them turn left then right. Squeezing with their legs the Searchers guided the horses up to the road and began walking towards their destination.

About one length later Curry looked over at Dale and asked, "When the Cosmos created the horse why didn't it put more padding on his back?"

Looking back Dale said, "I think I have had all the enjoyment I can stand from riding a horse. I prefer to walk." Agreeing, both dismounted and sent a thanking aura to the horses. The horses left the road and entered the wood line and began grazing.

As the Searchers began walking they had a peculiar swagger to their walk. As time passed, the soreness passed and they began to walk in a normal manner again. How a horse guard from a castle does this day after day they would never know. All they knew was that their two feet were better that four hoofs for traveling.

Two leagues later they stopped to let their companions rest under the shade of an oak tree. Sitting and leaning against the tree they listened to the cool breeze blowing the leaves above their heads. Blue skies with small puffy clouds and a cool breeze, they couldn't think of a better time to rest. It was a wonderful feeling to let the breeze blow against their faces. Looking up through the branches Curry watched as the wind made noises in the leaves moving them around. Closing his eyes he listened to these relaxing sounds. Listening to the constant rustling sounds, Curry again opened his eyes. The leaves were not moving and the wind was not blowing.

Sitting up, he quietly said, "Listen."

"What?"

"The noise, hear it?"

Looking up into the tree, Dale then looked towards the wood line. "Running water."

Moving towards the sound they came upon a small stone gorge. At one end was **a** waterfall at a height of about six paces.

The water fell into a small pool about five paces wide at its widest point. They were unable to determine the depth of the pool. The remarkable thing about the pool was that a layer of white foam covered it. Slowly they worked their way down the side of the gorge where they found the travel stones that the Searcher Warren had fallen on causing his death.

Crossing the stones they stopped in the middle of the pool and looked at the peculiar foam. Curry reached down and put his fingers into the foam and stood. Rubbing his fingers together he realized what it was.

He asked Dale, "Look over here next to the cattails, see it?"

"What?" Dale replied.

"Soap root." Curry went on to further explain. "When you pull up that plant with the small purple flowers and crush the root it foams into a soap when mixed with water. The foam on the pool is the result of the soap root being pounded by the waterfall. It's a pretty sight but it kills all the fish and nothing can drink from it.

"Come," said Curry, "we need to talk and standing in the open is not in our best interests." Agreeing the two and their companions crossed over the travel stones and went and sat under some laurels bushes.

Petting their companion's necks the two Searchers came to one quick decision. They had to separate. Should one be attacked the other may have a chance to deal with Kane while he was distracted. Looking about they saw another laurel thicket near by that Dale volunteered to occupy. It had quick access to the travel stones if they were needed to escape or come to the aid of Curry. He looked to the other side of the pool and examined the walls of the small gorge. Up high was a small concave depression that Curry felt he could hide in. He would have an excellent overview plus remain unseen. Both knew that if Kane came seeking auras they would have no chance. Hoping that his ego was such he would walk with no fear, they went to their ambush locations.

Curry thought for a moment that once they jumped out and yelled "Surprise!", what would they do next? Each was on their on with the skills he had acquired from his travels. The advantage they hoped would be with the one not being attacked by Kane. Whatever happened they would have to be quick.

Curry got up and crossed the travel stones to the other side. When he arrived at the other side he looked about. The bottom was littered with stones the size of a pebble to the size of a horse. Thinking back Curry absentmindedly reached back and rubbed his backside remembering his ride. Making his way to the side he followed a small foot trail back to the top.

At the top, he walked along the rim until he came above the depression he saw from below. Looking over the ledge he could not see it, this would be perfect. Hidden from above Curry would be alerted to any presence above him by a signal from Dale. The same applied to Curry. From his high view he could see deep into the woods behind Dale and could give him a warning should Kane come that way. Dale sent his companion, Kyle the timber wolf, along the stream below the pool. Curry mentaled Ral to climb with him and stay above the falls. Curry knew Ral's nose would tell him if the water was safe to drink.

Looking about to make sure he was not being watched, Curry took his hand staff, grabbed a rock outcropping then levitated himself. Using the rock outcropping he pulled himself to the edge and over. After passing the edge Curry allowed himself to be lowered by removing part of the levitation. When his feet touched the lip of the depression, Curry released the levitation and backed into the opening.

Looking up he was hidden from view but he could still see where Dale was hiding. Kyle could not be seen, neither could Ral. Curry knew they were both alert and ready for anything. He knew that both wolves would give their lives for their companions and the same was true of the Searchers.

Curry settled back against the wall, finding the Sun and determining the East, West line, he knew that the path of the Sun would not shine into his tiny depression and revel his position. Now it was a waiting game.

To Curry it seemed as if some unknown force had grabbed the Sun and delayed its travel across the sky. Moments seem to drag on forever. Curry constantly scanned the position of Ral, to Dale then onto Kyle then returning to Ral. Curry's greatest fear was for Ral. Ral had no powers and his own ability was to alert Curry if Kane came. He feared that would end Ral's life. Even though a Wizard, any kind of Wizard, could not directly injure anything of blood, that did not mean he could not manipulate the rule to his advantage. As with any rule it was sometimes left to your own interpretation.

Curry had been taught by Warlick and accepted the teachings that he could not touch, throw or project anything towards anything of blood to cause injury. Accepting this, his aura physically prevented him from doing injury to anything of blood.

Light became dark, became light, and again became dark with no sign of Kane. Olen sent the three Searchers here and knew that Kane would be here at some time. Patience Curry, patience he kept telling himself. Curry settled back and began reciting his list of auras.

Slowly Curry's eyes began to close. Jerking upright Curry realized that he had not slept for two leagues and two nights of time. Tiredness had overcome him and this was not a place for a fuzzy mind. All his attention must be focused for his encounter with Kane. If he allowed himself to enter into a natural sleep, it would be lengths before he awoke. Dale may need his help so Curry could not allow this.

Taking a small rock Curry tossed it towards Dale. Hitting in the pool near Dale, Curry saw Dale's face appear through the green leafs. Bringing his hands together palm to palm and placing them beside his head in a sleeping position, Curry looked at Dale. Dale nodded and withdrew into the brush. Curry leaned back against the wall and enveloped himself in an intense sleep.

Waking three hundred heartbeats later, Curry stretched and was fully alert and rested. Looking about he saw that all was as it had been. Taking another small rock Curry again tossed it into the pool. Dale did not appear. Again he threw another rock with the same results. Dale must have misunderstood Curry's message and entered into sleep himself. Fortunately Kane had not come and no damage was done. Briefly Dale would awake and be alert for their expected visitor.

Hearing a change in the sound of the falls, Curry glanced over at the falling water. The center of the falls began to divide and spread. Suddenly a figure in black having black hair and beard levitated through the opening about a pace above the pool. The water behind him closed and resumed its normal path. The figure glanced at Curry and suddenly their was a rumble below him. The solid wall face broke into pieces and began to fall. Curry was surrounded by rocks as he fell. His hand staff, that was laying beside his foot disappeared into the pile of falling rubble. Tumbling downward, Curry repeatedly hit against the gorge wall bruising and cutting himself from head to toe. At the base, Curry' side hit heavily on a outcrop of rock. He felt several of his ribs give, then break. Deep within his chest a terrible pain erupted. Coughing from the dust, Curry saw a faint bright red mist spray come from his mouth. He knew this was not a serious wound, this was lethal.

Above, a large rock dislodged and fell. Grabbing his injured side he rolled away as best he could but not far enough. The falling rock fell crushing his right foot. Curry emitted a scream that seem to tear the lining of his throat. With the scream also came more blood that began to trickle down his chin onto his tunic.

Curry would die like this if he didn't put up some kind of a fight. Through tearing eyes Curry focused on Kane. Kane remained in the center of the foaming pool looking at him. Brushing the tears from his eyes, Curry called for his hand staff. There was a movement to his left as the rocks began to vibrate.

The hand staff suddenly burst from the rocks and came to Curry's outstretched hand. Holding the hand staff before him, he began to envelope a shield to give him some protection from Kane. Instantly his hand staff was ripped from his hand by some unseen force and flew towards Kane. Stopping a pace from Kane, he glanced at it briefly then let it fall into the foaming pool.

Curry glanced towards Dale and hoped he could envelope something while Curry distracted Kane.

Kane smiled and said, "Your friend and his wolf lacks mobility at the moment, as you slept I froze them for a period of a length of time. He shall become my next host and the wolf will take a swim. I weary of this body and seek another." Continuing on Kane said, "Your body would have been an excellent host but regrettable it appears to be just less than perfect for my needs." Curry's coughing began to increase and he started to become lightheaded. "Yet I," said Kane "am a merciful Wizard and will allow your death to come quickly, I shall change you into a fish and lower you into the foaming pool." Curry knew that nothing could live in the pool and death would come quickly.

Curry said, "Anyone of Wizardry cannot injure one of blood."

Kane's voice took on an edge of anger, "Stupid child, that rule must be interpreted by each and accepted within himself. Apparently you chose to not directly injure anything, I didn't. I choose not to injure anything by touching my flesh to another's flesh. As you found out the rocks touched you not my flesh." With a look of disgust Kane said, "I tire of this and have many journeys to make. Farewell my stupid little friend." Kane raised his hands above his head and began lowering them towards Curry.

From above the falls came a sound that seem to come from your deepest and most terrifying nightmares. Eyes wide, Kane stopped his hand motions and looked up to see Ral launching himself from the top of the falls towards him. Quickly Kane levitated to the side and Ral plunged into the depths of the pool.

Laughing, Kane turned saying, "Some pair, one without skills and one of brut force. Both of you will swim together." Kane again raised his hands and began lowering them to change Curry into a fish.

Curry instantly thought of the word slow and said the word "Time." Kane's hands slowed and almost appeared to stop. Curry then brought his bare bloodied hand forward and enveloped the freezing of stone for a year. Kane's face of evil and hatred froze, as did his body, even his hooded cape froze. Suddenly Kane fell into the foaming pool. Curry's eyes glazed over and he was swept up into a cape of darkness.

Ral surfaced and paddled to the pools edge. Climbing from the pool, he shook the water from his coat. Sniffing quickly he could not scent the evil one. He saw Curry laying very still on the rocks. Running to him he leaned close and sniffed Curry's breath. He found the smell of blood there. Ral had smelled this many times before when he had made his kills. Sitting back and arching his neck he released a howl that traveled a length of time. Never so mournful a sound has ever been heard. Lowering his head, Ral licked the blood from Curry's face and lips. Stretching out he laid his head on Curry's thigh, he would remain and protect his friend until his aura went to the void.

The day passed to night and Ral heard that Curry's breathing was slowly becoming more labored and slower. Hearing a familiar sound Ral turned his head and saw a Mintz. Ary flew towards them and landed on Curry's back. Ary sensed that there was almost none of Curry's aura let in his body.

Ral, in desperation mentaled to Ary, "Help him, please." Jerking her head around Ary looked into Ral's eyes. Taking her dagger she dropped it on Curry's back and she was gone. Ary would need all the speed she had to save her Searcher. Faster and faster she flew. The daisy petals were ripped from her horsehair belt by the speed that she flew. This didn't matter, her only goal was to reach the only one who could help.

Ral's situation didn't change, he would not sleep, eat or drink until the Searcher's aura went into the void. Two lengths into the night Ral heard movement on the other side of the pool at the travel stones. Raising his head and gazing into the dense shrubs, the moonlight revealed a Grand Boar. Twice the height at the shoulder than Ral and weighing at thirty stones. His ivory tusks were the length of a large hand. Peering at Ral with tiny pitch black eyes the Grand Boar began snapping his tusks and making dominate grunts. The Grand Boar had been attracted by the smell of blood and was preparing to attack. Ral rose to his feet and released a snarl that had never been emitted from his throat before. Hearing this, the Master Boar immediately turned and charged through the thicket to safety. Brush and saplings were ripped from the ground in his hast to leave the area. The boar had heard many attacking snarls in his lifetime but those sounds were always ones of those hunting him for food. This snarl was a sound made from one that only wanted to make a hatred kill. This pool he would never venture to again.

Just past dawn, Curry began to have the smell of death about him. His breath and heartbeats were shallow, weak and struggling. Ral knew Curry's time had come. With all his strength and size there was nothing he could do but wait. Looking at the still form of his friend he noticed a shadow passed over the two of them. Looking up Ral saw a gift from the Cosmos, Kiliac the Dragon. Circling twice, Kiliac glided into the pool causing a loud splash. Standing on her rear legs and one front leg she extended her front leg towards Ral. Opening her talons, Olen levitated to the ground.

Walking quickly to Curry, he began to seek out his aura, barely was there a hint of one. Olen sent his own aura into Curry to hold his aura from the void. With a wave of his hand the wall of the gorge exploded leaving a slab of rock the size of a bed. Olen levitated Curry over to the slab and slowly lowered him to the slab. Placing his palms close to him he checked for injuries and deep heat of internal bleeding. Placing his hands near his chest he found that he had broken ribs and a punctured his lung. Olen sent a strong healing aura and the ribs pulled from the lung and return to their position and began healing themselves. The lung sealed and the blood vessels began pulling the spilt blood back through the walls of the veins and arties. Finishing they sealed themselves. Placing his hand over Curry's mouth he forced an aura of air into his lungs to expand the collapsed lung. The coloring of red and purple began to slowly fade from his chest. Reaching out to his crushed foot the torn skin also began to heal, the bruise faded and the bones began to gravitate back to their original position and heal. Passing his hands high over Curry all the scraps and cuts began to heal. The red dried blood turned to brown, then black, then to a powder and dropped to the ground.

Taking a seat at Curry's head, Olen pulled his head onto his lap. Closing his eyes he placed his hands on Curry's head. Sensing deeply he sought out any excess heat. Deep behind Curry's right ear was a warming spot. Olen asked with most respect that the vessels open and allow the blood and fluid to return to the heart. Slowly the heat began to fade then it was gone. The vessels sealed and Curry's breath and heartbeat returned to normal.

Looking down on Curry, Olen said to himself, "Could he be the one?, Is he the one? The one who will end Wizardry." Curry's eyes fluttered and looked into Olen's eyes and stared at him for a moment.

In an instant he jumped up yelling, "Kane!"

Grabbing his arm Olen said, "Sit Searcher, the threat of Kane is no more. Below in the pool he stands frozen thanks to you."

"What of Dale?"

Calming Curry, Olen said, "He is fine, all are fine even Kelly. Dale is still frozen and Kyle is with him. It is impossible for anything to harm him in that state. I will release him shortly."

Curry said, "I need to tell you what happened."

Olen held up his hand, "No Searcher, Ral and Ary told me

everything. Now is the time for me to tell you what has happened." Turning Olen mentaled to Kiliac the dragon, she turned and dove into the pool. Twenty heartbeats, thirty heartbeats then she broke the surface. Clutched in her talon was Kane. Olen mentaled to Kiliac again and she took to wing circling once then headed for the Cavern of Sulferic, her home and to her unborn daughter.

Olen began, "Ary came to me first since I was close by, barely breathing she was, she lies now with Warlick and is recovering. She was near death when she arrived, she will be fine shortly. I called Kiliac to bring me to you, it was the quickest way." Continuing on Olen said, "Searchers have died from accidents and a very few from Kane. These killings were when the Searcher crossed him by accident. No Wizard ever died of an accident. All of their deaths were from Kane or Lord Shan who you vanquished.

At the Calling when the Searchers passed through the gauntlet, I felt that Kane would be looking for a Wizard, not a Searcher. This might give a Searcher the edge he needed. Sending you three out for a possible certain death was the hardest journey I ever assigned. What you have done no other has ever done and I hope by the Cosmos it never happens again. Kiliac will take Kane to the Cavern of Sulferic. There Guardian Wizard Shane will watch over him. On the eleventh month of each year a Wizard will travel to the caverns and again envelope Kane in the freezing of stone for a year. This second Wizard will be sent just in case anything ever happens to the Guardian Wizard. With Kane we cannot be too careful. He must never journey again.

"Searcher," Olen asked, "you had a question about your hand staff, do you have an answer?"

Curry thought for a moment and said, "It is not the staff in the hand that has power but the hand on the staff," Curry then asked, "Why even bother with a hand staff Olen?"

Olen smiled and replied, "A new Searcher has to develop his

skills quickly to survive. The hand staff forces him to concentrate on it and direct his enveloping correctly.

Surprisingly the first thing a Searcher learns is to call his hand staff. If the hand staff has the power then how could you call it to you. It is so simple that no one ever realizes the truth. It is very rare that a Searcher ever reasons this out. The last Searcher, before you, to accomplish this was Warlick"

"Warlick?" Curry said in astonishment.

"Yes, a Searcher has always had the power, he only had to discover it and learn the skills." Of course a Searcher is never told of this, a rare few learn this own their own. You should feel privileged.

The hand staff, walking staff and leather cap are all symbols of rank, nothing more. Those with evil hearts fear the staffs and think they posses their own power. These people should keep thinking that. When one earns the rank of Wizard they are told the power lies within themselves not their staffs. I ask that you keep this secret from the others, their lives may depend on them developing their own skills correctly.

"Done," said Curry.

"Call your hand staff and lets be own our way."

Standing, Curry called his hand staff and watched as it exploded from the water. Grasping it with a new understanding he stuck it in his belt. Pulling it out again he asked Olen, "These writings on the hand staff, what do they mean?"

It's your name written in the first language of the Cosmos. Take this," Olen handed Curry something tiny, "this is Ary's dagger, return it to her." With a puzzled look on Curry face, Olen said, "She will explain it to you later, after she has rested." Turning the three walked across the travel stones to release Dale and Kyle from their freezing of stone.

THE END

EPILOGUE

Sitting on the ground leaning against a fallen log, Curry sat scratching behind Ral's ear. Curry watched the cool flames of the companion fire as Ral began to doze. The memory of the pain from the encounter with Kane was fading. The challenges of the Serpents, Krill of the Watkils, the Kligget, Gnomes and a friend he had made in Kiliac the dragon helped him mature and develop the skills that he was conceived for. Now was the time to relax and wait for the next visit from Ary.

Ral's head jerked up and a snarl developed deep in his throat. Somewhere outside the light of the fire was something, and it was coming towards them. Curry reached for his hand staff, more out of habit that need, and eased up onto the log. Ral slowly began walking forward, just as Curry was going to call him to stop, Ral sat and looked up into the tree branches. Looking into the tree tops Curry saw nothing. Looking back at Ral he saw the hair on the back of his neck start to move. He wasn't raising his hackles, it was something different. Then a hooded caped figure materialized. His was the hand that was scratching Ral's neck.

Curry was startled but not afraid. He didn't know who the figure was but he knew who it wasn't, Kane. Pulling the hood back the figure revealed himself, it was Olen the Master of all Wizards.

"Olen," Curry addressed him, "welcome to my fire."

"Curry I have a message for you," Olen said.

All messages before were given by Ary. For Olen himself to deliver a message, in person, it must be important as the one for the Falls of Foam. Curry stood and waited for Olen to continue.

"Guardian Wizard Shane's time grows near, soon his aura shall enter the void. You are to go to him and do what is required," Olen said.

"Of course I will do anything asked of me."

At the calling, Curry was told that Wizard Shane had asked to be assigned as the Guardian Wizard to the Cavern of Sulferic to guard Kiliac's egg.

With a solemn look on his face, Olen said, "You are to assume his duties."

Shocked, Curry looked at Olen and said, "Olen, I am but a Searcher, how could I assume the duties of a Guardian Wizard?"

"A Searcher cannot assume a Guardian Wizard's duties, only a Wizard can," Olen said then smiled. Curry could only stand and stare. "I called a council of Wizards and you were recommended by all, as his replacement. Guardian Wizard Shane will teach you those things that are needed and the rest you will acquire on your own as you have done so far."

"Olen do you feel I am ready for this?"

Olen replied, "Your aura was sensed by all, yes Curry you are ready to walk with a staff."

Hold out your hand staff." Curry held out his hand staff, the symbol of a Searcher, in front of him at arm's length. Olen opened his hand and passed it across the hand staff. A feeling of vibration began in Curry's hand then the staff started to lengthen. When it had reached about a pace of length it stopped. Olen then raised his hand and closed his eyes. For the space of ten heartbeats he stood motionless, then he lowered his hand and opened his eyes. "You now have the powers of a Wizard, use them rightly as you did as a Searcher."

"Take this," Olen said and a book materialized and began to

float towards Curry. Taking the book Curry saw it was bound in a black cover something not of cloth and not of leather. A leather thong was wrapped around it to keep it closed, the ends of the thong were sealed in a black wax against the cover.

"When Guardian Wizard Shane enters the void, open and read the book carefully and slowly, it can only be read once." Curry knew not to ask what Olen meant by this, he had learned that in time he would have the answer. Curry took the book and placed it in the small of his back under his belt. "Last of all take this." Olen handed Curry a round orb. Looking closely he saw it was about the size of a small egg and was the color of black. Not just black but black within black. The outside was polished as smooth as melting ice. Looking at it, you felt you could actually see deep inside of it because it was so black.

"Place it inside your cape, you will find a secret pocket there." Reaching inside his cape Curry found a small pocket that had not been there before. Obeying, he secreted the orb in the pocket.

"Tonight your journey ended as a Searcher and began as a Wizard."

Looking down at Ral, Olen said, "Watch over this Wizard Ral," looking up he added, "you too Ary." In a distant tree a tiny glow flashed. Then Olen vanished.

In the morning a Wizard would begin his first journey…

Printed in the United States
44029LVS00005B/70-114